ENTER A GLOSSY WEB

McKENNA RUEBUSH

WITH ILLUSTRATIONS BY JAIME ZOLLARS

Christy Ottaviano Books

Henry Holt and Company • New York

Henry Holt and Company
Publishers since 1866
175 Fifth Avenue, New York, New York 10010
mackids.com

Library of Congress Cataloging-in-Publication Data
Names: Ruebush, McKenna, author. | Zollars, Jaime, illustrator.
Title: Enter a glossy web / McKenna Ruebush ; with illustrations by Jaime Zollars
Description: First edition. | New York : Henry Holt and Company, 2016. | "Christy Ottaviano Books." | Summary: "A fantasy adventure about a young girl on a magical quest to rescue The Timekeeper in order to protect the future"—Provided by publisher.
Identifiers: LCCN 2015050733 (print) | LCCN 2016023316 (ebook) | ISBN 9781627793704 (hardback) | ISBN 9781627796576 (ebook)
Subjects: | CYAC: Fantasy. | Magic—Fiction. | Time—Fiction. | Adventure and adventurers—Fiction. | BISAC: JUVENILE FICTION / Fantasy & Magic. | JUVENILE FICTION / Action & Adventure / General.
Classification: LCC PZ7.1.R84 En 2016 (print) | LCC PZ7.1.R84 (ebook) | DDC [Fic]—dc23
LC record available at https://lccn.loc.gov/2015050733

First edition—2016 / Designed by Anna Booth
Printed in the United States of America
by R. R. Donnelley & Sons Company, Harrisonburg, Virginia

1 3 5 7 9 10 8 6 4 2

For my mother, who got me started;

my sister, who kept me going;

and my father, for his vivid imagination

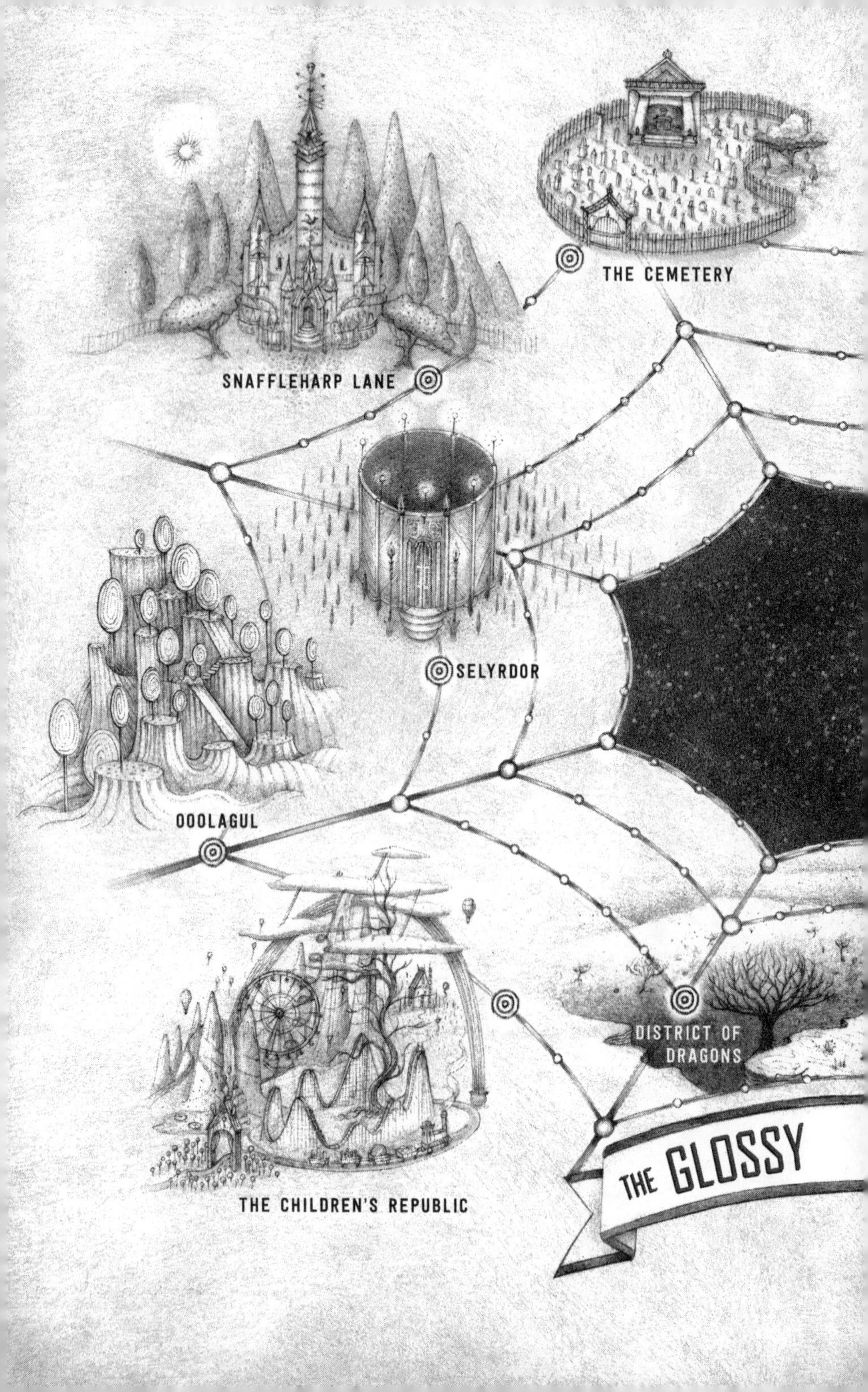
THE CEMETERY
SNAFFLEHARP LANE
SELYRDOR
OOOLAGUL
DISTRICT OF DRAGONS
THE GLOSSY
THE CHILDREN'S REPUBLIC

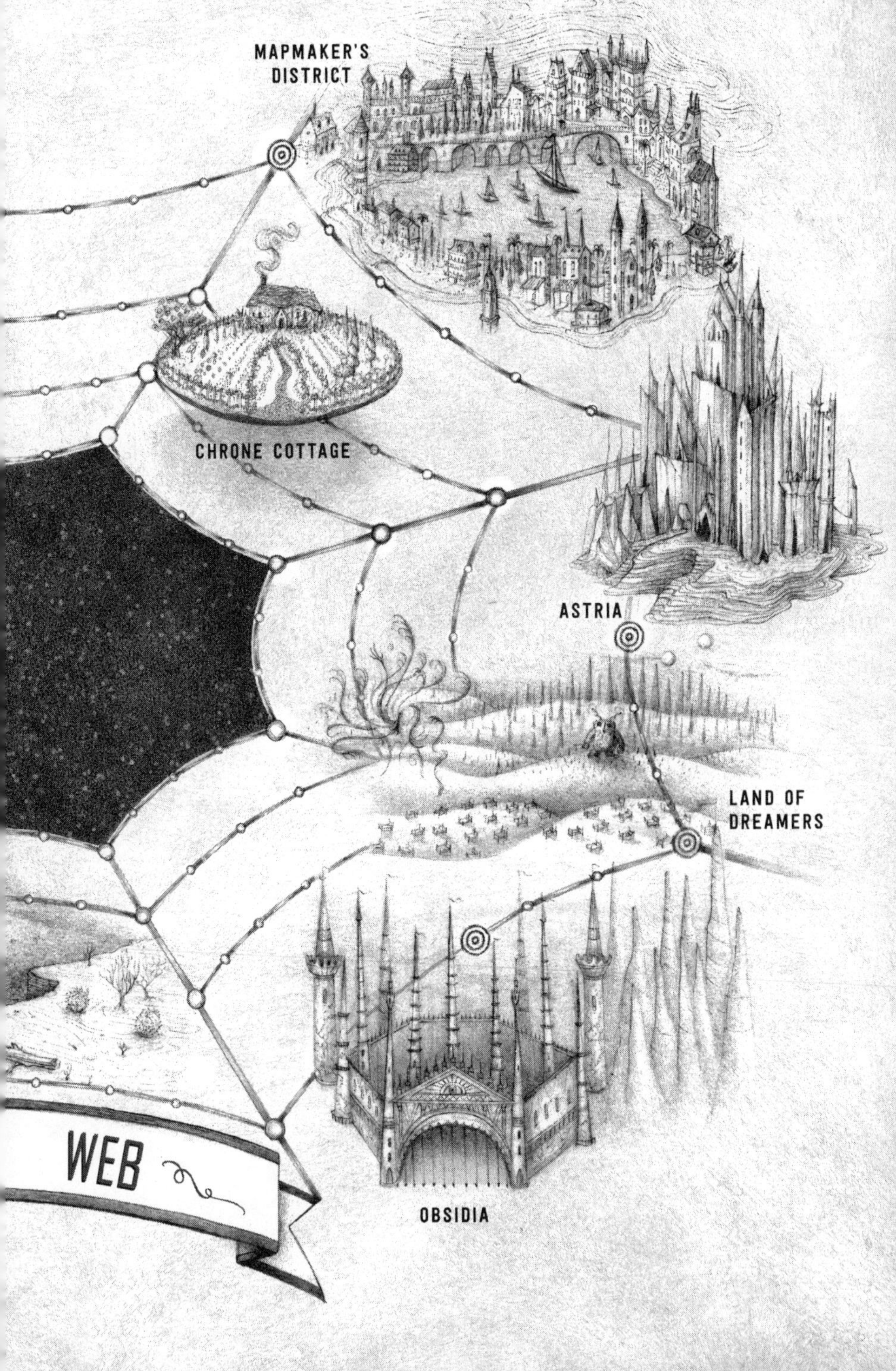
MAPMAKER'S DISTRICT
CHRONE COTTAGE
ASTRIA
LAND OF DREAMERS
WEB
OBSIDIA

CHAPTER ONE

THERE ARE PLACES IN THIS WORLD THAT are not meant to stay where they have been forgotten. You may come back to where you last saw them and find they've wandered off, regardless of how it might inconvenience you. I know of such a place, and it was there that a girl named George kissed her mother good-bye on a Saturday evening not long since past.

"We'll be back as soon as we can," her mother said, tucking a frizzy lock of orange hair behind George's ear.

George said nothing, only stared at a mailbox leaning against one of the cherry trees that lined both sides of the deserted road. Written on the mailbox in flaking letters were the words #1 SNAFFLEHARP LANE, C. & H. SNAFFLEHARP. George looked left as far as she could see, and then right, but there were no other mailboxes, or homes for them to belong to. She stood before the only one.

Her mother's worried eyes darted to the solitary house and then back to George. "I'm sorry we can't come in. We have to get back to the search. Give Constantine and Henrietta our love." She patted George's freckled cheek, but her gaze lingered on the toy frog George held against her chest. "Be good." She turned and hurried to the vehicle.

"But I want to help . . . ," George said, blinking back tears as the door slammed and gravel crunched. The car disappeared behind spring-colored hills, and she watched until the last of the cherry blossoms drifted to the ground in its wake.

George took a deep breath and turned again to face the fading Victorian cottage lurking behind the trees. It was all weather vanes and spires. A fat round tower rose from the center of the house, appearing impossibly tall. George felt a quiver of anxiety as she squared her shoulders and began to drag her suitcase along the cobblestone path, stepping carefully over the brave dandelions sprouting through cracks in the stone.

As she climbed the steps, she saw that every window was covered with glossy nets of silken thread from which hung generations of plump spiders. She shivered as a breeze caught the ends of her scarf, whipping them against the peeling paint of the front door. She tugged them straight and noticed an unfamiliar symbol carved into the wood just above the knocker. She traced a fingertip over the strange mark, a looping circle attached to a line pointing down with two strikes through it. 

Then the door was yanked open and slammed against the wall. George gasped and stumbled back as the wind pulled the scarf from her neck and blew it through the entrance, down the hall, and out of sight. She was too busy staring at the person before her to care.

In the doorway was a frazzled and curious-looking old woman. She wore a safety harness over a polka-dotted apron, and her blue eyes were huge behind a pair of goggles. The woman threw her arms around George, embracing the girl against her massive bosom.

George dropped her suitcase, stiffening in surprise before returning the hug warily.

A man's deep voice boomed from inside the house, "Let her breathe for heaven's sake, Henrietta!"

"My goodness, I know. I'm just delighted to see you! We've been looking forward to your visit so much." Giving her one last quick squeeze, the woman released her and then called loudly, "Constantine? Constantine, come out here!"

A very distinguished old gentleman stepped from behind Henrietta. "I'm here, Chicken," he said, resting one hand on Henrietta's back as he looked at George kindly.

George's mouth fell open as her eyes followed the man from his red shoes up, up, up to little round spectacles perched over the bridge of his nose, wide handlebar mustache, and bushy white eyebrows.

She cleared her throat and stepped forward with her hand outstretched. "Hello, I'm George. Thank you for having me."

"Goodness, would you listen to her?" Henrietta said, her eyes twinkling with laughter. "Why, I haven't seen you since you were knee high to a June bug, and here you go greeting us like we're the king and queen of

England. Isn't that the most precious thing you've ever heard?"

"We're very happy to have you," Constantine said. "Though we're very sorry for the circumstances."

Henrietta's face fell, and she reached out to take George's hand in both of hers. "Yes, we were so terribly sad to hear about your little brother. Imagine, a seven-year-old boy all alone in that great city. . . . How long has he been missing now?"

George stared hard at her feet. "Daniel's been gone for ninety-seven days," she said in a small voice. "My parents let me help look for him at first, but I guess I got underfoot, so they brought me here."

Henrietta glanced at Constantine before smiling sweetly back at George. "How old are you now, Georgina? I could just swear you have a birthday coming up. Oh, would you listen to me going on and on while you're standing in the cold. Come in, come in!"

"I'm twelve," George said as she stepped into the house, hauling her suitcase with her.

"So grown up!" Henrietta said. "Now, dinner is ready if you're hungry. Just drop your things there by the staircase; we'll take them up later."

George paused a moment to appraise her surroundings.

Hanging from the ceiling of the foyer was a massive crystal chandelier casting rainbow shadows upon the walls. She could see a large dining room through open double doors on her right, but the matching doors on her left were closed. The staircase Henrietta had referred to was made of gleaming black wood, which curved into ornate spirals at the foot of the stairs.

George obediently stacked her belongings near the steps. She counted softly to herself as she did so. "Toad is number two, backpack is number three, and suitcase is number four. Nothing's missing." She placed the toy frog on top of the suitcase gently. "Wait here, Toad."

Henrietta exchanged a quizzical look with Constantine, but he just shook his head.

"How did you like Istanbul, dear?" Henrietta asked. "Are your parents heading straight back there to continue the search for Daniel?"

"You're going to wear out her tongue, Chicken," Constantine said.

"Nonsense. I'm just interested." She looked at George anxiously. "Your tongue is all right, isn't it, dear?"

"My tongue is just fine, thank you."

"Ha! She doesn't mind my questions at all. Now, let's skedaddle. Dinner will get hot if we don't hurry. You're just going to love it! I made it special. Applesauce sandwiches and pickled eggs. Your father's favorite when he was a boy, you know."

George began to wrinkle her nose but then remembered to be polite.

Henrietta wiped her hands on her apron, pulled off the goggles, and hurried through the open doors. George lagged behind, concentrating hard on her luggage. Constantine waited patiently as George counted again: "Toad is two, backpack three, suitcase four. Nothing's missing."

Constantine counted too. "You're right. Nothing's missing."

George smiled shyly and allowed him to usher her after Henrietta and into the dining room where dinner was already laid out. Constantine pulled Henrietta's chair out for her and then did the same for George.

George was placing her napkin in her lap when a soft quacking sound drifted from beneath the table. Her forehead wrinkled in confusion as she leaned over in her chair, lifted the white tablecloth, and peered under. She sat up again.

"Aunt Henrietta," she said tentatively, "do you know there are ducks under your table?"

Henrietta took a sip of water, waving one hand

dismissively in the air. "Don't mind them, dear. They're just pets."

An indignant series of quacks sounded from beneath the table, causing Henrietta to sputter. "Goodness me! I do apologize. They're not pets; they're my friends!"

George burst out laughing but immediately clapped her hands over her mouth as her face flushed with embarrassment. "I'm so sorry. I didn't mean to be rude."

Constantine chuckled deep in his throat. "No need to be sorry, Georgina. We can laugh here. Now, will you pass the pickled eggs?"

She handed him the heavy bowl. "I actually prefer to be called George."

"But why, dear? Georgina is a lovely name," Henrietta said.

"And so is George," Constantine said with a wink.

George smiled at him gratefully before taking a bite out of a soggy applesauce sandwich.

AFTER DINNER CONSTANTINE HELPED GEORGE recount her luggage. They both agreed nothing was missing and followed Henrietta upstairs to George's new bedroom. As they climbed the steps, Henrietta casually mentioned that George would be staying just across the hall from the ducks' room, and the ducks in question appreciated their privacy after ten PM.

Constantine raised his bushy eyebrows and smiled at George, who earnestly assured Henrietta that she wouldn't disturb the sleeping fowl.

They entered a room with matching beds. Above each was a large porthole framing the many constellations of the night sky.

George went immediately to the bed closest to the door and placed Toad lovingly on the pillow. "Two for Toad." She moved to the far side of the room and claimed the bed nearest the mirrored closet for her own.

Constantine hefted the suitcase onto a dresser and left George and Henrietta to unpack while he went back downstairs to tidy up.

George opened her backpack and pulled out a multitude of velvet bags. From each bag she removed a hard, glistening ball the size of a goose egg and in varying shades of brown, black, gray, and even rusty red. She placed each ball in the window while counting under her breath. "Two is Venice, three is Moab, four is Easter Island, and five is Giza." This went on until she reached "Twelve for Istanbul," which was not shiny like the others, but dull and dirty looking. She stood back to admire them.

Henrietta looked up from where she was placing George's socks in a drawer. "What are those pretty stones, dear?"

"They're my *hikaru dorodango*."

Henrietta looked confused. "Why, yes, I suppose they are."

George smiled at Henrietta. "They're balls made of mud and then polished with dirt or sand until they shine. I make them. I haven't finished twelve for Istanbul yet."

"But how do you keep them from crumbling right to pieces?" Henrietta asked, moving closer to get a better look. "And how long will they stay pretty?"

"You just have to be really patient when you're forming them. And as long as I don't get them wet or drop them, they'll stay pretty forever."

"Absolutely fascinating! They are lovely *hikaru doro* . . . They are lovely." Henrietta turned to hang several of George's scarves in the closet and then shut the door tightly. "You're quite brave. Most children prefer to sleep as far from a closet door as possible."

George shrugged. "I always take the bed nearest the closet."

"Yes, of course you do," Henrietta said, glancing across the room at Toad. "How silly of me. Why don't you go get washed up, dear? The bathroom is down the hall, the yellow door, you can't miss it. You'll find towels and a new toothbrush and everything you need."

"Thank you, Aunt Henrietta." George took the pajamas offered to her. She washed and brushed quickly. She patted her face dry and left the bathroom, moving quietly down the hallway so as not to disturb the ducks. As she neared her bedroom, she heard Constantine and Henrietta speaking in hushed tones. They were so intent on their conversation that George was able to enter the room completely unnoticed.

"—poor girl left the bed farthest from the closet for her little brother, bless her heart," Henrietta said. "It was thoughtless of me to put her in here. We should move her down the hall where there isn't an extra bed reminding her constantly of who's missing."

"Chicken, ignoring it won't make it any better. She's already afraid Daniel's disappeared forever, and we both know there's still hope. If we pretend he never existed, we'll just make her worst fear feel like it's coming true," Constantine said.

George shifted uncomfortably and coughed.

"My, you're a fast one," Henrietta said, her hand fluttering to her chest.

George nodded. "I skedaddled."

Constantine chuckled, and it made George relax to hear it. "So you did."

"Now, what do you say you hop under the covers?" Henrietta said, turning down the sheets. "Maybe we can talk your uncle into a bedtime story."

"It's possible . . . ," he said, glancing at a silver pocket watch hanging from his coat.

George noticed the watch didn't have any hands on it.

Constantine nodded. "Yes, we have time. If a certain young lady is ready, that is?"

George climbed into bed and leaned against her pillows. "I'm ready. But how can you tell time on that watch, Uncle Constantine? It doesn't have any hands!"

He closed it with a snap, and his eyes settled on the polished clay balls in the window. "That, my dear, is not the story I've chosen for tonight."

Henrietta sank into a chair and fished a screwdriver and an old clock out of an apron pocket as Constantine settled down next to her.

"Do you know what a meteor shower is, George?" Constantine asked.

"Yeah, it's a night when there are a bunch of shooting stars. Mom and Dad and Daniel and I got to watch one near Giza once. It was the best night ever. I used some of the dirt from where we camped to make one of my *hikaru dorodango*. Five for Giza."

"That's right. Some meteor showers last only one night, but some have been known to last much longer. The story I have in mind is about one that lasted for seven whole nights. So many stars rained down from the heavens that people started drowning in them!"

George raised her orange eyebrows at this. "That's an awful lot of stars, Uncle Constantine."

He nodded solemnly. "It is, indeed. Shall I tell the story, then, or would you prefer to hear about Jack and the Beanstalk?"

"No. I would like the star story, please."

"Good choice," Constantine said. "Now, it first happened a very long time ago, when there were more worlds than this one and they were a bit emptier. All life was new and had yet to find order. People, nature, and time itself operated in a hopeless chaos.

"One dark evening, throughout all of the worlds, a sprinkling of stars fell from the sky. The inhabitants had never seen anything like this before, and they were frightened. When no harm came, they crept cautiously from their homes. At last, they realized there was no danger, and they rushed outside in droves and began gathering the shimmering spheres.

"The meteors came again the next night, and the people were still excited and again gathered the fallen stars. On the third night, even more came down, and the citizens grew concerned. Every night the stars fell harder and thicker, until the people were terrified and fleeing for the high ground. Many were swept away by the glowing orbs.

"By the seventh evening, those who endured knew they had to do something, or surely the stars would continue to rain fiery destruction down upon the worlds until nothing was left of heaven or earth. From the small group still living, the people chose seven of their kindest, wisest, and bravest. They named them the Council and charged them with bringing order to the worlds. When the members were sworn into their new positions, the meteor showers ceased, for the election had brought the first semblance of order to a topsy-turvy universe. This happened at exactly eleven eleven at night."

"Which is a very curious time," Henrietta said.

"It is. Once the immediate danger had passed, the members of the Council of Seven embraced their new talents and responsibilities, and they began to set out laws of conduct, as well as tend to their individual jobs."

"What were their jobs?" George asked.

"Let's see, the Timekeeper was in charge of reining in time, as you can imagine. Before that, time had just been jumping around higgledy-piggledy, and it was his responsibility to set things up in the chronological order we enjoy today. The Judge was charged with the task of enforcing law, and the Guide was responsible for whispering softly in the ear of the people and acting for them as a conscience until they developed their own. The Engineer began to design various procedures to encourage friendship between worlds, and the Recorder kept a written history of all people. The Innocent provided much-needed childlike wisdom and was a special friend of nature."

"I think the Innocent had the best job," Henrietta said.

"But that's only six people," George said. "You said they chose seven."

"She's right, Constantine," Henrietta said.

"So she is! The seventh was the Unlikely, and her job was to offer just a bit of chaos."

George held up her hands. "Wait, wait. I thought the Council was made to put things in order, so why have a member especially to make chaos?"

"You're a good listener, and that's a very good question. The Unlikely was just as important as all of the rest because everything has its place, even that."

"I guess so," George said, but she didn't sound

convinced. "Were there any stars left when the meteors stopped falling?"

"Yes, but very few. They slowly regrew as the Council did their job. Now, every one hundred eleven years, the Selyrdorian meteor showers return, but only for seven nights, and they no longer threaten to destroy the worlds. Thanks to the Council, the eighth morning always dawns bright and clear."

"Sell-er-door-ee-yan," George said slowly.

"Yes," Constantine said. "And guess what?"

"What?"

"Tomorrow night they begin again!"

George's green eyes grew wide. "Can we watch them together?"

Constantine leaned back in his chair and folded his hands over his belly. "We can. Many people live and die without seeing them. You're a very fortunate girl."

George thought about that for a moment and then frowned. "Uncle Constantine, if the worlds were new, where did the people come from? And how do stars grow?"

Constantine smiled as he got to his feet and helped Henrietta up. "I don't know all of the stories, George. Just some of them."

Henrietta leaned down to kiss George's forehead.

"Sweet dreams, dear. We'll be just down the hall if you need anything, anything at all!"

George sighed and snuggled into her blankets. "Thank you, Aunt Henrietta, and thank you for the story, Uncle Constantine. Good night."

"Good night, George, and you're very welcome," he said as he pulled her door closed.

George lay awake for a long time staring at Toad on the empty bed across the room. She wondered if her parents might get Daniel back in time for him to come watch the Selyrdorian meteor showers with her. Then they could make a *hikaru dorodango* together if any stardust fell at their feet.

CHAPTER TWO

LOUD QUACKING WOKE GEORGE. SHE ROLLED over and covered her head with a pillow. The noise continued, this time followed by an enormous splash. She threw back the covers, climbed out of bed, and hurried to the nearest window.

George looked down to the yard, where she saw a

garden shed next to a slow-flowing creek. An enormous wading pool dominated the center of the lawn. A duck emerged from under the water and began grooming itself furiously as it bobbed on the surface. As George watched, three more ducks plopped in next to it. She squinted and leaned outside on her elbows to get a better look. One of the ducks dunked the one preening itself, and George laughed.

"I see my friends have already been entertaining you this morning," Henrietta said from the doorway, a bright smile on her face.

George turned to her and grinned as she tucked her hair back behind her ears. "I think they're playing!"

Henrietta joined George by the window. "So they are."

"Why did you give them a pool when the creek is right there for them to swim in?"

"It was their idea." Henrietta then lowered her voice to a whisper. "To be honest, I'm afraid my friends are terrified of heights, and there's that big drop-off into the creek. They don't realize they can fly! Don't let on that I told you." She looked over her shoulder suspiciously.

"My lips are sealed," George promised.

Henrietta nodded contentedly and wandered out of the room.

George dressed and went down to breakfast, but not before grabbing Toad by the leg and carrying him along.

After tidying the kitchen, Henrietta showed George to the parlor. It was a spacious room filled with dusty antiques, and there were at least seven different doors, all of which were closed, but only four of which were mounted in the wall. Two leaned against the sofa, and one lay flat upon the floor. Light streamed through windows draped in glistening cobwebs, and the smell of musty upholstery and lemon furniture polish tickled George's nose.

Henrietta gestured to a spacious brick fireplace. "That's where we roast our marshmallows."

"I like mine burned black," George said as she inspected the room curiously.

"Why, so do I!" Henrietta said.

"What are all these doors for? Where do they go?"

"Oh, you know, here and there."

"Okay . . . Hey, isn't that what you were wearing when you met me yesterday?" George asked, pointing to a safety harness hanging in the middle of the room. It was connected to a thick rope and attached to an oak beam on the ceiling.

"Yes, I like to tinker. It's when I do my best thinking. The gears in that fan up there have been acting up for the past few weeks." She tilted her head and frowned. "I would have finished it days ago, but my ladder just up and disappeared."

"Maybe Uncle Constantine borrowed it."

Henrietta shook her head. "No, it wasn't Constantine who borrowed it."

George looked confused. "Who else would have moved it?"

"Oh, them and they," Henrietta said vaguely.

"I'm very proud of Henrietta's tinkering," Constantine said as he stepped into the room and came to join them. "Her mechanical skills put me quite to shame."

Henrietta patted her hair and blushed. "Heavens to Betsy, Constantine. You're embarrassing me."

"It's true, Chicken."

"Well, I did have a very good teacher . . ." She trailed off and pursed her lips together.

Constantine leaned down to kiss her cheek. "Yes, you did." Then he glanced to a clock, which was off center on the wall, and to the pocket watch in his hand. He nodded to himself and closed the watch with a loud snap before turning to George. "Good morning, George! I trust you slept well?"

"I did, thank you. But why do you call Aunt Henrietta Chicken?"

Constantine frowned and looked up at the ceiling.

"That was such a long time ago. I know there was a reason. Henrietta, do you recall?"

Henrietta tapped her chin thoughtfully, and then she clapped her hands together. "I do! Chicken is short for Henrietta." She smiled and nodded, proud of herself for remembering.

"She's right, of course. Chicken is long for Hen, which is short for Henrietta."

A bashful smile spread over George's face. "I like that. Chicken is a good name."

"I must admit that I'm partial to it," Henrietta said, and then changed the topic. "As you can see, Constantine's portrait is there above the mantel. It was painted on our anniversary over fifty-five years ago!"

"Fifty-five years ago? You mean he's always been that old?" George asked incredulously, and then blushed so deeply that her red freckles disappeared. "Sorry, Uncle Constantine."

Constantine's laughter boomed through the dusty parlor. "No need to apologize, George. You see, I *am* that old."

"Old?" Henrietta looked at Constantine. "Yes, I suppose so. It's the nature of his work, you know." She then began dusting the mantelpiece with a stray duck feather.

"His work? What do you do, Uncle Constantine?"

"Oh, I dabble a bit," he said. "Are you excited for the meteor shower tonight, George?"

George nodded eagerly at the reminder. "I can't wait."

THUD! There was an enormous bang from behind one of the many closed doors, and at the same time, a cloud of ash erupted from the chimney. Henrietta, who had been standing next to the fireplace, was black with soot.

Constantine rushed to her side and dabbed at her face with a handkerchief. "We really ought to do something about that draft, Chicken."

Coughing and sputtering, she patted her dress, which caused more ash to erupt into the air. "Apologies, child. We have a call."

"Yes, George, why don't you run along while your aunt and I take this?"

George looked around the room in confusion. "I don't see a phone." She sneezed twice as she bent over and tried to look up the chimney. "And what was that bang? Should I check?"

"No! Don't check. As your uncle said, it's just that pesky draft." Henrietta swiftly ushered George from the parlor as Constantine began tugging the curtains closed. "Check the mail tree, dear. Maybe there's a postcard from your parents!"

"But I hate postcards," George said as she was hustled into the hallway and the door shut behind her. "And I didn't see a phone!"

After a moment of silence from within the parlor, George headed outside. She skipped to the mailbox and pulled out a stack of letters. She riffled through them, but there was nothing for her. Her shoulders drooped ever so slightly. "Like I said, I hate postcards."

George left the mail on a side table in the foyer and gazed at the parlor doors for another moment. Finally she sighed and started up the stairs. When she was halfway up, she heard Henrietta speaking loudly to someone.

"Why, I never! Can you repeat that? Oh my. Constantine, say hello to you-know-who."

George paused to listen with her hand on the smooth wooden banister. The low rumble of Constantine's voice leaked from the room. George crouched behind the railings as the door cracked open just enough to allow a plump white duck to be shoved through.

The duck quacked indignantly and then made its way up the stairwell. It hopped clumsily up each step, clucking to itself, a piece of paper held securely in its bill.

"Do they seem a little crazy to you?" George asked as it passed.

The duck reached the landing, ignoring her except for a quick shake of its tail feathers. It waddled briskly down the hallway.

George burst into laughter. "Yeah. They're totally crazy. But I must fit in, because I'm the one talking to a bird." She met the same duck just a moment later coming out of her bedroom as she was going in. She stepped aside to give it room to pass. "Excuse me."

George dropped Toad on the spare bed. "Two for Toad," she said as she took number twelve for Istanbul from the windowsill. She sat down and rubbed gently at the clay ball with a rag. As the *hikaru dorodango* developed a faint sheen, George's mind began to wander.

SOMETIME LATER, GEORGE WAS JERKED abruptly from her reverie.

"There you are!" Henrietta said as she came into the room carrying a small suitcase. "I've been calling and calling for you! Didn't you hear me, dear?" She hurried back the way she had come.

George blinked and shook herself, then followed Henrietta down the stairs. "No, I'm sorry. I didn't hear anything." She noticed a label on the side of the suitcase. PROPERTY OF C. SNAFFLEHARP. PLEASE RETURN TO NEAREST

ACTIVE PORTAL IF FOUND UNATTENDED. "What is an active portal? And where's Uncle Constantine going?"

"He has a business trip scheduled."

"A dabbling trip?" George asked.

"What's that, dear?"

"When I asked Uncle Constantine what he does for work, he just said he dabbles a bit. Is he leaving right now?"

"No, he'll be leaving tonight after the meteor showers. He promised to watch them with you, remember?"

George smiled. "I remember. How long will he be gone?"

"Not very, I hope!" Constantine said as he bounded down behind them on his long legs. When he reached the foyer, he took his pocket watch out of his waistcoat and examined it.

George noticed again that it didn't have any hands.

"Uncle Constantine—" George was cut off by the shrieking of a teapot.

"Just in time," he said with a satisfied smile, snapping the watch shut. "Are you ready for banana splits, George?"

"For dinner?" George asked, surprised.

"Of course! There's no better time for banana splits!"

Henrietta nodded her agreement as she straightened his jacket.

"I don't know how my parents would feel about banana splits for supper. . . ."

Constantine patted her on the shoulder. "Don't fuss, don't fret, my dear. Why . . . don't fress! We'll have to add that one to our dictionary, Chicken!"

Henrietta smiled indulgently at Constantine. "Don't worry, George. When your father was a boy, we always had banana splits one evening per week."

Constantine led the way into the dining room, muttering to himself, "Fress! Why, don't fress," and chuckling at his own cleverness.

GEORGE BRUSHED HER TEETH AND PREPARED for bed without having to be reminded, eager to watch the meteor showers. When she returned to her room, Constantine was busy plumping her pillows, while Henrietta opened the porthole skylight as wide as possible.

"Two for Toad," George said as she put Toad in his usual spot and then bounded onto her mattress. "I'm so excited!"

"Oh, me too," Henrietta said, dimming the lamp before joining George on the bed and stretching out beside her. "It feels like we've been waiting forever!"

They made room for Constantine, who lay down next to Henrietta.

George snuggled into Henrietta's plump arms as they watched the sky above, waiting for the stars to begin their fall. She smothered a yawn behind one hand. "Can you tell me a story while we wait, Uncle Constantine?"

"I can. What would you like to hear? How about 'The Princess and the Pea'?"

"No . . . how about the story from last night? Is there any more of it?"

"Indeed there is. Do you remember where we were?"

"The Council had just been made up of seven people, and they each had important jobs to do," George said. "There was the Timekeeper, who made sure time ran in the right order; and the Judge, who made sure people didn't break the rules." She began ticking off on her fingers. "There was the Guide, who helped people make good choices; the Engineer, who invented things so the people in different worlds could be friends; and the Recorder, who wrote down the stories of all the worlds. The Innocent was smart in ways only kids could be. The Unlikely was last, and she made chaos, because you said that everything has its place, even that."

Henrietta's mouth fell open in surprise at this quick recital.

"Good gracious!" Constantine said. "All right, then. So the creation of the Council of Seven brought a stop to the Selyrdorian meteor showers, which had ravaged the worlds and killed countless people. As long as the Council performed their duties, order was kept. There was peace and the people prospered. Everyone had enough to eat, children had long childhoods, and there was friendship between worlds, times, and even dimensions. The Council operated in harmony for eons, and every one hundred and eleven years, they would come together again at the very place and time they were elected all those millennia ago to re-form their bonds, thus renewing the magic that kept the falling stars, and the destruction of the Flyrrey, at bay."

"The Flyrrey?" George asked.

"All life, worlds, eras, and dimensions are in the Flyrrey. It's everything that exists."

"Like everything inside our universe?" George asked.

"Bigger even than that," Henrietta said. "All universes are part of it. Even ideas are a part of it. Can you imagine something so vast as to contain every thought ever conceived on every world that ever lived?"

George shook her head slowly as she tried to believe something that large could exist.

"Sometimes it boggles even my mind, and I've had a lot longer to think about it than you have," Constantine said. "And as big as that is, consider how difficult the jobs of the Council members must have been. The pressure to keep order was intense. That's why the Council had been made up of seven different people, and not one single person. It was vital that no individual have too much power or responsibility, so as not to be crushed by their obligations. Unfortunately, that didn't work out the way it was intended, and soon a certain member began to feel the strain of his position. That might be enough to explain what happened next."

"What? What happened?" George asked.

"It all began to fall apart," Constantine said. "Though the people who elected the Council had intended that each member have only one task, they had unwittingly given the Judge the jobs of *three* individuals. As the Judge, he was responsible for acting as Justice, Critic, and Mercy. It was up to him to determine not only if someone had broken the law, but why they had broken it, and whether or not they were due mercy, and exactly how much mercy they deserved. It was truly an unintentional curse, for he was but one man after all—"

"That's no excuse, Constantine," Henrietta said, and there was an edge to her voice.

"I know, Chicken."

"What happened to the Judge?" George asked.

"Throughout their long lives, the members of the Council of Seven had all been the dearest of friends. The Timekeeper and the Judge had been children together, and they became closer as the years went by until they were as brothers. The two had become the unofficial leaders of the little group. But the Judge's great power had planted seeds of madness in his soul. There were disagreements between him and the other members—small at first, but then they grew. The Judge wanted something that was not permitted. When the Council voted against his wishes, the Judge began to resent them. His fevered mind reasoned that, with his wisdom and experience, it was possible for him to act as the entire Council. He decided there was no need for the other six members. He was the Judge. He controlled who was punished and for what. He doled out mercy as he saw fit, and the more insane he became, the less mercy he distributed. And so, the Council of Seven broke."

There was a long pause.

"Is that the end of the story?" George asked.

"I'm afraid not," Constantine said. "The Judge was mistaken, of course. In his greed for power, he overlooked how very vital were the positions of the Timekeeper,

Guide, Engineer, Recorder, Innocent, and Unlikely. It wasn't long before his madness ran away with him. It began as a small dispute with the Unlikely, but it quickly grew in ferocity, until in a rage, the Judge shoved her from a cliff into the sea far below, where she perished, her body never to be recovered."

George gasped in dismay, and Constantine nodded sadly.

"The Timekeeper, horrified by this act of betrayal, pursued the Judge in hopes of preventing further violence. The remaining members of the Council fled into hiding, except for the Innocent, who refused to leave the Timekeeper and insisted upon joining his efforts.

"The Timekeeper knew there was little he could do for the Judge, for he had committed the vilest of sins, after all. He had taken a life, and in so doing, he destroyed what could have been. The Timekeeper and the Innocent spent years tracking the madman they had once called friend. Imagine their shock, the agony and crushing sense of failure they must have felt as the Judge countered their every move."

George realized she was holding her breath, and let it out in a whoosh.

"The Judge found the Guide, the Engineer, and the Recorder, and he demanded they provide him with forbidden information. When they refused, he tortured them. When they did not break, he killed them. Perhaps he felt that by extinguishing the lives of the other members of the Council, then he could assume their power and authority." Constantine stopped to clear his throat.

"He was wrong," Henrietta said, her voice quavering. "Wasn't he, Constantine?"

George grasped Henrietta's hand and squeezed it. "Don't be scared, Aunt Henrietta. It's just a story."

"He *was* wrong," Constantine said. "But that knowledge didn't help the Timekeeper, who almost went mad himself, with grief, when he discovered that his companions had been murdered. Only the Innocent remained alive, and the Timekeeper would have been alone if not for that. It seemed improbable, though, that either of them would live through the Judge's savage campaign. But then, in the midst of a great crowd, the Judge was caught in a fiery explosion. Where he had stood, nothing was left but a blackened smudge and the compass gifted to him long ago by the Council of Seven as a symbol of his position. He had never been without it, but now it was cracked and clouded with soot. It was all that remained of him.

"At first the Timekeeper thought it was a trick, and he searched and searched to be certain it wasn't. Eventually he accepted that the Judge must really be gone, and the Timekeeper and the Innocent went on with their lives. They did their best to keep the world on her now-tilted and imperfect axis, and always after that, they searched for those special individuals who could help rebuild the Council of Seven. And tonight the showers return for the first time in one hundred eleven years, and for the first time since the breaking of the Council."

"Did they ever rebuild it?"

"I'm not sure," Constantine said. "I've not yet reached the end of that story."

"I know it's just a fairy tale but . . . the falling stars aren't going to destroy the worlds this time, are they?" George asked.

"Don't be afraid, child," Henrietta said. "I'm sure the Timekeeper and the Innocent have it all under control."

George gasped and pointed to the sky above. "Oh! Did you see that? It's started!"

Henrietta shook her head. "I must have blinked."

"Don't worry, Chicken. There's still time." Three more stars shot across the heavens before Constantine could even finish his sentence, and Henrietta gasped in delight.

"They're so big," George said. "I've never seen them so bright before, not even in Giza."

"They do like to show off," Constantine said.

The trio watched in silence for a while before George spoke again. "Do you think these stars can be seen from Istanbul?"

It was a moment before anyone answered her.

"Perhaps not right now, George, but the same stars are falling over your parents as are falling over you," Henrietta said.

"And Daniel too?"

"Yes. Daniel too," Henrietta said.

They watched for what seemed like a very long time. George was drifting in and out of sleep when Henrietta and Constantine wished her good night.

"Two for Toad, three for Aunt Henrietta, four for Uncle Constantine," George said sleepily as she rolled over to face the spare bed. "Good night, Toad."

CHAPTER THREE

THREE DAYS LATER, CONSTANTINE STILL hadn't returned from his business trip.

George sat at the dining room table polishing twelve for Istanbul as Henrietta tinkered with a glitchy outlet. She flinched as a loud *POP!* sounded from her aunt's direction.

Henrietta frowned at a trail of smoke coming from the wall and adjusted her safety goggles. "Goodness. You are a temperamental one, aren't you?"

"Do you need any help?" George asked tentatively.

"Thank you, but I've just about got it."

"Right . . . Aunt Henrietta, would it be okay if I went exploring?"

"Of course, dear. Maybe today you can find the library. It does meander about so."

George's forehead wrinkled in confusion, but then she just shook her head, remembering that sometimes her aunt wasn't at all logical. "Thanks!" She tucked twelve for Istanbul into her pocket, grabbed Toad by the leg, and sprinted from the room.

George wandered for a while; upstairs and down, through forgotten bedrooms, into a cluttered music room, out of a dusty nursery. She finally found herself in the parlor, with no idea of how she had ended up there. She swiped her hair away from her sweaty face.

"Is it just me, Toad, or is this house way too big on the inside to make sense for the outside?" Toad didn't answer, but his silence gave George a sudden inspiration. The library would have to wait.

She scanned the room quickly to make sure all the

doors were shut tight. She placed Toad on the sofa and began tiptoeing around the parlor. She opened cabinets and looked under armchairs. She dropped to her knees by the fireplace and peered up the chimney. She even checked the back of the piano, but a telephone was nowhere to be found.

"I knew there wasn't one in here!" She flopped onto the sofa next to Toad. "Ouch!" She jumped right back up again. Sticking out from between the cushions was the corner of a book.

George tugged on it, but it was stuck. She pulled harder and stumbled backward when it came free. A black-and-white photograph fluttered, unnoticed, from between the pages. The tome was bound in rich mahogany leather. On the cover, above the word *Candidates,* was stamped the same odd symbol she had seen on the front door.

George began to open the book, but then a slight cough came from behind her. She stopped dead, and turned to face Henrietta. "Oh . . . hi," she said sheepishly. "I found this book."

But Henrietta wasn't looking at George, and upon her face was a devastated expression.

"What's wrong, Aunt Henrietta?"

Henrietta bent and, with a shaking hand, retrieved the fallen photograph from the floor. She stared at the nine smiling faces within.

George peered anxiously over Henrietta's arm. "Who are those people? Isn't that you and Uncle Constantine in the middle? Who is the baby that pretty lady is holding? Are you okay?"

Henrietta skimmed her fingertips over the glossy paper, the corners of her mouth wrinkling in a faint smile. "Yes. I'm okay. That was us with several of our colleagues many, many years ago. The baby's name was Carl." She looked a moment more before blinking rapidly and tucking the photograph into her apron pocket. She cleared her throat. "I came to see if you wanted to roast marshmallows. Would you like that?"

"Yes, please." But George's eyes were still on Henrietta's apron pocket.

"Run along to the kitchen and see if you can find some lurking about in the cupboards. I'll get the fire going."

George did as she was told, and when she returned, Henrietta was her usual smiling self.

"Which roasting stick would you like, dear?" Henrietta gestured to a bundle of sharpened twigs leaning against the wall.

"Actually, I have one upstairs. It folds up. We go camping a lot, so Daniel and I each got our own. Mine is purple. I'll go get it." George hesitated a moment, twisting the ends of her scarf. "Aunt Henrietta? I'm sorry the picture made you sad. Is there anything I can do for you? I want to make you happy again."

Henrietta stroked her soft palm over George's frizzy hair. "It isn't your fault the picture made me sad, and just having you around makes me happy. Now, hurry along or I might eat all of these marshmallows myself!"

George grinned and ran upstairs. She placed Toad on the spare bed and went to the closet. She dropped to her knees and reached back into the darkness, retrieving the roasting stick quickly from her camping supplies. She was startled as her fingers brushed against a hard, cool object. Pushing the clothes aside, she followed the object with her eyes up along a smooth length of yellowed ivory. George found she was gazing into the face of an enormously tall and very bewildered skeleton, who was watching her with its head tilted curiously to the side.

George shrieked and scrambled away from the closet. Before her was an honest-to-goodness skeleton, lurching clumsily into her very own bedroom, clutching something in its bony hands.

"Heavens to Betsy!" George said, holding the roasting stick before her like a sword.

Henrietta barreled into the room and skidded to a halt, looking around wildly before her eyes settled on the skeleton. Her mouth dropped open as she stood there holding a crooked stick with a half-roasted marshmallow dangling off the end. Then she smiled.

"Hello, Yorick," she said.

"Aunt Henrietta, what do I do?!" George's voice was edged with panic as she clambered onto the nearest bed, never taking her eyes from the creature. "It's a monster!"

The skeleton was absolutely shocked at such an accusation and promptly burst into tearless sobs. It dabbed at its empty eye sockets with the ends of a familiar-looking scarf.

George's mouth opened and closed again before she managed to sputter, "That's mine!"

The skeleton grasped the scarf protectively, unwilling to part with this pilfered treasure.

"Finders keepers, George. And don't call him a monster. You'll hurt his feelings."

George still held the makeshift sword aimed at the skeleton as she tried to decide whether she wanted her scarf back after it had been claimed by the living-impaired. "How do you know it's a he?"

Aware of her disdain, but with a job to do, the skeleton diligently advanced on her.

Henrietta shook her head in amusement. "Isn't it obvious? Besides, he's an old friend of the family, and your uncle's most trusted helper. And look, he's got a note."

As Henrietta stepped up to the jumble of bones, the gooey marshmallow slid off the end of her stick, plopping onto the carpet unnoticed. "I do apologize for the unfriendly welcome, Yorick. It isn't George's fault, you see. I simply forgot to tell her that you occasionally drop by." She patted the sniffling skeleton awkwardly and took the letter he held.

George relaxed slightly as Yorick, task completed, turned to leave. He looked down with obvious disgust as his foot came into contact with the sticky marshmallow. He gave his leg a good shake and ambled back to the closet with one last sigh and a dirty look.

"Oh dear," Henrietta said. "I'm afraid you've offended him. I suppose it can't be helped. It isn't like you're used to this sort of thing yet." She waved as he disappeared behind the hanging clothes, shutting the mirrored door behind him.

"*Yet?* Right . . . ," George said. "Do you think he's really gone?"

"I'm sure of it. He leads a very busy life. Er, death. Now, hurry down off that bed, you silly squirrel. This letter is addressed to you!"

George eased down, still glancing suspiciously across the room.

Henrietta handed her the note. "Open it! Do hurry! I'm very excited to see what it says!" But she didn't look excited. She looked nervous.

George took the note but then gazed at Henrietta with a look of bafflement on her face. "Aunt Henrietta, you do realize a skeleton just strolled out of your closet, right? A skeleton? A dead person's bones? And you're okay with that?"

"Like I said, he drops by from time to time. Read it!"

George opened her mouth to say more, but then she gave up and opened the note. "It's from Uncle Constantine."

Dearest ~~Georgina~~ George,

My plans have been interfered with in a most dastardly fashion, and I find myself in need of immediate assistance. Circumstances are dire, and I cannot proceed alone. You must set out at once to find the Eldest of the

Els, where you will be instructed further. Swiftness is imperative, and caution is crucial. Farewell!

—Uncle Constantine

P.S.: Dear Chicken, 1G + 2B = 3 to Flee. Forecast: Generous Rain!!! Be a duck, have a plan.—Love, C.

George squinted and then looked at her aunt. "I think this weird P.S. at the bottom is for you. What's it mean? And do you know who the Eldest of the Els is?"

Henrietta took the letter from George. "Of course. Everybody knows of the Els; they're rather infamous. The Eldest, though, she's a real character."

"Do you know where to find her?"

"Hmm, no. She's rarely in the same place twice, dear. Well, she's in the same place, but that place is never in the same place. Her sisters are more predictable in their travel habits."

"That doesn't make any sense, Aunt Henrietta."

But Henrietta only murmured under her breath, "Ge*nerous* . . . Now, what could he mean by . . . ?" Then she glanced at George's earnest face, and her eyes grew wide with alarm. She came to life in a flurry of motion. "Oh my! Quickly, dear. Swiftness is imperative!" She shoved the note into George's hands and grabbed the backpack from the foot of the bed.

George slipped the paper into her pocket, and her hand brushed against twelve for Istanbul. "Aunt Henrietta, is this a joke?"

But Henrietta had stopped listening and was now scurrying from the room. "Raincoats, we have to get the raincoats!" She returned seconds later carrying three brightly colored slickers, which she frantically stuffed into the backpack.

"Aunt Henrietta?" George grabbed Toad from the bed and hugged him to her chest. "You're scaring me."

Henrietta paused and took a deep breath. She hurried to George and wrapped her in a tight hug. "Don't be afraid, dear. There isn't time."

"I don't understand what's—" George said.

"Hear me, Georgina," Henrietta said sternly, taking George's freckled face in both hands. "There isn't time to be scared. There are villains afoot. Listen to the note. Locate the Eldest of the Els. Hopefully, she will lead you to Constantine. I have complete faith in you."

"But I don't know how, or where," George said in a tiny voice.

"The Eldest will be looking for you." She released George and pressed the backpack into her arms. "Don't lose this. The raincoats are vital to your method of transportation, so don't take your eyes off them for a minute."

"But they're just raincoats!"

"You'll understand later, dear. Don't argue. And remember, when in doubt, always go left!" Henrietta stopped dead and cocked her head to the side. "Did you hear something?"

George just shook her head mutely, but then there was a creak in the stairwell that was too heavy to be a duck.

The color drained from Henrietta's face. "Hide!" was all she said as she shoved George down and under the nearest bed.

George huddled with the dust bunnies, silently obedient in her fear and confusion. She clutched Toad and her backpack as she watched Henrietta in the closet mirror.

Henrietta stood breathing shallowly. She smoothed the front of her dress and then patted her hair before perching serenely on the edge of a chair as if waiting for something.

Nothing happened.

"Aunt Henrietta? Can I come out now?" George asked in an anxious whisper, wondering if this was all part of an elaborate game.

Henrietta met George's eyes in the mirror and gave her head a sharp shake. Then the bedroom door creaked open.

GEORGE CLASPED BOTH HANDS OVER HER mouth as a ridiculously large man entered the room. He was dressed in a black slicker, and there was a red bandanna tied around his bulging neck. His head and face were completely free from any hair, and there were bloody scabs covering his scalp and where his lashes and brows should have been.

Even Henrietta, sitting there so calmly, gave a start as his ghastly blank eyes fell on her.

"Move aside, Arlo," a hidden man said, his cultured voice entirely empty of emotion. "We have a deadline."

Henrietta stiffened ever so slightly at the sound of that voice.

Arlo grunted and obeyed, exposing a dapper gentleman with crooked eyebrows and hair just beginning to gray at the temples. He was wearing a plaid raincoat over his suit and holding an elegant cane.

"Hello, Henrietta."

Henrietta didn't reply, but her hands tightened to fists on her lap.

The man moved about the room, his fine leather shoes trailing drops of muddy water. His cane thumped the ground with every step, and the floorboards groaned. He walked to the window between the two beds and pulled the curtains back to look at the ducks swimming in the sunny garden below. "Such a peaceful home you have." The smell of his spicy aftershave drifted down and stung George's nose.

His bored gaze fell upon the shining clay balls on the sill. He touched one delicately, relishing the smooth texture. "You know how they say that history repeats itself?" he asked, and then, with a twitch of his finger, he gently pushed two for Venice over the ledge. The *hikaru dorodango* crashed to the ground and shattered into a dozen glistening shards. "Sometimes I like to make sure that's still . . ." He paused, and then three for Moab followed two for Venice and burst upon the floor. "True," he finished with a placid smile.

George's heart lodged in her throat as he reached down and smoothed his palm over the mattress directly above her head.

The broken pieces of clay cracked beneath his heels as he strolled to Henrietta.

George couldn't swallow, couldn't blink, couldn't do anything as she lay hidden and listening.

"Nothing to say to me?" the handsome man asked. "But it's been so very long."

"I have plenty to say to you. Just nothing fit to be overheard."

"What, you mean Arlo? Don't mind him. He isn't quite all there. He's been rather a disappointment to me. Now, do you know why I'm here?"

"I believe you're here to kidnap me. Is that right?"

The man laughed softly. "*Kidnap* is a rather harsh term. It will do admirably."

"Then get to it, won't you?"

"If you insist. Arlo, bind her hands. Tightly. Don't be gentle."

George, eyes wide with horror, watched as Henrietta was yanked to her feet and her hands pulled back to be tied.

Henrietta mouthed a single word to George in the mirror: "Left."

George nodded, barely a tuck of her quivering chin.

Henrietta flinched ever so slightly as she was jerked backward and dragged cruelly from the room, down the stairs, out the front door, and away from Snaffleharp Lane.

GEORGE WAS STIFF AND SORE WHEN SHE finally got the courage to leave her hiding place. She crept silently down the stairs, Toad in one hand and her backpack in the other. She checked the kitchen, dining room, and finally the parlor, but it was true. Henrietta was gone.

George sank onto the sofa and stared blankly at the wall for a very long time. When her eyes finally came into focus, she saw she was staring at Constantine's portrait over the fireplace.

"Uncle Constantine," she whispered. "This can't be real. What do I do?"

The portrait didn't reply.

"I should have done something to help Aunt Henrietta. Now I've lost her, just like Daniel. Those horrible men have her, and I don't know what to do. There's no phone, so I can't call my parents. It's just me and the ducks. You would know what to do, Uncle Constantine, but I don't know where you are."

She pulled her knees up to her chin and rested her forehead on them. She stayed like that until her neck ached. Then she looked back up at Constantine. She jumped to her feet and pulled out the crinkled note. "Aunt Henrietta said the Eldest of the Els might lead me to you."

She stood indecisively for a moment and then straightened her shoulders. "I suppose there's only one thing I can do."

George tucked Toad under her arm. "Three for Toad." She shrugged on her backpack "Four for backpack." Then she put the note in her pocket and walked out the front door.

CHAPTER FOUR

When George reached the end of the driveway, she turned left. She walked for a very long time before the road stopped being a road. A well-trodden path took over, leading to an open meadow on the right and disappearing into an overgrown forest on the left. She hesitated, but remembering Henrietta's final word of advice, she turned left again and reached the shelter of the woods just as fat raindrops started plopping onto the path behind her. The light was dim, and moss hung from the branches of towering redwoods. Crickets chirped behind boulders as big as cottages, and the scents of pine and damp earth permeated the air.

Gradually the trees began to thin. A rusty iron fence cropped up along the left side of the road. Behind the fence were grave markers and faded plastic flowers.

George stiffened her resolve and continued. She rounded a bend and came to an abrupt stop. Her mouth dropped open in dismay, and she wiped sweaty palms on the front of her dress.

An ominous black gate cut directly across the path, and the fence lay on either side of it. The only way to go on was to cut through the cemetery.

George took a deep breath and hitched up her backpack. "It's okay. I can do this. Dead people aren't so bad. They're perfectly lovely, in my experience. Of course, I've only ever met one of them, but it's living people I need to watch out for. A dead person never kidnapped my aunt Henrietta."

After a moment of misgiving, she stepped up to the gate and pushed gently on the cold metal. When it didn't budge, she gave it a firm shove, and it swung forward soundlessly.

"There must be a groundskeeper," she said, looking around at the orderly monuments and manicured lawns. "Either that, or very handy corpses. . . . Oh, don't try to be funny, George. You're not funny."

She pressed bravely on as the sun sank behind the hills. She was humming nervously to herself when a rhythmic scraping drifted by on the light breeze.

George rolled her eyes in exasperation. "Great. Hearing something in a cemetery. How original." She peered through the hazy twilight in the direction of the noise and saw a shadowed building. Two lights flickered on. Could the Eldest of the Els live in a place like this? She crept silently forward. The lights grew brighter, and George saw that it was an enormous mausoleum.

Two lanterns were sitting beside a freshly dug grave. George ducked behind a tombstone as a shovelful of dirt was thrown out of the hole.

"Watch it!" a boy's voice grumbled. "You got dirt down my collar."

An older boy's voice came from inside the ground. "Sorry, I wasn't looking."

George's brow shot up at the sound of kids' voices. She decided to play it safe, though, and wait a few minutes to be certain she wasn't witnessing a grave robbery. She was glad she did, because the head that popped out of the pit a second later didn't look at all like it belonged to a young boy, for it had hair as silver as a new dime.

"Hey, Mikal, where'd you go?" he asked. "You're awful quiet. Come give me a hand." He threw the shovel out of the hole and watched it land with a clang next to the lanterns.

"I'm here, Caleb." A dark-haired boy appeared from behind the pile of dirt. He looked to be no older than eight and was wearing a tattered, oversized coat. "I was grabbing our dinner before the rats did." He dropped a large basket to the ground. He bent over and grasped his friend's hand, then leaned backward, straining to help him up.

The friend sprang out of the hole, sending the small boy tumbling back to the grass.

George shifted against the tombstone to get a better look at the silver-haired person's face. She sagged with relief when she saw that, although he was tall and lanky, he was clearly around her age and not a man after all.

The small boy frowned from where he sat sprawled in the dirt as the tall boy chuckled and offered him a hand. "Sorry. You okay?"

"Fine," the small one said, dusting off his bottom.

Then, with a sharp crack, the aged cement George had been leaning against crumbled away. She squeaked with alarm as she lurched to the ground, landing right before the strangers.

THE TWO BOYS WERE SHOCKED SPEECHLESS as the redheaded demon tumbled out of the dark.

The taller boy put one arm protectively in front of the smaller boy as he bent to retrieve the lantern. He held it up to see George more clearly, and then he grinned and tilted his head, causing his silver hair to shimmer in the light. "Check it out, Mikal. We've got a live one here. We had better catch it and put it back in the ground."

George jumped to her feet, trying to maintain as much dignity as possible.

"A quiet one too," the small boy said, his eyes glittering. "Are you sure it's alive?"

"Don't be ridiculous. Of course I'm alive," George said as she straightened her dress.

"Well, that's a relief!" the tall boy said.

"I'm not so sure," the small boy said. He peeked out from behind the tall boy. "Who is she, and what's she doing here? Living people aren't supposed to be here."

"Hmm. You're right, Mikal," the tall boy said.

"But you're here," George said.

"Hmm. She's right, Mikal," the tall boy said with a crooked smile.

Mikal scowled ferociously and moved closer to his friend.

"Speaking of that," George said, swallowing hard, "what exactly *are* two boys doing in a cemetery alone at night? You are alone, right?" She threw a nervous glance over her shoulder.

"We live here, and except for you, we are totally alone," the tall boy said.

"Caleb! You shouldn't tell her that," the small boy said urgently. "She may be a bad guy!"

"I don't think she's a bad guy." Caleb looked George up and down. "You're not, right?"

George shook her head so quickly her hair flew back and forth. "I'm not. Are you?"

Caleb shook his head too, but Mikal just glowered at George. Caleb nudged him playfully with an elbow, and he jumped nearly out of his skin. "Don't mind Mikal. He just really doesn't like strangers."

George took a moment to inspect them both. The small boy, Mikal, was wearing a hand-me-down white dress shirt. Bright red suspenders held up faded black pants. His eyes were dark as coal, like his slicked-back hair, and his narrow face was suspicious.

Caleb, the tall boy, was wearing clothes that perfectly matched Mikal's, except for yellow suspenders. His eyes were gray and sparkled with good humor in a pleasantly plain face. The only remarkable thing about him was that odd hair: shaggy, almost touching his collar, and the color of moonlight.

"I'm not fond of strangers myself," George said, fidgeting with the ends of her scarf.

Caleb nodded. "Yeah, we haven't had good experiences with them. But my name is Caleb, just Caleb. And that's Mikal . . . What's your last name again, Mikal?"

Mikal frowned at Caleb. "We've discussed this before, but since you can't seem to remember . . ." He turned to George, and though he still glared with mistrust, there was pride in his voice as he said, "I am Mikal Stanopolistravinsky, also known as the Soaring Penguin." With a flourish, he bowed low at the waist. Then he ducked behind Caleb.

George blinked at the mouthful of syllables.

Caleb grinned at Mikal approvingly, then turned back to George. "Now tell us who you are, and we won't be strangers."

"Hi. I'm George Snaffleharp, and it's very nice to meet you." She gave a tiny wave.

Caleb grinned and waved back. "Hi, George! I've never heard of a girl called George."

"And what is a Snaffleharp?" Mikal asked. "It sounds dangerous."

"Well, I'm a girl, and I'm called George. I don't know what a Snaffleharp is, but that's a really good question. I'm not dangerous, though." She stepped a bit nearer to the boys. "How old are you guys? You didn't tell me what you're doing out here. Are you okay? Are you lost?"

"You ask a lot of questions!" Caleb said.

"I don't like people who ask questions," Mikal said.

Caleb rolled his eyes at Mikal. "I'm thirteen . . . ish. Mikal's eleven."

George looked at Mikal in surprise. "I thought you'd be nearer my brother's age."

"How old is your brother?" Caleb asked.

"He's seven," George said.

"I'm just small for my age," Mikal growled. "I *am* eleven."

"I believe you," George said. "I'm twelve, by the way."

Caleb reached up to rub the dirt out of his hair and noticed George staring at it. "It's always been silver like this," he said shyly. "I really am only thirteen."

George blushed and started to apologize. “I’m sorry, I didn’t mean—”

But Caleb interrupted. “We’re out here because we work here. We’re not lost. What about you, are you lost?”

“I am, a little. But you said you were alone except for me, so what do you mean you work here? Is your house close by? Are your parents the groundskeepers?”

Caleb grinned. “Yes, our house is close by. No, our parents aren’t the groundskeepers. Mr. Chinchinian is.”

“Where is he?” George asked.

“No idea. Mikal, do you know?”

Mikal just shook his head moodily.

“Where are your parents?”

“Don’t have any,” Caleb said.

“What do you mean you don’t have any?” George asked, her face full of concern. “Where do you live?”

“I told you, we live here.”

“Here?” George asked stupidly, looking as hard as she could for a house nearby.

“Right here,” Caleb said, pointing to the mausoleum.

Understanding dawned on George’s face, followed by dismay. “Oh . . . I see. But why would anyone want to live in a crypt?”

Caleb gave that same lopsided smile. “Believe me, it wasn’t our first choice, was it, Mikal?”

Mikal just shrugged.

George's face was blank with confusion.

"I'm not making much sense, am I?" Caleb asked. "Sorry, but we don't get much company out here. Like I said, we're here because we work here. I really don't know where Mr. Chinchinian is. He goes into town for days at a time. We don't know when he'll be back."

"And we're the only people around?" George asked.

"Except for the ones in the ground," Mikal said, kicking at a clump of dirt.

"Did you mean it when you said you don't have any parents?"

Caleb nodded. "That was true too. We don't have parents. I never have, and Mikal's—"

Mikal coughed sharply and narrowed his eyes at Caleb.

"And Mr. Chinchinian just leaves you out here in the middle of nowhere to do his work for him?" George asked.

Caleb shrugged. "We don't mind. It's better than the last place. Not as good as the place before that, but he feeds us well. He leaves baskets of food for us to find every few days."

"How many places have there been?" George asked curiously.

Mikal interrupted. "I'm hungry, Caleb."

"Oh, right. Are you hungry, George? Would you like to eat with us?" Caleb asked.

"I am hungry, but . . ." George blushed and looked away.

"But what?"

"I don't have any food," she admitted.

"Psh. We have plenty. Don't we, Mikal?"

Mikal retrieved the basket and stomped off toward the mausoleum.

"Are you sure you don't mind?" George asked, watching Mikal go.

"Definitely. Don't worry about Mikal. He'll warm up to you . . . eventually. You can stay with us too. There's nowhere else around for miles."

George smiled and relaxed slightly. "I'd really like that. Safety in numbers and all."

"Come on," Caleb said, picking up the shovel and holding the lantern high as he led her to the crypt. "We normally sleep outside, but when that started"—he gestured to the night sky above—"we decided it was time to move indoors."

George looked up to see what he was talking about. Overhead, dozens of bright stars were trailing across the darkness. "Oh, those? My uncle just told me a story about them."

"We love stories!" Caleb said, and ushered her inside.

The mausoleum was well lit but not empty. The air smelled stale, and a huge tomb stood in the middle of the floor. Caleb spread a tablecloth over the stone as Mikal arranged tin plates and mismatched spoons, forks, and knives.

"Welcome to the Café Crypt. This will be our table," Caleb said.

George smiled nervously. "I'm thrilled to be here, really."

Caleb pointed his fork to the bountiful supply of sandwiches and fruit Mikal had unpacked from the basket. "Help yourself."

Mikal dug in immediately, and George sat for a moment, fascinated with how thoroughly he seemed to be enjoying the simple meal.

"Earlier you said that this place is better than the place before, but not as good as the place before that. What did you mean?" George asked as she peeled an orange.

Mikal grunted and swallowed his food before grabbing another sandwich and saying, "The circus, it was better. The butcher, not so good."

"You worked at a circus?" George asked. "A real one?"

"I was an acrobat," Mikal said proudly. "The Soaring Penguin, and I was the greatest in the land . . . for my size."

"He *was* pretty good," Caleb said with a grin.

"Wow. And what did you do?"

"I didn't do anything nearly as exciting as that. I just tended the animals. Although once, when the lion tamer was sick, I got to go on and perform his act for him."

"Heavens to Betsy! You tamed an actual lion? Was it scary?"

"Who is Betsy?" Mikal asked suspiciously. "Is she with you? You said you were alone."

"I am alone, I promise. I don't know who Betsy is. It's just something I heard my aunt say, and I liked it," George said.

"Take it easy, Mikal," Caleb said, and turned back to George. "The lion was already tame, and we were friends. I basically just stood there while he performed. I only got to do it once, but it was pretty sweet."

"How did you end up here?" George asked.

"Well, Mikal's dad . . . he was an acrobat too, and he took care of us. There was an accident. . . ." Caleb glanced at Mikal, who kept his eyes firmly on his plate. "Mikal's dad died," Caleb finished softly.

"Oh no." George's eyes brimmed with compassion as she looked at the small boy.

"When we woke up the next morning, everyone was gone. The performers, the ringmaster, the animals, the tent . . . blammo. Not a word, just gone," Caleb said. "I guess they thought we would be too much trouble without Mikal's dad to look after us."

"What did you do then?"

"We didn't really have a lot of options. Luckily, we were near a big town, so we were able to find work with a local butcher. He was the only one who could take us both in. We didn't want to be separated. That worked out for a little while, but he was mean. Once Mikal accidentally dropped a leg of lamb, and the butcher threatened to beat him, so we left."

Mikal grunted and continued eating.

"We couldn't find any other work, and things were kind of rough for a while. We didn't have a whole lot to eat. We traveled around for a long time, just looking for something better. Then the police found us. They took us to an orphanage. We stayed there for a few months, and it wasn't that bad. Then a family wanted to adopt Mikal."

Mikal made a disgusted face, and Caleb frowned.

"I was all for it, but Mikal said if they took him home with them, he would just run away and come find me again. He doesn't have a very good sense of direction. . . . I was afraid he'd get lost. So we bailed from there. We dodged the police for a while, and then we found the groundskeeper for this place, and he brought us here. He doesn't pay, but he feeds us and leaves us pretty much alone. All we have to do is dig the graves and keep the hinges oiled and the place tidy, and we can stay together and do whatever we want."

"I'm so sorry. That sounds really terrible," George said.

"I wouldn't say that." Caleb looked protectively at Mikal. "It could be worse. We've got each other. As long as we're together, it's okay. What about you? What were you doing wandering around out there?"

They had finished eating, and Mikal was gathering the leftovers.

George leaned back as he took the dishes from in front of her, piling them all up to be washed under the spigot outside. "It's a long story."

"Like I said, we love stories."

Even Mikal seemed reluctantly interested.

"Okay, well. I'm looking for the Eldest of the Els, because the note said to find her, and Aunt Henrietta said she might lead me to Uncle Constantine, and then two men came and kidnapped Aunt Henrietta, and I didn't know what to do except to try to find Uncle Constantine, and that meant finding the Eldest of the Els, so I went looking for her, but I found you." She took a deep breath and glanced up to see both boys watching her with their mouths hanging open.

"What?" she asked self-consciously as she tucked her hair behind her ears.

"Maybe you'd better start from the beginning," Caleb said.

"You said it was a long story. Make it longer," Mikal said.

And George did. "It all started when my little brother, Daniel, disappeared from Istanbul. My parents decided to leave me with relatives so they could concentrate on finding him. I was really sad at first, because I wanted to help—I mean, I still do, but then I met my bizarre aunt and uncle. . . ."

Then she told them about how funny and gentle Henrietta was, how kind and patient Constantine was, and about the ducks having their own bedroom. She shared the stories Constantine had told her about the meteor showers and about the business trip he had delayed just because he had promised her they would watch them together. Then she told them about the giant skeleton bringing the note, and how alarmed Henrietta had been. Finally she confessed that she'd been too paralyzed with fear when the men had come to even try to help her aunt, and how she had decided the only thing she could do was find Constantine because surely he could fix it, and she had to do *something* to make up for being such a scaredy-cat.

When she finished, the boys exchanged a glance. Then Mikal lifted his hands helplessly in the air, and Caleb cleared his throat.

"Well, I don't think you're a scaredy-cat. She told you to hide, and there's nothing you could have done except get yourself kidnapped too. Who would have been left to help your uncle then?" Caleb asked. "But you're definitely in a little trouble."

George's breath whooshed out of her in a half laugh. "A *little* trouble?" But she was relieved they didn't think she was a coward, and that they believed her, even about the skeleton.

"And it seems like a pretty big job for a kid to take on by herself," Caleb said. "You'd be crazy if you weren't afraid."

"I *am* afraid," George said. "But it isn't like I have a choice. I have to help my aunt Henrietta. She's too good and kind to be left with those horrible men. They were just . . . ghastly." Goose bumps broke out on her arms at the memory of the handsome man's voice.

Caleb nodded. "I believe it. So Mikal and I are going to help you."

Mikal gave a tiny sigh of resignation as he folded his hands on the top of the table and rested his chin on them.

George blinked in surprise. "Help me? How?"

"I'm not sure, but we can't let you go off on your own. It goes against our code. So we're going to go with you. We'll help you find the Eldest of the Els so she can help you find your uncle."

George looked down at the table. She tried to swallow, but her throat felt tight. Finally she managed to say, "I would really like that."

Caleb gave his lopsided smile. "We were getting bored anyway, weren't we, Mikal?"

Mikal just rolled his eyes as he got up and climbed into a sleeping bag.

"Good idea. We need to get an early start," Caleb said, then lay down in his own sleeping bag. "There are extra blankets in the crypt. Just be careful not to disturb Linus."

"Um, Linus?" George asked with a touch of alarm. "There's a . . . body in there?"

Mikal smirked, but Caleb just chuckled and said, "Only one about the size of your fingernail."

George braced herself and looked warily into the tomb, but she didn't find a dead body—only a small green spider lurking next to a few supplies. "Oh. You must be Linus. Hello," she said before fishing out a blanket and spreading it on the floor. She pulled Toad from her backpack and stuffed him under her head as a pillow.

"Aren't you a little old to be sleeping with a toy?" Caleb asked.

"Toad isn't mine. He belongs to Daniel."

"Then why isn't Toad with Daniel?" Mikal asked.

"Because if I find Daniel, he's going to want him. He loves Toad."

"Makes sense to me," Caleb said.

George lay quietly, listening to the crickets chirp as she tried to fall asleep.

"George," Caleb said. "What kind of name is George for a girl anyhow?"

"It's one I like," she said. "If you never had parents, how did you get your name?"

Caleb remained silent for so long she had almost forgotten her question. When he spoke, it startled her. "I named myself. I heard a man calling for his son a long time ago. It was his son's name. I liked the way it sounded when his dad called for him. Good night."

"Good night," George said softly. She lay awake for a long time wondering what it might be like to be born without a name, and to live without one until you decided to take matters into your own hands.

CHAPTER FIVE

"RISE AND SHINE!" CALEB SAID EARLY THE next morning. "It's a beautiful day, and we have a long way to go!"

George covered her eyes with her hands to block the sunlight streaming through the mausoleum doorway. She squinted through her fingers at Mikal, who was perched on the crypt with his arms crossed over his thin chest.

Mikal stared back at her blankly.

"Good morning!" Caleb said with a wide grin. He was busy folding spare clothes and shoving them into a dirty knapsack that had different lengths of rope, a flashlight, a canteen, and other useful things hanging off it.

"Are you always this cheerful in the morning?" George asked.

Mikal made a face like he had just bitten into a lemon.

"Yep!" Caleb said. "Well, most mornings. Unless I've just spent the night somewhere unpleasant."

"We just spent the night in a cemetery," she said.

Caleb only smiled and continued packing.

Mikal sighed and hopped down to help, still shooting grumpy looks George's way.

"Is he okay?" George asked Caleb.

Caleb laughed. "Mikal? He's fine. Just isn't a morning person. And like I said, you'll grow on him."

"If you say so," George said, but she didn't sound convinced. She folded up her blankets and began helping the boys pack. "Do you have a broom?"

"A broom?" Caleb asked.

Mikal gave her a funny look.

"Yes, you know, so I can sweep the floor."

"But it's a crypt," Caleb said. "And we're leaving. What do you wanna sweep it for?"

George glanced away bashfully. "I like to leave everywhere I go better than it was when I got there." She wandered outside and came back a moment later with a pine branch, which she used to sweep up as best she could.

They ate a quick breakfast, and then Caleb and Mikal took a moment to trade suspenders. Mikal put on Caleb's yellow pair, and Caleb put on Mikal's red pair.

George collected her belongings, counting as she did so. "Three for Toad, four for backpack." She looked up and saw the boys watching her.

Caleb was chewing a thumbnail, and Mikal was scratching behind his ear.

"Whatcha doing?" Caleb asked.

George looked down at her hands. "Just keeping track."

"By counting?" Caleb asked.

"I don't like to lose things. There are consequences to losing things."

"Okay, yeah. I get that. But you know you missed one and two, right?" Caleb asked. "You started at three. You missed numbers one and two."

"Oh. No, I didn't. I lost them. I can't count them again until I find them."

Mikal stuck out his bottom lip and nodded like this made sense to him. Then he led the way out of the mausoleum.

"Home, sweet home," Caleb said, shutting the mahogany door and giving it a farewell pat. "Take care, Linus!"

George dawdled by the water spigot to wash her face and hands. She stood up from the tap, her face bright red from the freezing water, and straightened her dress. "Have you guys tidied up yet this morning?"

Mikal scowled. "I washed last week."

George raised her eyebrows and sat down on the nearest tombstone. "I'm not going anywhere with the two of you until you clean up." She watched two robins twittering over a worm in the dew-dampened grass.

Mikal crossed his arms over his chest, the expression on his face mutinous.

Caleb grinned and began to roll up his sleeves.

Mikal leaned close to Caleb. "Do you think she's always so bossy?"

Caleb laughed softly as he knelt by the cold tap and began to scrub his face and hands. When he had finished, he looked back and forth from Mikal to George, as if trying to determine who would outlast the other. They both looked equally stubborn.

"Please, Mikal?" George asked.

Mikal squinted at George, but then his shoulders slumped in defeat. He marched to the spigot and began to wash up. "Bossy girl," he said under his breath.

George smiled approvingly at the boys when they stood before her clean. "Super! You look much better. Everyone ready, then?"

"Sure am," Caleb said.

Mikal just grumbled something that sounded rude.

Caleb led the way back to the entrance of the graveyard. It was the same one George had come through the night before.

"Isn't there another way out?" she asked. "I've already been this way, and it seems silly to retrace my steps."

"Nope. This is the only path around here. We'll follow it back to where it forks at the road, and from there we'll just go wherever you haven't already been."

"We should leave Mr. Chinchinian a note, Caleb," Mikal said.

"I doubt he'll notice we're gone," Caleb said.

"That doesn't matter." Mikal fished out some paper and a pen. He wrote quickly, and then he closed the gate behind them, wedging the note next to the lock.

George saw black ink bleeding through the back of the note. "What's it say?"

"That we'll be back soon, and not to forget the Smith funeral coming up next Friday."

"Does he often forget funerals?"

"Let's just say that several times before we got here, hearses would pull up with a body and have no place to put it," Caleb said.

"How morbid," George said.

"The funeral business is a morbid one," Mikal said gloomily.

IT WAS A BEAUTIFUL SUNNY DAY, BUT IT soon became uncomfortably warm. They were grateful to reach the shade of the damp forest. George was humming as she walked when Caleb accidentally stepped on the end of her scarf, which was trailing in the pine needles.

He grinned at her. "Sorry. So . . . any idea where we're going to find this Eldest of the Els?"

"Not a clue," George said, gnawing on her lip. But Aunt Henrietta said that she would be looking for me."

"Are we just gonna wander around hoping to run into her?" Mikal asked. "That doesn't sound like a good plan."

But then Caleb came to a stop in the middle of the

path and let out a low whistle. Mikal ducked behind him, and George's mouth fell open in surprise.

"Okay, maybe I was wrong," Mikal said in a nervous whisper. "Maybe it was a good plan."

A rickety old shack had taken up residence directly in the middle of the trail. The faded blue paint was peeling off the building, and it was surrounded by a white picket fence. Inside the fence was a lovingly tended garden filled with blooming flowers. There were two pomegranate trees, one on each side of the little white gate, and their branches twined together, forming a perfect arch over the entrance to the yard. Honeysuckle vines had been trained to spell out the words *Chrone Cottage.*

"Heavens to Betsy," George said. "I was just through here yesterday, and this wasn't here. Does this forest grow houses or something?"

A paper-thin voice drifted from the yard. "No, it certainly does not. This forest grows silence on a good day. Today ent a good day."

An ancient humpbacked crone straightened from behind a rosebush. Her bones creaked and popped with age as she hobbled over to the gate, holding a rusty pair of garden shears in her crinkly, blue-veined hands.

"You children are late," she said.

"YOU CHILDREN ARE VERY LATE. I HATE IT when people are late. I wanted you to see me while I was pretty," the old woman said, attempting to smooth her frizzy white hair. "This is such a bad age for receiving company. Oh well, beggars can't be choosers. You had better come in."

She held open the gate, shuffling impatiently as George stood rooted to the ground. Caleb gave her a gentle shove, and she came back to life, stepping forward reluctantly. The honeysuckle vines clung to the children's clothes like sticky fingers, their cloying scent intensifying with every step as each child passed beneath the pomegranate archway. George shuddered as the leaves brushed against her skin.

The children followed behind the woman as she doddered up the cobblestone walkway toward the shack. George saw a tiny symbol etched in the wood of the doorframe. It was the same mark she had seen on the door at Snaffleharp Lane and on the mysterious book in the parlor.

The woman led them inside, where shovels and rakes hung on the wall. A rusty chain dangled from the ceiling, and she pulled it. A light flickered on, and then off, and back on again.

"Take off your shoes," the woman said.

George and Caleb looked at each other uncertainly but did as they were told.

"Caleb?" Mikal said in a panicked whisper. "We said we would help her find the Eldest of the Els. We helped her find the Eldest of the Els. We can go now, right? Why are you taking off your shoes? Stop it."

"We can't leave her alone, Mikal," Caleb whispered back. "It's against our code. You know that. You're the one who decided we needed a code!"

Mikal hesitated, groaned, and then kicked off his shoes.

The woman had been watching. Now she opened a hidden door on their left by thumping on the wall. She stepped through, ducking to avoid the hanging garden tools.

They descended a creaking spiral stairway, which ended before large double doors with silver knobs. A glistening spiderweb hung delicately suspended in the upper corner of the frame, and within that web was woven the now-familiar symbol. The woman turned the knobs, opening the way into a huge library filled with towering bookcases complete with shiny silver ladders and runners. The smell of old paper hung in the air as they stepped into the room. A polished cherry desk stood in the corner, a yellow bicycle leaned next to an empty fireplace, and the ceiling contained a glass dome through which they could see the garden growing above. Light shimmered down into a circle on the floor.

George glanced at the bookshelves and read titles such as *2,357 Dangerous Districts in the Door Way: A Tourist's Guide,* by Finn Philo, and *Letters on Dragons,* by Gabe Jacobi.

George cleared her throat. "You have a very lovely library . . . Ms. Eldest? Ms. Els? What should we call you?"

"The library ent mine," she said. "Much too cheery for my tastes."

"Oh. Are you from England?"

"Now, what kind of question is that? I ent from nowhere."

"You talk like you're from England. I'm just trying to get to know you."

"I talk how I want! I'm old! When you've been around as long as I have, you try to keep things interesting. Last time I was this age, I sounded Greek. Next time I reckon I'll sound Finnish."

"Oookay." George tried again. "Well, your bike is pretty, Ms. . . . ?"

The woman scowled. "My name is Lucretia, but to you I'm the Hag. The bike ent mine either. It belongs to my younger sister. Stop chattering and come along."

"The Hag?" George asked. "We're looking for the Eldest of the Els. Are you her?"

"I am! I am. And when I'm the Eldest of the Els, I'm also Lucretia the Hag."

"Oh, thank goodness!" George said, hurrying to keep up. "I got a note from my uncle Constantine saying I needed to find you, and my aunt Henrietta is in trouble, and do you know where my uncle is? I have to find him so we can help Aunt Henrietta. I didn't know what else to do but to look for you. Do you know where I can find him?" The questions poured out of her so fast she had to stop to catch her breath.

But the Hag didn't even look in her direction when she said, "Whatsit with you children always blathering away? Hush up now, all of you, or I'll throw you in a pot." She let out a high-pitched giggle then, and George looked at Caleb and Mikal helplessly.

"Better to do as the nice lady says than to end up in the pot," Mikal said nervously.

The Hag opened another door, and this time the symbol was carved into the knob. She led them down a steeper, darker flight of stairs. The stone steps were covered in moss, and the walls seeped moisture.

George put a hand out for balance, only to yank it back covered in slime.

They entered a dark chamber, and when their eyes adjusted to the light, they saw they were in a dungeon. The air smelled of mildew, and water dripped from the shadows. Chains hung from rafters, and shelves of jars filled with teeth, hair, herbs, potions, and mystery liquid lined the walls. The center of the room was taken up by an enormous cast-iron cauldron, so tall there was a stepladder standing next to it so that the top could be reached.

"Heavens to Betsy," George said, stepping closer to the two boys.

Mikal gasped in disgust as he backed into a mismatched skeleton, pinned together and dangling from the ceiling by a frayed rope. "This is not okay," he said to himself, brushing bone dust frantically off his shoulder.

Caleb whistled softly through his teeth as he surveyed the room's contents.

George cleared her throat. "Excuse me? Um, Hag?"

"Whatsit, whatsit, whatsit?! You children and questions. Always talking! Talking! Talking! Never listening!"

"You weren't saying anything," Caleb said.

The Hag gave him a dirty look. "I was not saying anything *yet.* I am about to tell you things. Dark things that you don't want to hear. But you had better listen because they are important. Unless you want to end up dead, hanging from a tree by your own entrails!" She nodded firmly as Mikal shook his head in mute denial.

"You are *not* a very nice person," George said in awe.

"Nice? You want nice? You should have met me a week ago if you wanted nice." She coughed wetly and spat on the floor at their feet. She stepped up to George and shoved something smooth and cool against her palm.

George recoiled as the crone's clammy hands cupped her own, refusing to release her.

"You'll be wanting this," the Hag said with a toothless grin. She turned her back to George and started shuffling bottles on an old, rotting table.

George opened her hand and saw a pocket watch. "How did you get this?" she asked, her voice taut with anxiety.

The woman ignored her as she hummed off-key, occasionally singing an unfamiliar word.

"What is it?" Caleb asked, glancing back to the door to gauge the distance.

"It's Uncle Constantine's pocket watch," George said.

The Hag began to ramble to herself. "I have a younger sister, you know. A younger sister, a younger sister, I have a younger sister la la de da da."

"How do you know it's your uncle's watch?" Mikal asked.

"It doesn't have any hands," George said. "How many watches don't have hands?"

"She's been so naughty lately," the Hag said absently, wiggling her fingers in the air.

George swallowed hard and closed her fist around the watch. "Where did you get this?"

"Never you mind, child. Now hush up—we have a ritual to perform."

George stamped her foot. "I'm not going to hush! I have to find my uncle Constantine so we can help Aunt Henrietta. Do you know where he is? Did he give you this?"

"Oh, child, you *will* hush, and you'll help me perform this ritual. Only when you've helped me will I answer your questions."

"A ritual?" Caleb asked nervously. "What kind of ritual?"

"Just you wait. You're an important part of it." She

laughed to herself and then lost her breath, bending over and clinging to the table as she coughed and sputtered. "Drat. This body ent what it used to be."

Then she skittered up beside Mikal, whose eyes grew impossibly wide as she leaned in close. "Are you afraid, boy?" the Hag asked slyly, looking at him through wisps of white hair.

Caleb bravely stepped forward to stand between the Hag and the other children. "We're not participating until you tell us what you're on about."

"Young man, I *will* tell you what I'm on about." She began speaking in a singsong voice as she ground herbs on the pockmarked table.

"Ghostly shadows on the wall, brought to life by
heathen call.
Out of darkness beasts will come, awakened by
a pagan tongue!
Summoned to that speaking fire, awaiting orders
oh so dire.
Leagues of goblins not so small, waiting still for
those who fall.
Impatient for the loathsome spell, the hopeless
gather round the fires of hell!"

By now, Mikal was as pale as the skeleton swinging from the rope behind him.

Caleb moved closer to George until they were positioned in a tight little knot.

The Hag continued mercilessly.

"But then . . . from the shadows of forgotten
places, spirits shall be awakened!
Over my cauldron I will bend and stir, times and
events will begin to blur!"

The Hag gestured to the ceiling and then began to twirl.

"My chants will grow louder and louder! Into my
brew I'll toss magic powder.
From the spongy bowels of the earth, putrid
corpses of the dead will emerge!"

With a soft sigh, Mikal collapsed, falling to the floor in a dead faint.

The Hag cackled with glee, clapping her gnarled hands and dancing around madly.

George was absolutely shocked as the boy landed at

her feet. She shook Mikal's shoulders, pinched his arm, and demanded that he wake up immediately.

He did not obey.

"Do you care to explain this, Caleb?" George asked, her voice high and alarmed.

Caleb shrugged as he patted Mikal's cheek. "I told you, he doesn't like strangers. Well, he doesn't like witches either, apparently."

"I ent a witch!" the Hag said.

"Oh good grief!" George said.

Mikal's eyes fluttered open just as George slapped him sharply against the cheek. He yelped and looked around frantically.

"Jeez, George," Caleb said as he helped Mikal to a sitting position. "You didn't have to hit the poor guy."

"I'm sorry. I was just trying to wake him up. Is he okay?"

Mikal grimaced. "Did you have to wake me up so hard?" He saw the Hag grinning maniacally at him, and he buried his face in his hands. "So, not a nightmare, then."

"Tee-hee," the Hag giggled.

George jumped to her feet and advanced on the Hag. "You're an awful, wicked old woman! He's just a little boy!"

"I'm eleven," Mikal insisted pitifully. "I'm just small for my age."

"Oh, pish posh! I was just joshing him about the corpses. I can't do all that anyway. Besides, I wasn't even to the good part." The Hag sullenly began collecting bottles and vials and little satchels of herbs.

"Maybe she doesn't know anything about your uncle. Maybe we should go," Caleb said.

"I had the watch, didn't I?" the Hag asked.

"She did have the watch," George said. "I have to find out what she knows."

Mikal swayed a bit as George and Caleb helped him to his feet. "I think I'm going to be sick," he said, holding his stomach.

"Of course you're not, Mikal. Pull yourself together. She's just trying to scare us," George said, glaring at the old woman.

"You should be scared! You should be terrified!" The Hag swore as she tossed a lit match on the kindling beneath the cauldron. It erupted in smoke and flames, barely missing her as she danced backward out of its reach, surprisingly agile for her old age.

Mikal waved his hand in front of his face as the smell of burning hair stung his nostrils.

The Hag batted at her singed eyebrows and then began digging through her apron pocket. She pulled out a crumpled piece of parchment and shoved it at George. "Read this for me! Loudly! Come on, now, all of you, read! At once!"

"Why should we help you?" Mikal asked faintly. "You're horrible and mean."

"Because, child, if you don't help me, I shall go against my orders and keep you all as ingredients for my potions!" She waved a hand in the direction of the rusty cages lining the wall.

George swallowed hard. "I think you'd probably prefer that."

The old woman nodded her head vigorously with a toothless grin and tottered up the stepladder, carrying an apronful of bottles and vials.

George narrowed her green eyes at the woman. "You promise you'll answer my questions if we read for you?"

"Yes! Together, now!"

"I can't read that," Mikal said. "It could be a curse to kill us all. Don't do it, George!"

Even Caleb shook his head at the idea.

George hesitated a moment and then held up the parchment. "I have to." She cleared her throat and began to speak.

"The eyelid of an eagle, and the tongue of a liar.
The spit of a fool in a circle of fire."

As she said the words, the Hag tossed matching ingredients into the cauldron.

"I need your help, guys. Please be brave, Mikal," George said.

Mikal gave her an odd look, and he stood undecided, but then he began to whisper along, his voice wavering.

"The kiss of a comet, the dark of the moon,
Blood of innocence from a silver spoon."

The old woman gave up trying to pour congealed blood from a vial onto a silver spoon and just shoved the spoon into the vial, throwing them both in the fiery cauldron. "Louder! You must speak louder!" Her voice, though she shouted, was faint under the noise of the fire roaring and the sizzle of the ingredients landing on the hot iron.

Caleb, who had remained silent, looked at George and Mikal as if he was afraid they had gone insane. After a moment of indecision, he grabbed the paper and bravely started yelling the words to the spell.

"A hair of newt, four hen's teeth,
Seven eggs of a sparrow, twelve butterfly wings!"

The children began to shout together.

"The hiss of a viper on a small pebble stone,
Three tears of a widow, and a knife carved
from bone!
The petals of a rose and two small fleas,
Two wings of a raven stir the sweat of a priest!"

Mikal clenched his fists tightly against his sides.

"A tail and a half of two separate mice, one
pint of glowing fireflies.
The breath of a snail, the scab of a wound,
A handful of straw from an old witch's broom!"

"I'll take it from here!" the Hag shrieked.

"Sands from an hourglass let fall to the floor,
The time comes near with this mixture I pour!
Rhythmic chants to all four winds,
Good is born, and all good ends!

One glossy web and a dove set free,
Completes at last our recipe!"

The room fell into a silence so thick it felt as if it could crush bone.

The Hag thrust herself over the boiling cauldron, stretching up on her tiptoes to reach a tiny blue drop that flew out of the concoction. She caught it safely in a glass vial and swayed, off balance, at the top of the ladder.

The children gasped, thinking she would fall in and be boiled alive, but she caught herself and straightened.

She wobbled slowly back down to solid ground.

CHAPTER SIX

THE HAG LOOKED WEARY AND AS DOG-eared as an old book as she handed the vial to Caleb. Her face was sunken, and her hair was falling off her scalp, landing on her humped shoulders. "This will help you," she said, her voice weak.

Caleb reluctantly took the vial, holding it between his thumb and forefinger. The blue drop was transforming into a shimmering pink vapor before their eyes. "That's . . . it?" he asked.

George shook her head in disbelief. "All that hare-brained hoopla for common fog you could find in a grave-yard? We just *came* from a graveyard!"

"Shh. You'll make her mad," Mikal said desperately.

"What's she going to do, turn us into fog?" George asked.

"It's for later. It'll help you later," the Hag said, waving her hand to silence them. "Now, hush. I must tell you things. Things which you will not like, but things which will help you. I must first have tea. Rituals always take the strength from my bones." She hobbled over to a kettle sitting on a cookstove in the corner of the room.

She poured steaming gray liquid into a chipped china cup that cracked a little more as the heat touched it. "Would you like some?"

"No, thank you," they said in unison.

"I must apologize for my earlier behavior," the Hag said. "It comes and goes these days." She settled into a wicker chair and pulled a ratty afghan over her lap. "Come. Sit with me."

They didn't budge.

She waited, and they edged nearer to her, being care-ful to maintain a safe distance.

The Hag nodded, satisfied. "Let's see, where should I begin?"

"You could start by telling me where my uncle Constantine is. You said you would if we helped you. I need to find him because my aunt Henrietta is in trouble."

"Yes, yes, I know all about it. Poor Henrietta, abducted by that awful man."

"How do you know about that?"

"It was only to be expected that the Judge would retaliate when he found out what your uncle was up to."

George blinked twice. "Wait, what did you say?"

"The Judge, child. Or rather, let's call him Nero. He is no longer the Judge. He is now only Nero. Didn't Constantine tell you about him?"

"He told me some bedtime stories about the Council of Seven, but I don't see how . . . Are you saying the Judge is real?"

"Call him Nero. Yes, he's real. Henrietta and Constantine are real too."

George just stared at the Hag.

Mikal nudged her with an elbow. "I think the Hag is saying that your aunt and uncle are the Innocent and the Timekeeper."

"No," George said slowly. "I don't think she *is* saying that. Because the Innocent and the Timekeeper are characters in a *story,* not a sweet old lady who keeps pet ducks and a funny-looking man who makes up words and has a handlebar mustache the size of a banana and a watch with no hands!"

"Think about it, child. Isn't that exactly the kind of people they would be?" the Hag asked.

George gnawed on her bottom lip. "Okay, so let's say the Timekeeper is Uncle Constantine and Aunt Henrietta is the Innocent. Does that mean the story about the meteor showers and the Council of Seven is true too?"

"Well, obviously," the Hag said, looking at George as if she wasn't all there.

"And you think it was the Judge—I mean, Nero—who kidnapped her?" George asked.

"Most certainly."

"But Uncle Constantine said Nero died in an explosion! And the Timekeeper—I mean, Uncle Constantine—searched and searched but couldn't find anything to prove it wasn't true. Aunt Henrietta didn't even look surprised to see him. So you must be wrong, and it wasn't the Judge after all."

"I'm rarely wrong. There's new evidence that Nero is alive and that he is responsible for taking your aunt, and more besides."

Caleb whistled softly through his teeth. "So he faked his own death?"

"Indeed," the Hag said. "There's a certain freedom involved in everyone believing you're no longer a threat."

"But why go through that trouble only to come back? And why kidnap Aunt Henrietta? She's good and kind, and I don't understand why anyone would want to hurt her!" George said.

"Because your uncle, the Timekeeper, is up to something, and Nero doesn't like it. By taking your aunt, Nero has gained some control of the situation. I assume Constantine told you about the destruction of the original Council of Seven? How the Judge—Nero, that is—went mad and murdered all of the members except for the Timekeeper and the Innocent? Well, ever since the Council of Seven broke, the Timekeeper and the Innocent have been trying to find people qualified to take the places of the fallen members. Do you know why?"

"Uh, I might know why," Mikal said, and cleared his throat. "In the story it was the creation of the Council of Seven that kept the worlds from being destroyed. Uncle Constantine told George that as soon as the members were elected, the meteor showers stopped. Every hundred and eleven years the Council would meet at the same place, at the same time, where they had originally been brought together, because that would renew the magic that kept the Flyrrey safe."

The Hag nodded and gestured for him to continue.

"If this is the first time the Selyrdorian meteor showers have come back since the Council broke, then the Timekeeper and the Innocent must be trying to rebuild the Council in time to renew the magic that keeps the falling stars from drowning the worlds and killing everybody."

"*Is* it the first time since the Council was broken?" Caleb asked.

"Uncle Constantine said it was," George said. "Is that what his business trip was about? Rebuilding the Council in time?"

"Yes. Constantine and Henrietta had found five very special individuals who they believed were worthy of filling the positions of new Engineer, Recorder, Guide, Unlikely, and Judge. You remember, of course, that Nero murdered the original members of the Council of Seven because he was mad with ambition. He thought that by killing them he would gain power, but he was proven wrong. With the destruction of the Council of Seven, the Judge lost power rather than gained it. I believe that the reason he is interfering now is not to *prevent* the re-forming of the Council, but rather to prevent it from being done without him."

"Without him? You mean he wants to be the Judge again?"

"Yes. He has discovered how lonely the worlds are without companions and how little he can do without great influence. He wants the Council rebuilt as much as we do. And that is why Nero has kidnapped Henrietta."

George shook her head back and forth in denial and gripped the ends of her scarf so tightly her fingers turned white. "This is so much worse than I thought. My aunt Henrietta is being held captive by a murderer."

The Hag took a sip of tea. "I don't think he will harm Henrietta. Don't forget, the Council cannot be rebuilt without an Innocent. He took your aunt not to hurt her but to use her as leverage against your uncle. Nero knows that Constantine will not easily allow him to reclaim his old position as Judge. With Henrietta's safety at stake, perhaps Nero thinks Constantine will be more . . . cooperative. But Nero is very thorough. He also took steps to make his replacement unsuitable, and that is very dangerous for us all. That is why Constantine sent that note asking for *your* help, Georgina."

"My help? But what can I do?"

"There is a talisman that is vital to the rebuilding of the Council of Seven. Nero, through his machinations and manipulations, caused that talisman to fracture into three pieces. When this happened, those pieces went to the place where all precious things go when lost, the world of Astria. You and your friends must fetch those three pieces. If you fail and they are not reclaimed and repaired, the Council is lost. The new Judge will not be eligible to take her position, and the old Judge cannot be reinstated."

"That seems like a pretty big job," Caleb said.

"Can't the Timekeeper get the pieces?" Mikal asked.

"It's a bigger job than you know, for if you fail, the Council will not be rebuilt in time. The stars will crash down, and we and all the worlds will be crushed beneath their weight."

She leaned toward them now, her eyes bright and intense as she stared into their faces. "Constantine cannot do this, for he is occupied elsewhere. Three pieces have been lost, and three people are needed to get them back. You are those three people! You must retrieve the pieces and return them to Selyrdor, where it all began, or we are lost and will all fade into the gray."

"But what about Aunt Henrietta?" George asked. "How will we save her? We can't just leave her to Nero."

"Nero knows the rules. He knows the Innocent must be in the Circle at eleven eleven at night, on the seventh night of the showers, or we all die. He knows that he must be there too if he is to be reinstated. He will be there, and he will bring her. You need not worry about Henrietta. If you return the pieces of the talisman to Selyrdor, you will be reunited."

"So the only way to save Aunt Henrietta is to collect the pieces and then take them to Uncle Constantine," Caleb said. "How will we find him?"

"Follow the path provided. It will lead you to him."

"But why should we believe you?" Mikal asked, still suspicious.

"If I do not help you, I am stuck here, all alone, until I drown in a shower of stars, just like everyone else," the Hag said in a harsh whisper.

George wiped her sweaty palms on her dress. "We're only kids. I mean, we're just kids. Isn't there anyone braver, older, bigger, out there?"

"Oh, you stupid girl. It hardly matters that you're *just* kids. There's no one else. You're all there is!"

"That doesn't sound very hopeful," Mikal said.

"Yeah, shouldn't there be something here about it being our destiny and stuff like that?" Caleb asked.

The Hag stuck out her tongue and blew a raspberry,

spattering the children with saliva. "Destiny? Hogwash. You are the children who are going to rescue the talisman, help rebuild the once mighty Council of Seven, and foil century-old plots. And why? Because of fate? No. Because there's nobody but you to do it. Destiny has no part in this. All it takes is *one* person making the right decision to change the entire course of the future, and you are *three* people."

Caleb casually wiped the spittle off his face. "Will it be dangerous?"

The Hag rolled her foggy eyes. "You're a ninny. Of course it's dangerous. If you fail, the worlds will be destroyed, and there are so very many ways for you to fail."

"But we can't fail," George said. "Because my aunt Henrietta needs us. And we can't let the worlds be destroyed, because my parents are out there, and Daniel too. I don't want them to die. And Uncle Constantine trusted me to help."

"Okay, so what do we do now?" Caleb asked.

"You must go adventuring, of course! You must find the keys to Astria," the Hag said. "Three have been left in hidden places. You must go to these places and collect the keys, for only with the keys can you access Astria, where you will find the lost pieces to repair the Council and save the worlds."

"That doesn't sound so hard," George said.

"Child, you have no idea. These places are not ordinary places. It's not like going to the market on a Sunday afternoon to get a fresh loaf of bread. No, these places are different," the Hag said.

"Different how?" Caleb asked.

"Different realms, different worlds."

George took a deep breath. "And how exactly do we get to these different realms and worlds?"

For the first time, the Hag smiled at George. "Mud puddles."

George said nothing.

Caleb blinked.

Mikal scratched behind one ear.

They all looked at the Hag as if she had grown another head.

"Can you please repeat that? This isn't my mother tongue," Mikal said.

"Mud pud-dles," the Hag said very slowly. "Puddles of water made from rain, child. You must travel through the mud puddles. Find a mud puddle and travel through it. Surely you've done this before?"

George closed her eyes and shook her head in exasperation. "No, we haven't done that before."

"How did you get here if not through a puddle?" the Hag asked, bewildered.

"We walked . . . like all the other people who can't drive yet," Caleb said.

The Hag wrung her hands anxiously. "I don't know how to explain it to first-timers. You must simply find a mud puddle and step into it. All the Flyrrey is contained within mud puddles."

"You really are crazy, aren't you?" Mikal asked, not sure whether to be frightened or impressed by the depth of her insanity.

"It's what the vial is for, you silly children! Not all worlds have rain. You will need it when you reach the world without rain. There are no proper mud puddles without rain!"

"Okay, and then?" Caleb asked.

"Follow the signs to the Mapmaker's District. He will direct you from there."

"Direct us from there?" George asked.

"Direct us to where?" Mikal asked at the same time.

"He will tell you where to go next. I'm finished having company now. You may go."

She waved them away.

"Wait," George said. "You didn't tell me how you got

my uncle's watch. Did he give it to you? Do you know him?"

"Of course I know him. Everyone knows him, and yes, I got the watch from him. That's enough questions. Let yourselves out. I have potions to brew and aging to do."

"Wait, wait. Just one more question," Caleb said. "Are you absolutely sure you don't have any more advice on this mud puddle travel?"

The Hag was silent for a moment, deep in thought. "I know that two things are required for it to work. The first is that you have to actually intend for it to happen. Imagine what it would be like if children jumping in mud puddles after a good rain just fell through them! Whoosh! Gone!" She threw up her arms to illustrate her point, but she looked suspiciously pleased by the idea.

"And the other thing?" George asked.

"Hmm. I can't remember what the other thing is right now. You shouldn't have been late! I would have remembered if I had been younger when you got here. Now, shoo! Out!"

George cleared her throat. "Right. Well, thank you."

They turned to go.

"And one other little thing I forgot to mention," the Hag said.

The children groaned.

The Hag frowned at them, her skin drooping a bit more than before. "Remember, if the Council isn't re-formed by the seventh night of the showers, we are without hope."

"But tonight is the fifth night," George said. "We only have two days!"

"Yes, you can count, child. Don't show off," the Hag said.

"Nothing like the threat of eternal nothingness to light a fire under a fellow," Caleb said.

"Thank you for your help . . . ," George began, but trailed off as the Hag's eyes began to shrivel within their sockets.

She shrunk away from them, pulling the afghan up over her face. "Get! Be gone! Away with you!"

They stumbled toward the door, tripping over their own feet in their haste.

The Hag's voice was dry and cracking as she called out, "When in doubt, always go left! Remember, Georgina. Left! NOW, GET OUT!"

The children scurried out of the dungeon, darted through the library, dashed up to the garden shed. When they finally reached the dingy room, they stood bent over and panting for air.

Caleb grinned widely and swiped the hair off his forehead. "Georgina, huh? That makes so much more sense than George."

"I don't like that name," George said, gasping for breath. "And I'd appreciate it if you never called me by it again."

"Good luck with that," Mikal said.

"If he knows what's good for him . . ." George trailed off as she opened the door to exit the building.

The garden was still there, but the forest had disappeared. They were in the middle of a windswept golden plain, and it was pouring down rain. The house had moved.

CHAPTER SEVEN

"IF ONLY THIS WERE THE WEIRDEST THING TO happen today," George said, ducking out of the rain and back into the Hag's shed. She dropped to her knees and began digging through her backpack.

"What are you doing?" Caleb asked. "Shouldn't we get going?"

"We need raincoats," George said.

"We don't have any," Mikal said.

"My aunt packed extras. I don't know why—she didn't say—but I'm glad she did." George stood up then and held out the three bright plastic raincoats.

"I like blue," Mikal said.

"Dibs on orange," Caleb said.

Purple was left, and George was glad of it. Purple made her happy.

When the children had shrugged the slickers on, Mikal examined his reflection in the cleanest metal shovel he could find. "I have never owned anything so nice. Blue's a good color for me. It brings out my dashing looks."

"Yes, very dashing," Caleb agreed, and then offered George the vial of pink vapor.

"Right, our precious graveyard fog," she said. She slipped it, along with the watch, into a spare plastic bag that she'd put twelve for Istanbul in that morning. "If we're lucky, they'll stay dry."

"Now what?" Caleb asked.

"Now we put this all behind us and go home?" Mikal asked hopefully. "I think that lady was a little crazy, and I've never wanted to get back to digging graves so badly."

"She was a little crazy, I think," George said. "But I don't have a lot of options. Those men who took Aunt Henrietta were terrifying, and now that I know one of them might have been the Judge . . . I don't care what the Hag says. I don't trust him not to hurt her. He's a murderer."

"And the Hag did have the watch," Caleb said.

George nodded. "And the stars do seem to be falling closer than they were. They look a lot bigger now. You saw them last night, that's why you guys have been sleeping inside, because you were afraid of them. I think the story is true. Aunt Henrietta isn't the only one in danger. I think we all are if we don't do what the Hag said and find the lost pieces of the talisman."

Mikal looked utterly miserable as they gazed out over the flooded wheat fields.

"I don't think you guys are going to be able to go home," George said. "I have no idea where we are. I understand if you want to try to find your way back, but I have to go on."

Mikal perked up and looked at Caleb.

Caleb just rolled his eyes. "There's no way we're leaving you to do this on your own. Even if we could go home. Isn't that right, Mikal?"

Mikal made a mutinous face, but then his shoulders slumped and he hitched up his backpack. "It's right. It's against the code. We must do what we can, for those we can, when we can." And then he muttered under his breath. "It's a dumb code."

Caleb grinned. "It was your idea. Chivalry and honor and all that, remember?" Then he said to George, "Mikal's dad used to tell the best stories about that kind of thing."

Mikal stared at the ground for a moment, but then his back straightened. "He did tell the best stories." And he led the way out of the shack.

George and Caleb splashed down the cobblestone walkway after him, clearing the honeysuckle vines and making it out of the gate just as the rain slowed to a drizzle.

"So, Georgina. Left or right?" Caleb asked.

George made a face at him. "We go left, and you agreed never to call me that."

"I didn't agree to anything," he said cheerfully, turning left and kicking at a rock on the muddy path. The rock landed in a puddle, and brown water splashed up at Mikal.

Mikal gasped and sidestepped. "Watch it! I don't want to get parasites."

"Don't fress, Mikal. I don't think you can catch parasites that easily," George said.

Mikal looked up sharply. "Fress? What's that word? I haven't heard it before."

"It's just a word my uncle Constantine made up."

Mikal stopped in his tracks, causing the others to stop too and stare back at him.

"What?" George asked.

"You're telling me you can just . . . make words up? Isn't that against the rules?"

George laughed, but quickly stopped when she realized that Mikal was dead serious.

"Yes, you can just make up words sometimes. You can make up whole phrases. Not everyone will know what you're talking about, but it isn't against the rules."

Mikal looked thoughtful. "That's wonderful. What does it mean? Don't fress?"

"*Fress* is just a combination of *fuss* and *fret*. It means not to worry."

"Ah, I see. Fressss," Mikal said slowly, tasting the word on his tongue. He smiled dreamily and started walking again.

Caleb grinned and shook his head. "Don't worry about him; he just likes new words. He's crazy smart. I think he speaks like six languages. They're all Greek to me. Last night you said that your parents left you with your aunt and uncle so they could go look for your little brother, Daniel. Won't they worry about you when they call to check in and you don't answer? Do parents do that? Call to check in, I mean? I've never had parents to call and check in. . . ."

"Yes, parents call to check in, but no, they won't worry about me. I don't think they'll even know I'm gone. My aunt and uncle don't have a phone, and my parents are on a completely different continent, so it isn't like they'll just stop by."

She was quiet for a minute but then said, "I was so mad at them when they wouldn't let me stay to help look for Daniel. But then I let my aunt Henrietta get kidnapped right in front of me, so I guess I wouldn't have been any use at all to my little brother. It was raining like this when he went missing, you know." She looked at the sodden fields and gloomy skies and sighed deeply.

"How did Daniel go missing?" Caleb asked. "I can't imagine how terrible it would be if Mikal just disappeared. Not knowing where he went would kill me."

George focused intently on the path at her feet. "I don't really like to talk about it. It makes my stomach ache."

Caleb skipped over a mud puddle. "Why? It isn't like it was your fault any more than those two men taking your aunt was. What, did you take him out and lose him or something?"

George stopped in her tracks, not even noticing that she was standing in the middle of a murky pool. Her face was stricken, her eyes wide with shock, and she opened her mouth to say something but then closed it again. She tucked her chin against her chest and walked rapidly away, leaving Caleb and Mikal standing in the road.

"Why did you say that, Caleb?" Mikal asked. "You should be more careful. Losing people hurts." He shook his head and hurried after George.

"But I just meant . . ." Caleb sighed and ran after his friends. "Look, George. I'm sorry. I shouldn't have said anything. I just meant it seems like you think everything is your fault, and it probably isn't."

George pushed her hair back. "I forgive you. But I don't want to talk about it anymore."

"Fair enough," Caleb said. "I won't bring it up again. Sooo . . . what's it like staying with the Timekeeper? Are there like clocks, everywhere? It must be pretty sweet to have a fairy-tale character for an uncle."

George laughed softly. "I haven't gotten used to that part yet, but I like staying with them. Aunt Henrietta's really good at fixing stuff, but she's an awful cook. She makes things like applesauce sandwiches and pickled eggs. But sometimes we have banana splits for dinner."

Mikal looked wistful. "She sounds very nice."

"Where did you live before you went to stay with them?" Caleb asked.

"My parents are archaeologists," George said. "We traveled a lot to different countries."

"What's an archaeologist?" Caleb asked.

"It's someone who digs up historical artifacts for museums," Mikal said.

George looked at Mikal in surprise. "Yeah, that's it."

"Told ya he was smart," Caleb said with a smug grin.

They walked on and soon came to a dip in the path where the rainwater had gathered, forming a miniature lake.

George took a deep breath. "Well, I guess now is as good a time as any to see if the Hag really was just a crazy old lady. Who wants to be first?"

Caleb smiled and shoved his hands into his back pockets. "It's your mission, Georgina."

She rolled her eyes but stepped to the edge of the water, placing one foot gingerly into the puddle. She waited and nothing happened.

"Maybe you're supposed to have both feet in," Caleb said.

George eased in, trying to stay close to the edge.

Mikal pointed to the middle of the muddy water.

"Maybe you're supposed to get all the way in there."

"And remember the Hag said you have to intend for it to work," Caleb said.

George put her hands on her hips. "Do you guys want to try? Because I'd be more than happy to let *you* get *your* ankles wet."

They both grinned, but Caleb tromped into the center of the mud puddle. "Let's do this."

George marched after him and crossed her arms over her chest. She closed her eyes and counted to nine. She could feel the mud starting to sink into her shoes.

"Come on, Mikal. You need to be here too. There aren't any parasites," Caleb said.

Mikal wrinkled his nose as he stepped into the water, and George hid a smile.

They stood in a little circle, and nothing happened.

"Maybe it has to get to know us first?" Mikal said. "It might not like strangers either."

"Okay, puddle," George said as she shifted awkwardly. "We're not strangers, and we're intending really, really hard. Aaand now I'm talking to a mud puddle."

Absolutely nothing happened.

George threw up her arms and started to mutter something about crazy old women and their silly stories.

Before the words had even left her mouth, there was a whoosh like a toilet flushing, and her feet dropped out from under her.

Nothing was left as evidence of the trio's departure except for tiny ripples on the dark surface of the water.

THE CHILDREN LANDED WITH A THUD.

Mikal yelped and threw his arms around Caleb's legs, causing Caleb to topple over onto his side.

"Heavens to Betsy," George said, her breath escaping in a cloud of white. The air was chill and damp with fog, and she rubbed her arms for warmth. She held out a hand to help Caleb up as she looked around in a daze.

"You can say that again," Caleb said as he disentangled himself from Mikal, who was crouched down with his eyes tightly shut. "You have got to see this, Mikal."

"No, I don't. I'm just fine not seeing it. I can't look. I just can't!"

"Yes, you can, Mikal," George said. "You thought you couldn't help us read the Hag's spell, but you did. You're getting braver. You can look."

Mikal hesitated but then gave in, and his mouth fell open.

The children were floating through an enormous

underground tunnel as wide as a football field and so long there seemed no end to it. Narrow passages forked off here and there, and traffic lights blinked green and red. Sailing promptly along, on every side of the children, were doors suspended in midair. They were of all shapes and colors, and they lay flat, with their knobs and handles facing up. There were wooden garden gates and old cellar doors, metal garage doors and pretty yellow pantry doors, glass doors and red church doors. They drifted by in an orderly fashion, all levitating over a shimmering silver mist through which the children could not see the ground.

They were startled to see that they themselves were balanced precariously on a solid oak hatch that must have once belonged to an attic.

George inhaled deeply and then let it out with a whoosh. "Do you smell that? It's like rain on hot pavement . . . and . . . oranges? Do you smell oranges?"

But the boys were too busy staring to answer her.

Upon various portals people and creatures perched, oblivious to the children. Some of these looked just like the sort of person you'd see at a supermarket, others looked like animals wearing costumes, but still others were threatening and unkempt. The latter hunkered down under long dark coats and watched with glittering eyes from behind lank and dirty hair.

Just then a man sped past, shouting at the top of his lungs, "I need to get to the haberdashery! We're going to be late!" But he could barely be heard over the clamor of traffic and the sounds of bells ringing, whistles blowing, and passengers hollering directions.

George saw that on either side of the main thoroughfare were even more doorways, and these at least had the decency to stand up in a normal fashion. They were not floating like the horizontal portals but seemed to stay in one place. Above each was a sign with the dimension, destination, date, and arrival time of the advertised location.

Caleb nudged George with his elbow and pointed at a dark blue door with a sign above it that read, 3RD DIMENSION, LOCH NESS, SCOTLAND, THURSDAY, APRIL 5, 4:32 PM DWT. Below it was a flashing advisory: *Please use extreme caution. Nessie is in a foul mood today and has already eaten three fishermen and two tourists.* And then, *Body count for April 5: 5. It has been 0 days since an incident.*

Mikal swallowed hard and pressed close to his friends.

The children came to an intersection where they stopped for a traffic light. A garden gate carrying a

funny-looking man with a miniature pet elephant pulled up beside them. George waved uncertainly, and the old man waved back. So did his elephant.

"Excuse me!" George said.

"Yes? May I help you?" the man asked.

"Could you please tell me how to reach the Mapmaker's District?"

"Indeed I can," he said, but then the light changed and his ride pulled away so fast they couldn't hear his instructions.

"Great, now what?" George asked.

"You could have just asked me," a sullen voice muttered from beneath them. "I mean, I *am* the one driving."

"What was that?" Mikal asked nervously, looking around.

"It was me, you ridiculous child!" And the voice was coming from the keyhole of the door they balanced upon.

Mikal was relieved that it was just a keyhole speaking, for he'd never met a bad keyhole, but George was so shocked that she stumbled backward, nearly falling into the mist. Mikal and Caleb grabbed the sleeves of her coat and hauled her back on.

"Ex-excuse me?" George asked. "Did you say something?"

"Yes! I said you could have asked me! Instead of just pretending I'm not even here. Children, these days. So rude."

"I'm very sorry," George said. "But I didn't know you were . . . alive? Are you alive?"

"How *dare* you. Of course I'm alive. Get off me at once. I won't take you another—"

"I didn't mean to insult you!" George said desperately. "I've just never met a talking door. We've never been here before."

"Never been here, eh? This is your first time? Fine. I accept your apology. I'll take you to the Mapmaker. But I'm not as young as I used to be! Can some of you please get off me before you smother me to death? You're heavy!"

"Hurry, we're hurting it," Mikal said.

"The little one can stay," the door said. "I like him."

"I'm eleven," Mikal muttered, but he stayed put.

George looked around and saw that several empty portals were traveling in the same direction as they. "I'm going to get on one of those, okay?"

"And I'm going to take that one," Caleb said, carefully jumping onto a cedar door.

"Wipe your feet," it snapped at him, the scent of cedar wafting from its frame.

"But you don't have a mat," Caleb said, and there was no reply.

George very cautiously stepped onto a white door.

"Hello there! It's such a pleasure to have you with us!" the white door said.

George looked around nervously. "Well . . . it's a pleasure to be here!"

"Where can I take you on this fine day?" White Door asked.

"We're going to the Mapmaker's District, please," George said.

"Swell. I'll have you there in a jiffy. Did I overhear you say that this was your first time in the Door Way?"

"The Door Way?" George asked.

"Look around you. This is the Door Way, the labyrinth of tunnels people use to get from world to world. The official name is the Xyla, but nobody calls it that."

"Oh, okay. Yes, you did overhear that."

"My goodness! I've never had the pleasure of meeting a newbie before. Are you enjoying yourself?"

"Yes, thank you, but it's quite a shock. I never knew you could ride doors," George said.

"Oh my, then let me be the first to tell you that you can't call us that. It just isn't polite."

"What would you like me to call you?"

"I'm a Tourie!" White Door said proudly. "All of us that are moving around are Touries. We're *mobile,* not like the ones that stand still."

Caleb tried to maneuver his door closer to George's so he could hear their conversation.

It grumbled and objected, bucking around a bit before scooting in close to White Door.

"What's the name for the ones that stand still?" Caleb asked.

"Them? They're Moors. And they are booorring. They're just stuck where they're built. They don't do much good for anybody except as entry points. But we Touries, we're special. We spend our lives going back and forth and thither and yon. We can go anywhere we want. We carry important people to special events and get to meet all kinds of interesting strangers. Why, just this morning I carried a very sinister chap—"

"You're such a gossip. Always telling tales," Caleb's cedar door said.

"It's not my fault! They asked!" White Door said.

"You're going to get us fired," Cedar Door said.

"Are you looking for a particular Mapmaker, or will any do?" Mikal's oak door asked, interrupting the spat.

"We were only told to find the Mapmaker," Mikal said.

"THE Mapmaker? Why didn't you say so!" White Door said.

They continued on, finally coming to a stop in front of a yellow door labeled 3RD DIMENSION, THURSDAY, APRIL 5, 4:45 PM DWT, PHINNEUS NEPTUNE.

Mikal was the first to ease off his Tourie, his knees wobbling a bit on the solid doorstep.

"All these Moors have the same letters above them, the *DWT.* What's it mean?" Caleb asked.

"It means Door Way Time. Now get off me," Cedar Door said.

"Okay, okay," Caleb said. He climbed onto the platform and offered a hand to George.

"Thanks for the ride," she called to the retreating Touries.

Mikal was holding his stomach and looking a bit green around the edges.

George paused for a moment to take off her raincoat and pack it away. "Three for backpack, four for Caleb, five for Mikal. Nothing's missing."

Caleb raised a silver eyebrow. "You ever gonna tell us what number one and two were?"

She ignored him and rang the doorbell.

Mikal rose up on his tiptoes to peek through the peephole and jumped back immediately as an enormous eye peered back at him.

The door still didn't open.

"There's somebody in there," Mikal said.

"I should hope so," George said.

"Maybe we should wipe our feet?" Mikal asked.

Before they could do as he suggested, the door swung inward.

CHAPTER EIGHT

THE CHILDREN STEPPED WARILY THROUGH Mr. Phinneus Neptune's door and found themselves within a cluttered study. Maps and charts adorned the walls, globes sat on various surfaces, and books were piled high on the floor.

A hairy little man was peeking at them from behind a stack of encyclopedias as tall as he. He wore an elaborate silk dinner jacket over plaid pants and a striped shirt. Around his neck was a blue tie decorated with longitude and latitude lines, and his watery blue eyes were made huge by a pair of thick glasses. His hands and face were covered in dark brown hair, but his head was so bald the children could see their reflections in it.

"H-hello there. You wouldn't happen to be the Snafflehar youth, would you?"

"Yes. Well, I am, at least," George said, peering around the pile of books.

"What about those other two? Who might they be?" he asked as he shoved the glasses higher up on his nose.

"We're her friends," Caleb said.

"Oh, I see, I see. Of course you are." He sighed with relief and eased out of his hiding spot. "I've been expecting you. I just wanted to be sure it *was* you."

"What were you hiding from, if you don't mind my asking?" George asked curiously.

Mikal looked at the man, his face suspicious. "I think that the better question is, why was he expecting us?"

"Both very valid questions, to be sure, and I will get to them eventually, but please, first allow me the pleasure of introducing myself." At this he threw back his shoulders, and his chest swelled pompously. "I am Phinneus

Neptune, distinguished author of more than seventy-three books in thirteen worlds and counting, as well as Mapmaker Extraordinaire. I provide services to those as esteemed as kings and queens, but most importantly, to the Timekeeper himself. Oh, and I do a fair bit of computer programming too."

"What sort of books do you write?" Caleb asked.

"And why haven't we ever heard of you if you're a famous author?" George asked.

"All kinds of books! Books on everything from the migratory patterns of the Bawlizanian Sun Gnat to the current whereabouts of Alexander the Great. And as for the second question—"

"I think you just answered the second question," Mikal said.

"Ahem." Phinneus Neptune cleared his throat, frowning at Mikal. "As for why you haven't heard of me, well, my books are far too advanced for mere children."

"Mere children, huh?" Caleb said quietly.

George offered her hand to the little man. "Nice to meet you, Mr. Neptune. I'm George."

Mr. Neptune grabbed her hand and shook it vigorously before gesturing to the boys. "And who might these young fellows be?"

Caleb extended his hand to Mr. Neptune. "Caleb."

Mr. Neptune shook Caleb's hand and looked at Mikal.

Mikal crossed his arms over his chest and glared back through narrowed eyes.

"Not very friendly, are you?" Mr. Neptune said with a strained laugh.

"He doesn't care for strangers," George said, stepping closer to Mikal.

But Mr. Neptune had lost interest. "Now, where did I put that list?"

Mikal watched the man as Caleb and George inspected the many charts and maps.

"Here it is!" Mr. Neptune pulled a tiny scroll of parchment from where it had been stuck behind his ear. "Oh, please! Don't touch that!" he cried as George began to spin a globe.

"Yikes, sorry." She slapped her hand onto it to stop its movement.

Mr. Neptune cringed as he hurried to its rescue. "It's quite all right. This is just a very rare piece. Why, it could spin off its axis at any moment and BANG!" He slammed his hands together so loudly they all jumped in surprise. "It would disintegrate into dust!" He dabbed at it delicately with a white silk handkerchief. "Yes indeed, very fragile this piece is."

"What planet is it supposed to be?" George asked.

"The earth, of course," Mr. Neptune said.

"It doesn't look like the earth to me," Mikal said.

"That's because it's a representation of the earth as it was when Pangaea was intact. Don't they teach you anything in school these days? Imagine!"

"Pangaea?" George asked.

"You know, before the continents split. There was just one big one," Caleb said, studying the orb, his hands deep in his pockets.

Mr. Neptune beamed at Caleb. "I see we have at least one scholar here. Marvelous!"

"How did you know that?" George asked.

"I *can* read," Caleb said with a bashful grin.

Mikal had been edging nearer to get a better look.

Mr. Neptune noticed him and stepped aside. "If you look riiiight here," he said, turning the globe gently and pointing with the tip of his index finger, "this is where you three are from. Or at least, that's where you would have been from before Pangaea split."

Mikal now stepped forward eagerly, nudging Caleb out of the way in his excitement. "What about Russia? Where would it be?"

"This blue area right here," Mr. Neptune said, pointing to an area near the top. "Have you ever been there?"

Mikal just shrugged.

George tilted her head to the side. "I wonder where the Hag is now. Her house doesn't seem to stay in one place."

"Now, that's a curious thing! A better question would be 'Where are the worlds?' In relation to Chrone Cottage, that is, the Hag's home."

"What do you mean?" Caleb asked.

"As the girl said, Chrone Cottage doesn't always stay in the same place. But that's complicated. It isn't the Hag's home that's moving. It's the worlds."

The children stared at him uncomprehendingly.

"Ahem. Well, you see, if you lightly place your finger here where Russia would be, and then you spin the globe, your finger stays exactly where you put it. However, when the globe comes to a stop, it's very likely that your finger will be pointing to a different location than Russia!" He demonstrated this, watching them to make sure they understood.

"She's always in the same place. It's just the worlds that are moving," Caleb said.

"Yes! Snaffleharp Lane is another one of these peculiar

locations that seem to have developed minds of their own and are often inaccessible through the Door Way. They can move about at will. Speaking of, how did you enjoy your first time? You were careful not to get separated, I hope. The Drifters can be dangerous if they find you alone."

"The Drifters, are they those mean-looking people we saw in the tunnels?" Mikal asked.

"Yes, I suppose *mean-looking* might describe them."

"We didn't get separated," George said.

"I thought the whole thing was pretty sweet," Caleb said. "Kind of like how I imagine surfing would be."

"I get doorsick," Mikal said sadly.

"It is a phenomenal creation," Mr. Neptune said. "The Engineer designed it all very brilliantly. All you need to access it is a mud puddle and a raincoat—"

"That's what the raincoats were for?" George asked.

Mr. Neptune frowned at this interruption. "As I was saying, it really is quite ingenious. The Engineer had a very difficult time configuring a process that would perfect interworld travel, until he thought up the Door Way. Time machines had so many glitches that anytime a person used one, he could very likely come out the other side with a goldfish for a head. Why, there was this one time—"

"Excuse me," George said. "I don't mean to be rude, but we really are in a hurry."

Mr. Neptune visibly deflated. "Very well. Come along." He scurried back to his desk.

Mikal looked up from the globe and frowned. "He hasn't answered our questions yet."

"What? Oh yes. Your questions. What questions were those again?" Mr. Neptune asked.

"How did you know to expect us?" Mikal asked.

"And why did it seem like you were hiding when we came in?" George asked.

"I knew you would be arriving because I was told by the Timekeeper to expect you. I was instructed to help you on your way."

"And the other question?" Caleb asked.

Mr. Neptune sighed. "It seemed like I was hiding because I was, indeed, hiding."

"Why?" Mikal asked.

"Because important people have been disappearing! You should know. George's own aunt was abducted just yesterday."

"So you were afraid that someone had come to kidnap you?" George asked.

"Yes, I was much relieved to see that it was only you,"

Mr. Neptune said, and then looked chagrined. "I'm only slightly ashamed to admit that I'm something of a coward." Then he nudged Mikal with an elbow and said, "But we cowards have to stick together, don't we?"

Mikal recoiled with indignation. "I am not a coward!"

"Apologies, I didn't mean to offend. You just seem rather afraid, that's all."

"Mikal is afraid," George said. "But that doesn't make him a coward, because he still tries to do the things that scare him. He's getting braver."

Mikal looked at the ground. He didn't speak, but his ears turned just the slightest bit pink.

Caleb cleared his throat. "Back to the topic. Aunt Henrietta is important, so I can see why she might be abducted. She's the Innocent. Why would anyone want to take you?"

Mr. Neptune frowned, trying to decide whether this was an insult. "I'll have you know that I too happen to be a very important person!"

"We're kind of important too, you know," Mikal said.

"Yes . . . you do seem to be our only hope." He looked at them doubtfully.

"We're a pretty good hope, if you ask me," Caleb said.

"Of course, my boy. Of course. But you *are* just

children, after all. Forgive me for being blunt, but children aren't good for much."

"I thought that too at first, but the Hag said it didn't matter. Look at Joan of Arc; she wasn't much older than we are when she led the French," George said.

"Pharaoh Tutankhamen was younger than me," Mikal said.

"Alexander the Great established his first city when he was only three years older than I am," Caleb said with a shrug.

Mr. Neptune took a step back, blinking and flabbergasted. "Yes, of course. You're all right. However, those are examples of the exception, rather than the rule."

George narrowed her eyes. "Anybody can be an exception if they try. If you don't think we can do it, why don't you go yourself?"

"Oh no, I couldn't possibly! No, never," he said, the color draining from his face.

She nodded as if she had expected this answer. "Then, that's enough about children not being good for much."

Mr. Neptune cleared his throat and gestured to his desk. "On to more pleasant things, then, shall we?" He dropped to his knees, crawled under the desk, and dragged out a large safe. He began to turn the dial, but then glanced up at them before leaning over it to block their view as he continued.

They averted their eyes and waited for him to finish.

"Two . . . ninety-seven . . . three . . . don't you look now!" he said irritably as Mikal leaned over the desk.

Mikal growled and turned his back. George grinned at Caleb as Mr. Neptune continued muttering the combination aloud. "Eighty-nine . . . five . . . eighty-three."

"Here we are!" he said, carefully placing a small square object wrapped in linen on the desk. He removed the covering to reveal a white rectangle roughly the size of a book and with a dark screen. The sides were decorated with intricate designs. He looked up at them expectantly, his face glowing with pride.

George tapped her fingers on the desk. Caleb chewed a thumbnail. Mikal shuffled his feet.

"What is it?" Mikal asked.

"What is it?! Why, it's a map, obviously! The very best map you can possibly find. The absolute height of technology. I should know. I designed it."

"How does it work?" George asked.

"You just enter the combination right here." Mr. Neptune pointed to a series of silver digits on one end. "And voilà!"

"Why does it have a combination?" Caleb asked.

"This map contains the location of every world, dimension, time period, and street address of anyone who ever did, or ever will, live. If it should fall into the wrong hands, mayhem would surely ensue! You must be very careful with it," he said, holding the map protectively to his chest.

"We'll be careful," George said. "Can we turn it on?"

"Yes, of course. The combination is two, ninety-seven, three, eighty-nine, five, eighty-three."

That's a long combination. How are we supposed to remember it?" George asked. "Should we write it down?"

"No! Are you insane?" Mr. Neptune asked, horrified.

"If we wrote it down and lost the paper and the map, anyone would be able to access it," Caleb said.

"Precisely," Mr. Neptune said.

"What if we each memorized two numbers," Mikal said. "Then when we need to turn it on, we'll go from oldest to youngest so we don't get them mixed up. Caleb, George, then me."

"Brilliant notion!" Mr. Neptune.

"Great idea, Mikal," George said.

"Thanks. Can I carry it?"

Mr. Neptune beamed at them. "Perhaps you children

will save us after all! Once you've entered the combination, simply command the map to turn on, then ask for your directions!"

"It responds to voice commands?" Caleb asked, intrigued.

"Yes, it is the most modern technology available," Mr. Neptune said smugly. "And it's just been newly programmed, and updated with a really interesting device that—"

"Show us," Mikal interrupted.

"Certainly! Map, wake up!"

The screen flickered.

Mr. Neptune tapped it firmly on the side. "Map, I said wake up!"

The screen slowly lightened to reveal a background that was white except for blinking red numbers and letters: *The time is now 5:00 PM DWT. You currently have 54 hours, 11 minutes until the destruction of all worlds.*

The children exchanged a nervous look.

"I've already programmed your journey from this location according to Constantine's research and specifications, so the map knows every place you need to stop along the way. You just ask it to tell you where to go next, and it will! Marvelous, isn't it?"

They nodded as Mr. Neptune returned his attention to the map.

"Now, map, show the Snaffleharp Company the location of their first key to Astria."

The voice of a young man drifted from the map's speakers. "What's the magic word?"

"Oh!" George gasped in surprise.

"*Oh* is not the magic word!" the map said in a snooty tone.

"I haven't quite fixed all the bugs yet," Mr. Neptune said sheepishly. "Please, map."

He leaned back to Caleb and whispered, "The magic word is *please*, by the way."

A picture slowly formed on the screen. It was a doorway with a sign above it that said LAND OF DREAMERS.

"Daniel would never believe this," George said.

"So we're supposed to go to that Moor?" Caleb asked.

Mr. Neptune nodded. "You'll find the first of your three keys to Astria in the Land of Dreamers. Map, off."

The map faded out and clicked off.

"Every time you turn the map off, it locks again. You'll have to reenter the combination whenever you wish to use it." He gave the map to Mikal, who held it reverently in both hands.

"Thank you, Mr. Neptune, for all of your help, but we really have to get going now," George said as she started for the door.

"What? Yes, of course you must be on your way, as must I."

"You? Where are you going?" Caleb asked.

"To the safest place of all! Where no one knows!" He ruffled Mikal's hair, grabbed a suitcase, gave a jaunty wave, and disappeared into the closet.

Mikal scowled and attempted to smooth his hair back down.

George shook her head. "Come on, we don't have much time."

They left through the door they had entered, and shut it tightly behind them.

A MOST UNPLEASANT GIFT

CHAPTER NINE

THE CHILDREN STOOD ON MR. NEPTUNE'S doorstep as the traffic rushed by.

"Any idea where to start?" George asked.

"Mr. Neptune said we would find our first key to Astria in the Land of Dreamers, which has to be through one of these Moors," Caleb said.

"Then we'll just ask some Touries to take us there," George said, hailing three.

The children mounted their rides carefully and then stated their destination.

"Daniel would love this," George said as they drifted through the orderly traffic. "He's obsessed with airplanes and magic carpets. He'd go bonkers for flying doors. I'll have to bring him down here when I find him."

"But the Mapmaker said there are dangerous people about," Mikal said nervously.

"Speaking of, look at that," Caleb said as they passed several dark tunnels leading off to the right. "I wonder where those lead."

"Those are the rough neighborhoods," George's Tourie said. "If you want to go there, you had better get a different ride, because I won't take you. That's a bad place."

They passed through several intersections before coming to a stop in front of a lilac Moor. The sign above declared 3RD DIMENSION, THURSDAY, APRIL 5, 5:17 PM DWT, LAND OF DREAMERS.

Caleb dismounted first and offered George and Mikal each a hand as they climbed off their Touries and onto the doorstep.

"Are you okay, Mikal?" George asked, noticing he looked a bit jostled.

Mikal clutched his stomach. “I’m okay. I just wish we could walk instead of ride.”

“It’ll probably get easier the more we do it,” George said as she rang the doorbell.

The Moor responded immediately in a feminine voice. “If you are not sleeping, you do not belong here. Go away.”

The children exchanged an uncertain look.

“This is our stop. I say we go for it,” Caleb said.

George nodded, took a deep breath, and stepped through the door into a dark rolling meadow. Rows and rows of little cots stretched as far as one could see, rising and falling with the hills. Two fat yellow moons hung overhead, and the air was warm and smelled of freshly washed linen. It was perfectly quiet but for the occasional snore and mumble coming from one of the many figures resting beneath their covers. Despite the fact that it was obviously nighttime in this world, it was surprisingly bright out.

“Look at that,” Caleb said, gesturing upward.

Stars were streaking across the sky in a frenzy of trailing lights.

“They’re even worse than last night,” George said.

“Do you think they’ll hit us and smash us into the dirt?” Mikal asked nervously.

“Don’t worry, Mikal,” George said, placing a hand on

his narrow shoulder. "It's still only the fifth night. We have two more days. We should be okay."

"If you say so. . . ."

"How about we find whoever's in charge here. They might be able to tell us where to look for our first key to Astria," Caleb said.

"I don't see anyone who isn't sleeping," Mikal said, squinting through the darkness.

"Me either, and I'd rather not disturb them," George said, and then tried to smother a yawn behind her hand. "This place is making me feel tired."

"It makes me feel . . . weird," Caleb said. "I don't like it. Let's break out the map. Maybe it can lead us to a supervisor or president or something." He took the map from Mikal and removed the linen wrapping. Then they each entered their numbers. "Map, turn on." When nothing happened, he looked at George and Mikal.

"Try tapping it, maybe?" George said.

Caleb thumped it soundly on the side, and it hummed on.

"I said tap it, not hit it!"

"It worked, didn't it?" Caleb asked.

Red words blinked threateningly against the white screen. *The time is now 5:25 PM DWT. You currently have 53 hours, 46 minutes until certain death."*

Mikal sighed at this and shook his head. "He isn't very cheerful, is he?"

"Map, where do we go to find someone in charge?" Caleb asked.

"Why should I tell you?" the map asked churlishly.

George glanced around in alarm. "Shh! Not so loud!"

"Keep your voice down. We don't want to wake anyone up," Caleb told the map.

"Why don't we?!" the map asked.

The children looked at each other.

"Yeah, why don't we want to wake anyone up?" Caleb asked.

Mikal scratched behind one ear. "Maybe they're cranky when they get woken up?"

"Because it would be inconsiderate," George said nervously as the sleepers began to stir. "Can you please help us? We need you."

"Really?" it asked, screen turning pink with delight. "Why?"

Mikal rocked back and forth on his heels, obviously thrilled to be having a conversation with a talking map. "Because you're the only one who knows where we're going or how to get there."

"I suppose that's true," the map said. "But that means

I'm important, and if that's the case, there are going to have to be some changes!"

"What kind of changes?" Mikal asked.

"For starters, I'm tired of being referred to as *map*. I have a name, you know."

"Mr. Neptune didn't tell us that. What is your name?" George asked.

"Hmm. Perhaps I don't *actually* have a name."

"We don't have time for this," Caleb said, glancing at the meteors above.

"Make time! I'm important!"

"What would you like us to call you?" George asked.

"No. I'm not telling you until *he* apologizes for rushing me," the map said.

Caleb's mouth dropped open in disbelief. "Apologize to something that runs on batteries? You've got to be kidding me."

The map gasped. "I do *not* run on batteries!"

"Really?" George asked. "What do you run on? Solar power?"

"Try to stay focused, George," Caleb said.

"I just thought Daniel would want to know. He's a total geek for all things techy. But I think you'd better apologize to the map. We do need him."

"Okay, okay. Sorry," he said, and then added very quietly, "that you run on batteries."

"I heard that!" the map shouted, causing the dreamers to stir and toss in their beds.

"Shh!" Caleb whispered, shoving agitated fingers through his hair. "That was the last one, I promise."

"All right then," the map said. "Now you must pick a name for me. I can't do it myself. A person cannot choose their own name."

"I chose my own name," Caleb said nonchalantly. "I liked the sound of it."

"That solves it! You must give me a name I like the sound of."

"Okay. How about Mary?" George asked.

"Mary? That's a girl's name! I am not a girl."

"You're an inanimate object, and the height of technology," George said. "You're not a boy or a girl."

"That's true . . . but I don't want a girl's name."

"Okay. What about Cavendish? He was an explorer, and you're a map. It works on some weird level, and it sounds very dignified."

"Caaaavendishhh," the map said. "Hmm. I think I like that!"

Caleb sighed with relief. "Cavendish it is."

"And who might the three of you be?"

"That's Caleb. The girl is George. I'm Mikal, and it's very nice to meet you." Mikal's black eyes were wide and sincere.

"How splendid. I'm Cavendish!" he said proudly.

"Yeah. We know," Caleb said. "So, Cavendish, we need to find whoever's in charge here so they can tell us where to locate a key to Astria. Can you help with that?"

"No. Definitely not. The person in charge is the Keeper of Dreams, and from what I've read, you do *not* want to vex her."

"Who is the Keeper of Dreams?" Mikal asked.

"The person who looks after the Dreamers, and I wouldn't want to be you if she catches you in here. She'd probably set your shoes on fire, with you still in them."

"Well, that's just delightful," George said. "Do you know anything else that might help? For starters, what is this place?"

"It's the Land of Dreamers, goofball," Cavendish said.

"That isn't very nice," George said.

"Okay, okay," Cavendish said. "Slightly longer version it is. This world is filled with Dreamers. They can be human, beast, or any type of creature who is capable of dreaming, because their purpose is to dream of the most wonderful things. Their dreams become your dreams, and as a result, you come up with all of the astounding things that make life grand. The dreams are eventually recycled, and the Dreamers dream them again for another person. So, there's that."

"That's good to know," Mikal said. "Anything else?"

"I'm getting to it! Just give me a moment to access the Door Way's daily newspaper. It should give us the most up-to-date information. Searching, searching. Here we go. Oh my. Well, that's off-putting."

"What is it?" George asked.

"Apparently, the Dreamers have been besieged. It says here that a horrible monster has invaded this world and begun wreaking havoc."

"Why would a monster do that?" Mikal asked.

"What am I, a psychiatrist? Why would a monster do anything monstrous?"

"The poor Dreamers," George said. "Maybe we should try to help them."

"We're on a tight schedule," Caleb said. "I'd like to get out of this place as fast as we can. It gives me the creeps."

"All right, maybe next time," George said. "It's too bad Cavendish can't just guide us right to the key."

"Oh, I could do that. But that isn't what you asked,"

Cavendish said. "Didn't my programmer tell you I've been equipped with a detection device that attracts me to items made from the iron sands of a forgotten beach in a long-lost world? That's what the keys to Astria are made from, you know. I could locate one within a hundred yards or so." He sounded very smug.

"No, he didn't mention anything like that," Caleb said.

"But it's very convenient. Would you please take us to find the key to Astria, Cavendish?" George asked.

"Absolutely!" Cavendish said. "But first, what's the magic word?"

"Please?" George said.

"Not you! I was asking *him*."

Caleb folded his arms over his chest and raised one silver eyebrow.

"Just get it over with, Caleb," George said.

"I'm not doooing it withouuutt the magic wooooOOOrrddd," Cavendish sang, his voice screeching on the high notes as he imitated an opera singer.

Caleb held up his hands to shush the map. "Shh! Okay, fine. Just keep it down. I don't want you to draw attention to us. Cavendish, will you show us the way . . . please?"

"Absolutely. But I can't just point to it, numbskull. You have to spin me around! Then when I locate the route and the picture starts to move, follow it."

Caleb started spinning in a circle.

"Not so fast!" Cavendish said.

Caleb slowed, and the picture moved forward. He stopped in surprise.

"Don't stop, birdbrain. Now follow!"

"You're pushing it," Caleb said, but he began walking in a straight line between two rows of cots, leaving a trail in the dew-dampened grass. He was careful to stay as far from the sleeping Dreamers as possible. "Stay close, guys. And don't get too near the beds. I have a bad feeling about them." His voice had a strange edge to it that neither George nor Mikal had heard before.

"You're right to be afraid," Cavendish said cheerfully. "That's where the Nightmares live, underneath the beds. If you're not careful, they'll reach out and grab you and drag you away, never to be seen again. They'll eat you right up, bones and all."

"The . . . Nightmares?" Mikal asked, going a bit pale around the edges.

"Yes. The Dreamers don't only have good dreams. They have bad ones too. That's okay, as long as they stay asleep. But sometimes a Dreamer has a particularly frightening dream and will wake up from the terror of it. That transports the Nightmare to this world and traps it here, which makes it very angry. The Keeper runs a tight ship, so she makes them live under the beds. They have to do what she says. I suppose she likes having them around, though, as they make a marvelously effective army against intruders."

"We're intruders," Mikal whispered.

"That must be how the monster got here, by being dreamed as a Nightmare," Caleb said.

Cavendish continued. "Of course. It wasn't always like this, but many of the worlds changed following the breaking of the Council of Seven, some for their own protection and some just because now they could get away with it."

"I wonder which one this is," Caleb said.

"Do you have any pointers on how to deal with a monster, Cavendish? Just in case," George said.

"Pointer number one, don't be food. Unfortunately, you are food, so that doesn't do you any good. At least I'll be okay. What monster would eat me when there's child flesh to be had?"

"Mr. Neptune really dropped the ball when programming your people skills," Caleb said.

THEY HAD WALKED FOR AGES AND STILL seemed no closer to finding a key. They had passed out of the meadow and were now skirting a dark forest that smelled of pine and woodsmoke.

"Maybe Cavendish is buggy?" George asked when they stopped to rest.

"Buggy?!" Cavendish said in a high-pitched voice. "I know exactly where I'm going!"

"Shh," Caleb hissed, clapping his hands over the map's speakers.

Mikal tugged on Caleb's sleeve and pointed to a series of huge footprints leading off through the trees. "It looks like a trail."

"That's the way the map says we have to go," Caleb said. "And if I had to guess, I'd say those were monster tracks."

Mikal squeaked a little and darted behind Caleb.

"Yep, monster tracks," George said. "You guys don't have to come any farther if you don't want to. I can go on by myself to find the key. . . ." But she looked at them hopefully.

"We're not supposed to get separated," Mikal said as he threw a longing glance over his shoulder, back the way they had come.

"I already told you, George, we're not leaving you," Caleb said, but there were beads of sweat on his forehead.

She breathed a sigh of relief and led the way down the path.

The trees thinned, and a clearing appeared before them. They reached the open space, and the picture stopped moving.

"Well? Where is it?" George asked.

"Look," Mikal said, his voice quavering as he pointed to the forest on the other side of the clearing.

Trees were mangled, their trunks splintered and tossed about. The enormous prints led off in that direction. It was so quiet you could almost hear the falling of pine needles.

Then the silence was broken by a great roar that crashed over the children, causing them to jump with fright. The ground trembled, and leaves fluttered down from the trees above them.

"Heavens to Betsy," George said, wiping clammy hands on her skirt.

"I think we found the monster," Mikal said in a choked voice.

Caleb just stood trembling, his face as gray as his hair.

They huddled together, their knees quivering like jelly, as the roaring came nearer.

Across the clearing, an enormous creature emerged from the thick trees, leaves swirling around it like a tornado as it thrashed through the underbrush, destroying everything in its path.

CHAPTER TEN

THE LEAVES SLOWLY SETTLED, ALLOWING them to see the monstrous beast. It was as wide as all of them put together. It had enormous red eyes, and its jagged fangs dripped foaming saliva. Its arms were long, knuckles almost brushing the ground, and on top of its head it had two squiggly antennae that spun madly. It was made only slightly less frightening by the fact that it was covered in curly purple hair, and hanging from its forehead was a bright red accordion. When the monster noticed the children, it stopped in its tracks and stood absolutely still.

The children took a horrified step backward, and the monster lunged at them, curling its lips to reveal more of those wickedly sharp teeth. With a trainlike bellow, it charged.

George's eyes widened in terror, and she screamed, "Run! It's going to kill us!"

"No! You mustn't run! It's an Ooglah! If you run, he'll chase you!" Cavendish said frantically, trying to raise his voice over the clamor.

Before they could decide whether to flee or not, the monster turned and flopped onto the ground. It buried its face in its massive hands and started to make a hideous heaving sound.

The children stood still, afraid to move as it continued to ignore them.

"Holy fire and hippos," Mikal said. He gripped Caleb's arm hard enough to leave marks.

George swallowed and pressed her lips together. "You can say that again."

"Can we run yet?" Caleb blinked as nervous sweat dripped into his eyes.

"Wait," George said. "Just a minute. I think it's . . . is it crying?"

"No, it couldn't be. It's an Ooglah. They don't cry," Cavendish said.

"I think it is crying," George said. "What's an Ooglah?"

"Why should I tell you?"

"If you don't, I'll tell it you said rude things about its mother," Caleb said.

Cavendish sighed. "An Ooglah is a special kind of monster. They're rare. Only the unluckiest of people ever meet one. They live in a world called OooLaGul. They're family oriented and eat shellfish and carrots and the occasional small child. This Ooglah is male, and around a hundred seventeen years old, I'd say, judging by the rotation of his antennae. That's young for them, by the way."

"You're so smart," George said. "I can't wait for you to meet my little brother, Daniel."

"My programmer gave me an encyclopedia program," Cavendish said boastfully. "But I did take a little creative freedom. The child-eating part is just a myth. It's never been proven."

Mikal relaxed ever so slightly upon hearing this, but he still trembled with fear.

"They're normally more intimidating. I've never heard of a purple Ooglah, or one with something like that hanging from its forehead, for that matter," Cavendish said.

The Ooglah continued to weep. He looked back at them over his shoulder, causing them to jump in surprise and huddle together. He sniffed and started sobbing again, louder than ever.

"What do you think is wrong with him?" Mikal asked.

"Beats me. They don't have feelings," Cavendish said.

"I think most things have feelings," Caleb said.

"Shows what you know," Cavendish said.

"Maybe we should try to help him," George said.

"Why in the Flyrrey would you want to do that?" Cavendish asked, obviously appalled.

"He's right, George," Mikal said. "It sounds risky."

"But he seems so sad. Besides, you're getting braver, remember?"

Mikal took a deep breath, but he didn't look completely convinced when George left the little group and began easing nearer to the beast.

"Jeez, Georgina!" Caleb said. "Are you crazy? Come back here!"

"She's not gonna listen," Mikal said, shifting back and forth on his feet.

"Oh, let her go. He probably needs a good meal," Cavendish said. "While he's feasting on her, we can run away."

"If it eats her, I'll feed you to it next," Caleb said.

Cavendish made an exaggerated gulping sound.

Caleb shoved both hands through his hair, the distress plain on his face. "Aw, jeez. Come on, we're going with her."

"Of course we are," Mikal groaned, but he didn't dawdle as he followed behind.

George crept closer and closer. The smell of crushed grass filled the air as she came to a stop near the front of the behemoth.

"Excuse me?" she asked, but her voice only came out as a hoarse whisper. She cleared her throat and tried again. "Pardon me, but are you all right?"

The Ooglah glanced up at her and sniffed loudly, causing the accordion to make a horrible musical sound. He then shuffled and scooted around, putting his back to her again.

George frowned and moved to stand directly in front of him. "You shouldn't ignore someone when she's speaking to you. It's very rude."

The Ooglah gazed at her through watery eyes. He blinked, hiccupped, and then sighed.

"That's better. Do you think you can settle something for us?"

The Ooglah tilted his head to the side and looked at her curiously.

"We were just trying to decide whether your kind has feelings. I'm pretty sure you do, or else you wouldn't be crying. You are crying, aren't you?"

Caleb and Mikal had been sneaking up behind the Ooglah, on their way to rescue George, when leaves crunched beneath Caleb's feet.

The Ooglah jerked his head in their direction and curled back his lips, hissing threateningly before scooting closer to George.

The boys stopped dead at the sight of his long ivory teeth.

"Stay back, he's about to talk to me," George said. "You are going to talk to me, right?"

"Ha! Ooglahs don't talk. They're notoriously stupid!" Cavendish said.

"Keep him quiet, Mikal," Caleb said through gritted teeth.

The Ooglah spoke then, and his voice was thin and

reedy. "My name is Thazel," he rasped. "We *do* have feelings, and we are *not* stupid." He shot a dirty look at Cavendish.

"Well, of course *he* doesn't think he's stupid," Cavendish said.

"Cavendish! Hush!" George said. "Now, why are you crying, Thazel?"

He sniffed and looked down. With a long claw he traced patterns in the dirt.

"Well? What could a strapping young monster like you have to cry about?"

"It's the Dreamers." He gestured vaguely over his shoulder with one hand, and the boys ducked as it whooshed toward them. "One of them dreamed about me when I was in OooLaGul. I was just fishing for carrots and minding my own business, but the Dreamer must have thought I was scary, because suddenly I had this horrible thing hanging from my face where my nose used to be." He pointed sadly to the red accordion dangling from his forehead. "That's what they do, you know, dream silly things onto monsters to make them less intimidating. But it must not have worked, because the next thing I heard was this terrible crying sound, and here I was! The Dreamer had woken up from fright and turned me into a Nightmare.

Now I'm trapped here, and I look so ridiculous that none of the other Ooglahs will ever take me seriously again."

George inspected him carefully. "I don't think you look ridiculous. The nose isn't that bad. It's just different. I'm different too. So are they." She gestured at Caleb and Mikal.

"How are you different?"

"I'm really small for my age," Mikal said, moving just a bit closer.

"I have hundreds of freckles," George said, settling into the grass beside Thazel. "Hundreds of them!"

"And I have this weird silver hair," Caleb said, pointing at his head.

"Er, Caleb?" Mikal said. "It isn't silver anymore. It's turning purple, like Thazel's. So are George's freckles, and look, my suspenders are too!"

"You've got to be kidding me," Caleb said, and tried in vain to see his own hair.

George touched her fingertips to her cheeks as if she could feel the tiny specks changing color. "Well, I guess now we're all different together."

"What about me? Check me! Am I different too?" Cavendish asked.

"No, sorry, Cavendish," Mikal said. "No purple anywhere."

Cavendish sighed his disappointment.

"I used to be green before I got here," Thazel said.

"Every world leaves a mark on the people of it. Even the Loeta who pass through. The mark usually fades after they've left, and sometimes it's not visible at all," Cavendish said.

"What are the Loeta?" George asked.

"*Loeta* means strangers from different worlds," Thazel said. "I'm Loeta in the Land of Dreamers. So are you. We don't belong here."

"I feel like that everywhere," Caleb muttered under his breath.

"It's the worst thing about being dreamed into this place," Thazel said with a heartbroken sob. "I want to go home! I miss my family, and I don't like it here. It's terrifying and full of Nightmares. When I first came here, the Keeper of Dreams made me live under the bed with those horrible creatures. I was too scared to stay there, so I ran away. But the Keeper didn't like me disobeying her, and she's hunting me with her wicked beasts!"

Caleb tugged uncomfortably at his collar.

"I miss my family too," George said, offering Thazel a handkerchief.

His hand dwarfed the small square of linen, but he blew solidly into it. The hanky dissolved under the pressure, causing him to splatter the boys with slimy lavender snot.

The boys yelped and jumped back, shaking themselves loose of the dripping substance.

George bit the inside of her cheek to keep from laughing.

"You have got to be more careful with that thing," Caleb said, pointing to Thazel's accordion nose as he wiped his face on the sleeve of his shirt.

"Not only does it look silly, but it's messy too," Cavendish said, tired of being neglected and feeling left out from being the only one without a mark.

Thazel's chin quivered.

"Cavendish! That's a mean thing to say," George said.

"He's just jealous we're not paying attention to him," Caleb said.

"I am not jealous!" Cavendish said, his screen transitioning from green to an angry red.

"It's okay, Cavendish. We still need you," Mikal said, patting the map affectionately.

Cavendish didn't say anything, but his screen faded into bashful pink.

"Thazel," George said, "how would you like it if we helped you get home?"

Thazel's eyes widened with hope. "I would like that so much. But how? The Keeper is hunting me to put me back under the beds, and the Nightmares are prowling."

"And we still have to find the key, George," Caleb said. "It must be close by; Cavendish said he can locate them within a hundred yards, and we're kind of in a hurry. Time, Cavendish?"

"The time is now seven fifty PM DWT. You currently have fifty-one hours and twenty-one minutes until you're smashed to smithereens. I say leave the monster and find the key."

"I don't like to agree with Cavendish, but that isn't much time at all to save the worlds from being destroyed, George. What about our mission?" Caleb asked.

"And Aunt Henrietta?" Mikal asked.

George fidgeted with the ends of her scarf. "Our mission is important. You know how badly I want to rescue Aunt Henrietta. But we can't leave Thazel here all alone. It would be wrong. It wouldn't be leaving this world better than it was when we got here. I think Aunt Henrietta would want me to help him. Daniel would. Daniel always wants to help everybody."

"Daniel must know the code," Mikal said. "We must do what we can, for those we can, when we can."

Caleb heaved a sigh of defeat. "Okay, you guys win. We'll keep Thazel with us while we search for the key, and then take him home after we've found it."

Thazel breathed an excited musical note. "I'm so

happy! I wish it was one of my keys you needed, and then you could take me home right now. I'm afraid if we stay here too much longer, the Keeper will find us."

"Your keys?" Mikal asked.

Thazel nodded, and his long nose flopped up and down. "I have lots. It's my job. I'm the Keyholder of OooLaGul."

Caleb's eyebrows shot up. "You, uh, don't happen to have a key to Astria, do you?"

Thazel reached up with his long arms and pulled over his head a necklace that had been hidden in his shaggy fur. Hundreds of keys hung from it, and they all looked very much alike, but Thazel instantly selected one that was made of a darker metal than the rest. He tugged at it three precise times and the links began to twitch and separate, for the chain was made of a myriad of golden spiders, their legs securely interlocking with one another.

"This is my family's personal key to Astria. It's been passed down for generations and generations. But we never lose anything, so we don't need it. You can have it, if you like."

George took the key reverently as the spiders reclosed the gap. "Thazel . . . you have no idea what this means to us."

"You're a lifesaver, Thazel," Caleb said.

Thazel looked very pleased with himself.

"I told you I knew where I was taking you!" Cavendish said.

"And you got closer than a hundred yards too! You're really good," Mikal said.

George got to her feet. "Yes, you did very well, Cavendish. Now let's get Thazel home."

Thazel clambered up, and the children stepped back to avoid his swinging arms.

George began walking back toward the Dreaming meadow. She stopped and turned when she realized Thazel wasn't following. She held out her hand to him, and he took it gently, his enormous purple mitts swallowing half of her arm.

"Lumbering oaf," Cavendish said.

"Go fly a kite, Cavendish," George said.

"Fly a kite," Thazel echoed.

"Why, I never!" Cavendish said, affronted.

"Everyone hush," Caleb said. "We need to be quiet if we're going to get Thazel out of here without being caught. I don't know if you've noticed, but he's kind of hard to miss, and the idea of tangling with those Nightmares makes me sick to my stomach."

They moved slowly to keep Thazel's enormous feet

from cracking branches and making a ruckus, and it took much longer for them to reach the place where they had first entered the woods than they had expected. The warm air had thickened, and the children were sweating when they stopped for a rest at the edge of the meadow.

George pushed the hair off her damp forehead and saw the trail they had made in the dew-dampened grass on their way to meet the monster. "At least we'll be able to find our way out."

"It's still going to take forever. Now we'll have to move even slower, since we're so close to the Dreamers," Caleb said.

"Maybe there's a shortcut," Mikal said. "Is there, Cavendish?"

Cavendish didn't reply, except to begin making a high-pitched beeping noise: *"Neep neep neep NEEP NEEP NEEP."*

"Cavendish, stop it!" George said. "You're too loud!"

"Turn off his speakers, Mikal! Do something!" Caleb said.

"I don't know what to do! I can't find his speakers. Cavendish, please stop!"

Thazel grabbed the map and held it against his furry stomach, muffling the noise until it faded away entirely.

"That was way too close," Caleb said.

"Why would you do that, Cavendish?" Mikal asked as Thazel handed the map back.

Cavendish whispered something so quietly Mikal had to lean close to hear it.

All the color drained from Mikal's face. "He says to run. . . ."

But then George lifted her arm and pointed a trembling finger to their right.

It was too late to run.

CHAPTER ELEVEN

THE WOMAN WAS TALL AND SLENDER. HER lavender hair was piled high atop her head, and her violet eyes cut through the night with a furious purple fire. That fierce gaze alone knocked the breath from their lungs and left George and Company staring in mute terror at the individual who could only be the Keeper of Dreams.

She stood on a small rise, close enough to smell her

sweet perfume on the breeze. As the kids watched, inky shadows began to rise from the ground at her feet. The shadows groaned painfully as they swelled and stretched into gruesome forms. They grew darker and began to thrash and multiply until the Keeper seemed to be standing in the midst of a roiling black ocean.

"No." Caleb's whisper was raw with panic. "No, no, no. Not this."

The Keeper didn't say a word, just lifted one lovely hand and pointed to the children.

The Nightmares surged forward in utter silence, and that silence was more horrifying than a thousand blood-curdling screams.

Caleb stood in a trance, eyes blank and mouth hanging open.

Thazel started to cry and tried to hunker down as low to the ground as he could get.

"Go! Go now!" George pushed Mikal toward the Moor far in the distance.

Mikal held Cavendish tight and bolted away over the meadow.

George grabbed Thazel by the arm and pulled as hard as she could. "Thazel, get up! You have to run! Caleb! Caleb, help me!"

Caleb snapped out of his daze, looking wildly around

to find his friends. "What are you still doing here?" he yelled as his eyes fell on George. "You have to get away! You don't know what they'll do to you if they catch you!"

"Help me get Thazel up! Please, hurry!" George said as the Nightmares drew ever closer.

"Thazel, get up, right NOW!" Caleb shouted. "Or we'll leave you to the shadows!"

That was all Thazel needed to hear. With an enormous bellow, he rose to his feet and thundered after Mikal.

"Run!" Caleb shoved George forward, and they dashed away through the rows of sleeping Dreamers.

The noise was too much for the Dreamers, and as they awakened, their little voices cried out. Their screeching wails stabbed daggers of pain through the children's heads.

As Mikal reached up to cover his ears, Cavendish fell from his grasp and tumbled to the ground between two beds.

"Wait! Don't leave me!" Cavendish squawked. "Please come back!"

Mikal spun around, almost smacking straight into Thazel, but Caleb had already skidded to a halt to retrieve Cavendish.

George caught up to Mikal and Thazel just in time to hear a shriek filled with horror. Her heart faltered in her chest as she turned and saw Caleb thrashing violently on the ground in the grasp of a shadow so black it seemed to pull all light into it.

"I have to help him," Mikal said, but his feet were heavier than stone.

"No, I'll do it. You take Thazel and find the Moor. Go! We need a way out of here!" George shot back over the meadow toward Caleb.

Mikal stood paralyzed with fear, watching her go.

"I just want to go home," Thazel sobbed beside him. "I'm so scared."

"I'm not a coward. I'm not, I'm not," Mikal repeated softly to himself. He gritted his teeth, and a fire started in his toes and rose swiftly up his body until it burst out of his mouth in a triumphant yell. "I'M GETTING BRAVER!" He clutched at Thazel's enormous hand, and together they sprinted toward the Moor.

George reached the place where Cavendish had fallen, and found him lying askew and babbling to himself. "They can't leave me, I'm the map. It got him. Dragged him right away."

George laid eyes on Caleb just as the shadow was

pulling him under the bed. Only Caleb's face was still visible, and his fingers clawing at the grass as he struggled to escape the creature.

"Help me, George!" Caleb pleaded. "Please don't let it take me!" And then with a jerk, he vanished into the darkness.

"Caleb!" George screamed as she threw herself to the ground and grabbed desperately for him. But he wasn't there. "Caleb! I'm here! I won't let it take you!" She slithered halfway under the bed trying to reach him, and then her legs began to kick wildly. But she wasn't being dragged in. She was fighting her way out, and in both hands she held Caleb's bony wrists. She pulled and tugged and yelled at the shadow that fought her, until suddenly Caleb sprang free.

They scrambled to their feet just before the horde of Nightmares converged upon them.

George snatched Cavendish and turned to run, but slimy black fingers tangled in her hair and scarf. She turned and began bashing at the Nightmare, using Cavendish as her weapon.

Cavendish, though slender and only as square as a dictionary, still packed a mighty wallop.

"GET. AWAY. FROM. ME!" George shouted, landing a blow with every word.

"THIS ISN'T. WHAT I. WAS MADE. FOR," Cavendish shouted back.

Then Caleb wrapped his arms around George's waist and pulled her out of the Nightmare's grip, leaving her scarf behind in its inky hands.

They ran as fast as you can only when pursued by Nightmares.

They reached Mikal and Thazel at a dark wall covered with pulsing bits of light. Thazel was huddled on the ground whimpering, but Mikal was running his hands over every inch of the flat surface he could reach.

"The Moor is hidden in the wall!" Mikal said. "I can't find the handle!"

The children looked back at the Nightmares pouring toward them, and then at Mikal. Their faces were bleak.

Then a crack of light appeared in the wall, and Mikal let out a jubilant holler as the Moor to the Door Way opened.

George and Caleb each grabbed Thazel by one arm, and they burst out of the Land of Dreamers and into the light.

THE KIDS SLAMMED THE DOOR BEHIND THEM and stood on the step, gasping for breath.

"Well, that was . . . an adventure," George said. "You guys okay? Are you hurt, Caleb?"

Caleb brushed his hair out of his eyes and shook his head. "I'm . . . I'm okay. I just never want to go back there. Ever."

"I definitely prefer the cemetery," Mikal said. "Give me a dead body any day over . . ." He waved a hand at the door. "Whatever that was."

"I sure won't be bringing Daniel here. He'd never forgive me," George said. "What's the time, Cavendish? And what were you thinking, making all that noise?!"

"The time is now nine forty-seven PM DWT. You currently have forty-nine hours and twenty-four minutes until you're reduced to rubble. And I was just trying to warn you that danger was approaching! Is it my fault that my alarm was turned up so loud? Doesn't anyone care about me?" Cavendish asked pitifully. "I've had a very bad day! First you hit me, then you dropped me, then you left me! Then you used me to fight off a Nightmare! Oh, the abuse. I don't think I can stand any more."

George rolled her eyes and handed Cavendish to Mikal. "Turn him off, Mikal. He's right. He's had a hard day and needs some time to recover."

"Why, of all the rude, insensitive people I've ever met,

you are surely by far the worst! Imagine! Using me to fulfill your needs and then just turning me off whenever it suits you after heaping abuse on me! You just wait till I—"

Mikal gave Cavendish an apologetic look and clicked him off. The screen faded out.

"Now let's get Thazel home," Caleb said.

It took a moment for Thazel to stop weeping. Finally he hiccupped and looked around in dismay. "What *is* this place? I don't like it!"

"This is the Door Way," Caleb said. "It's the way we get from world to world. It's how we're going to get you home."

"We have to ride the Touries now," Mikal said forlornly.

"We don't like riding the Touries?" Thazel asked, noticing Mikal's reluctance.

"Mikal gets carsick, er, doorsick. The Touries aren't so bad. You just need to be able to keep your balance," Caleb said.

George called for four Touries to stop, but it was hard to find one big enough for Thazel.

Finally two brown doors and a huge garage door pulled up.

It took some coaxing, and Mikal had to agree to ride

with him, but finally they managed to get Thazel onto the garage door.

George's brown Tourie informed the children that they would be unable to access OooLaGul without a special password.

"Do you know the password, Thazel?" George asked.

"Technically you need two passwords," the Tourie said. "One to get me to take you there and one to access the world."

Thazel scrunched up his face, deep in thought. Then he grinned. "I think I do! It's OooLaGul!"

"Rightie-oh, then. You heard the monster. Let's get him home."

"That isn't a very creative password. What if someone guessed it?" George asked.

"Why would anyone want to guess? Who wants to visit monsters?" Thazel asked.

Caleb chuckled. "I guess that it doesn't have to be creative when you put it like that."

They continued on until they came to a large steel-vault Moor. It was thick and heavy and looked like it belonged in a high-security bank.

"Is this it?" Thazel asked.

"According to my directions manual, it could be no other," the door said.

They dismounted and walked Thazel to his doorstep.

"It was nice meeting you, Thazel," Caleb said.

"It really was, and thank you again for the key," George said. "Oh, look! Your fur is turning silver, Thazel. And your hair has faded back to normal, Caleb. Are my freckles still purple?"

"No, they've faded to silver too," Caleb said. "So have Mikal's suspenders."

"That's slightly better, I guess," George said. "And you look very handsome in gray, Thazel. I'm sorry we couldn't help you with the nose problem. I hope it doesn't cause you too much trouble."

"I think I've decided I like being different," Thazel said. He then blew a rippling musical note out of the dangling accordion. "It makes pretty noise."

George laughed, and Thazel looked down bashfully.

"And now I have a mark that shows I survived the Land of Dreamers, just like you three."

"Not me," Caleb said. "My hair was already like this, so I don't have a mark."

"Maybe you've been to the Land of Dreamers before and that's when your hair first turned silver," Thazel said. "But I should be going. I'm eager to get home. Thank you for helping me. I don't know that anyone else would have."

"I think they would, because you're a good monster,

Thazel," Mikal said, holding Cavendish with one hand and his stomach with the other.

Thazel reached for the door handle but paused. "There was something strange in the Land of Dreamers that I forgot to tell you. The whole time I was stuck there, all of the Dreamers had the very same dream, night after night. Geese riding bicycles. Doesn't that seem odd to you? I don't know. Maybe that's a normal kind of dream for unmonsters."

"No," George said. "That does seem odd."

"Pretty weird," Caleb said.

Thazel turned to the door and mumbled the second password. "Thazel Thooflebottom."

Mikal giggled, and George elbowed him in the ribs as Thazel stepped through the Moor into OooLaGul.

GEORGE TOOK A DEEP BREATH. "NOW WHAT?"

"Now we sleep," Caleb said.

"Now we eat," Mikal said at the same time.

George grinned. "Both super good ideas. Which one first, though?"

"I say we find a place to make camp," Caleb said. "And then we can eat there."

Mikal groaned and looked longingly at the backpack

containing the food. "But it's been such a long time since breakfast. Long enough I can wait a little longer, I guess."

"Where do we camp?" George asked.

"How about we find out where we're going next? Maybe there will be somewhere safe to sleep," Caleb said.

Mikal's eyes brightened, and, hunger forgotten for the moment, he fired up Cavendish.

Cavendish's screen faded in light blue. "Are you still mad at me?" he asked timidly. "Because I can refuse to come on, you know!"

"Nobody is mad at you," Mikal said.

"Super! Now, what are we up to this fine evening?" Cavendish asked.

"We need to know our next destination," Caleb said.

"Ah, I see. And how's that working out for you?"

"It isn't, really, because you're the map and the only one who knows it," Caleb said.

"Hmm, I see, I see. That is indeed a problem."

"We were hoping you could tell us where we're heading," George said.

"Well, I suppose I could. Since you asked so nicely and all. Hmm. It appears you're headed for the District of Dragons, the Blue Planet, to be specific."

"I think I'd normally be more alarmed by that whole District of *Dragons* thing, but I'm way too tired right now," George said.

"And I'm too hungry," Mikal said.

"And I've always wanted to see a dragon," Caleb said, cautiously mounting a passing Tourie.

George and Mikal shared a Tourie, and as they settled down for the ride, George took a quick count. "Three for backpack, four for Caleb, five for Mikal. Nothing's missing."

"Hey! What about me? Don't I get counted?" Cavendish asked from Mikal's arms.

George shook her head. "Sorry, Cavendish, but I can't."

"Whyever not? Am I less important than a backpack?"

"Of course not. But you're not . . . mine. You know? So I can't count you."

"I see. And how would someone become yours? Not that I'm asking for me! I'm curious, is all."

"I'm not sure. It just happens. It's like someone sneaks up and ties one end of an invisible string to my stomach and the other end to my special people or things. It makes them mine, and then I can count them."

By now they had arrived at an orange door that was

slightly singed around the edges. A sign above it read 3RD DIMENSION, THURSDAY APRIL 5, 10:21 PM DWT DISTRICT OF DRAGONS: BLUE PLANET.

Caleb remarked on the impressive size of the doorstep and argued that it would be a good place to spend the night, until Mikal pointed out that it was probably so big to accommodate the dragons who lived within.

"Oh, they don't travel much," Cavendish reassured the kids. "Though the Engineer probably planned it that way when he created the Door Way. As long as you stay together, the Drifters probably won't bother you, and you'll be safer sleeping on the dragons' doorstep than inside their world."

"And there's the added bonus that we don't have to worry about being flattened by falling stars in here," George said.

Once they had agreed to stay put, the children dug out the leftovers from the previous night and ate ravenously.

Mikal propped Cavendish up against a backpack, and George and Caleb sat with their legs dangling off the ledge as they feasted on peanut butter sandwiches and cold grilled cheese sandwiches.

"Cavendish," Caleb said around a mouthful of peanut

butter, "you said the Engineer created the Door Way. That's the same Engineer from the Council of Seven, right?"

"Of course, dummy. How many engineers do you think there are who could create something this complex? None, that's how many. In fact, there's not a single person alive today who knows how he did it—not even his daughter. Nobody can figure out what keeps the Touries afloat, let alone how he managed to connect all of the worlds to a single place. Not even my programmer, and he's marvelously brilliant."

"What do you mean, keep the Touries afloat?" George asked. "Isn't there something under there that keeps them up and moving? Like tracks or rails?"

"Nope. Not a thing. The only thing under the doors is a great big nothing. An abyss, a void. You fall, you die."

"Wow, that's amazing. And kind of scary. Are you okay, Mikal?" George asked, noticing he had gone pale, and his mouth was hanging open and full of half-chewed sandwich.

Mikal blinked twice and then scooted back as quickly as he could, pressing himself against the orange door. He pulled his knees up to his chest and looked around wildly.

George glanced at Caleb, who also had stopped eating. "What's going on?"

"Please," Mikal said, his voice raspy and dry. "Please, come away from the edge."

Caleb responded at once, moving carefully away from the drop-off and closer to Mikal. "It's okay, Mikal. We're okay. George, will you please come over here? Slowly?"

"What in the Flyrrey are you on about?" Cavendish asked. "Are we under attack?!"

George did as Caleb asked, bringing the backpacks and Cavendish with her. "What's wrong, Mikal?" she asked, her brow furrowing with concern as she settled beside him.

Caleb had his arm around Mikal's shoulders and was talking to him so quietly George couldn't make out what he was saying. He looked up at George and gave a half smile. "Sorry to be weird, but Mikal has a thing about heights."

George reached out and took Mikal's clammy hand in both of hers. "Oh. It's okay, Mikal," she murmured. "Can I help at all?"

"A thing about heights? Is he afraid?" Cavendish asked. "Is this some kind of human problem? Are your fuses shorting? Logically, we are too far away from the edge to fall, which makes your fear irrational. My programmer didn't give me a protocol for this kind of nonsense."

Mikal said nothing, only huddled as close as he could against the door frame.

"I don't think it's something you can understand, Cavendish," Caleb said.

"But I *want* to understand!" Cavendish said.

It must have been the sincerity in his artificial voice that caused George to try to explain. "It *is* a human problem. Sometimes we just get scared. Logic has nothing to do with it."

"Yeah," Caleb said. "Like I'm scared to death of those things in the Land of Dreamers, and being in tight spaces gives me the heebie-jeebies."

George looked down at her lap. "Goldfish . . . I'm not saying I'm afraid of them! They just make me nervous. . . ."

"GOLDFISH? Ha. *I'm* not scared of anything," Cavendish said. "Except . . . perhaps . . . water. Water makes my circuits quiver." His screen faded pink at this admission.

"M-maybe it's not such a human problem after all, then," Mikal said.

"Do you think you can sleep, Mikal?" Caleb asked.

Mikal shook his head violently back and forth.

"What if we make your bed right here, as far from the side as possible?" George asked. "We'll sleep next to you to make sure you don't roll off, okay?"

"No!" Mikal said. "What if you fall off?"

"We won't, Mikal. In fact, I bet that if we fell asleep and got too close to the edge, Cavendish would let us know. Wouldn't you, Cavendish?" Caleb asked.

"You want *me* to keep watch?" Cavendish asked, surprised.

"If you're up to it," Caleb said. "And while you're at it, you could let us know if any of those Drifters show up."

"Oh, I am. I AM up to it!" Cavendish said.

Mikal nodded reluctantly, and George helped him make a pallet.

Caleb made his bed between his friend and the drop into the void.

George arranged her blankets at Mikal's head, and he squeezed his eyes shut, clutching Cavendish to his chest.

Cavendish, for a reason perhaps not entirely unhuman, kept up a steady stream of quiet chatter, and soon Mikal was snoring, secure in the knowledge that his friends would keep him safe.

"Caleb?" George asked softly. "Are you still awake?"

"Sure am," Caleb said. "What's up?"

"Can you tell me what that was about?"

Caleb didn't say anything.

"If it isn't too personal, I mean," she said, embarrassed.

"Remember how Mikal was an acrobat when we traveled with the circus?" Caleb asked. "And his dad was too, before he died?"

"Yeah, I remember."

"His dad was really good, and taught Mikal how to be really good. He and Mikal were doing a show together when his dad fell. That's how he was killed. That's the real reason why the circus left us. Mikal saw his dad die, and he couldn't go back up again. The people in charge figured we weren't worth the trouble if Mikal couldn't perform, especially without his dad to look after us."

George's throat was too tight to say anything.

"He was a good man. When Mikal found me wandering around half starved, his dad took me in and treated me like I was his boy too. *Truly* his. That's why I'll take care of Mikal for him, no matter what," Caleb said, sounding fierce and not at all like the laid-back boy George had met.

"Why were you wandering?" George asked.

"Dunno," Caleb said. "I don't even know how old I really am. Mikal's dad thought I looked to be around nine when he took me in, but I had no idea who I was, or even where I was. I'll find out someday, though. I have to. G'night, George."

"Good night, Caleb." She was still for a moment but then removed Toad from under her head, where she had been using him as a pillow. She tucked Toad into Mikal's arms next to Cavendish and lay back down. "Three for Toad, four for backpack, five for Caleb, six for Mikal. Nothing's missing," she whispered to herself.

"Ahem," Cavendish said softly.

George hesitated.

Cavendish sighed.

George broke.

"Seven for Cavendish," she said. "Nothing's missing."

"That's right," Cavendish said. "That's right."

CHAPTER TWELVE

CALEB TOSSED AND TURNED LONG AFTER the others were asleep. Suddenly he sat up and threw his hands in the air. "That's it. Can't sleep. No use trying. Need me to take over, Cavendish?"

"Don't be ridiculous. I happen to be doing a very good job. Don't you trust me?"

"I just thought you'd want a break. Maybe take a nap. If you sleep, that is. Do you?"

"I don't want a break, and no, I don't sleep. Do you?"

Caleb rubbed at his face. "No. Not really. Not for as long as I can remember."

Then they chatted quietly as they kept watch over their sleeping friends.

FINALLY IT WAS TIME TO WAKE THE OTHERS. Mikal opened his eyes, peeked out from under his covers, and groaned with dismay. He stayed pressed safely against the Moor as the children shared a quick breakfast of bruised bananas and apples.

When they finished eating, they gathered their belongings. George took a quick count, and Caleb reached for the silver knob.

George lingered. "Wait, Caleb."

"What is it?" Caleb asked.

"I know we were too tired to care last night, but am I the only one concerned about the fact that we're going into the District of *Dragons*?"

Mikal frowned and clasped Cavendish to his chest. "I can't decide what's worse, fire-breathing reptiles or heights."

"What do we know about dragons?" Caleb asked. "Cavendish!"

"Insomnia! Huh? What?" Cavendish asked.

"Give us some information on dragons, would you?" Caleb asked.

"Dragons . . . furry little creatures. Whiskers and cute pink noses . . ."

George raised her eyebrows. "Cute pink noses?"

"Cavendish, pay attention!" Mikal said, shaking the map a little.

"WHAT? Can't you see I'm doing research? What's a fellow got to do to get a little personal time around here?"

"Dragons! What do you know?" Caleb said.

"If I could roll my eyes right now, I would, and I'd roll them really hard too. I told you what I know. Well, partially. They vary, really. Some of them are cute like kittens. Others are massive as skyscrapers. In fact, that's where skyscrapers get their name. You don't really have to worry about those, though."

"So, we'll be okay?" George asked.

"You'll be fine. Unless, that is, you come across one of the Medium-Sized Variety. In which case, all you can do is think happy thoughts and try to escape your mind."

"What do you mean?" Mikal asked, smoothing his hair back nervously.

"Just as you're too big for the Small ones, and too small for the Big ones, you're just the right size for the Medium ones, and they'll eat anything that moves."

"Absolutely delightful," George said. "But we need our second key to Astria, so we don't have a choice."

"I wouldn't worry too much," Cavendish said. "Medium ones get into so much trouble that there aren't very many of them left. Besides, if you *do* meet a dragon of the Medium-Sized Variety, one of you can provide him with a wholesome meal while the others get away."

"First you said we should let Thazel eat George, and now you're saying we might have to let a dragon eat one of us. Why are you so eager to feed us to something?" Mikal asked.

"Because while something is feasting on one of you, the rest can escape. It's logic."

"We need to get going, guys. How are we doing on time, Cav?" Caleb asked.

"The time is now seven thirty AM DWT. You currently have thirty-nine hours and forty-one minutes until you're buried six feet under an avalanche of meteors. That's Door Way Time, in case you didn't know. And a nickname? I'm flattered!"

Mikal sighed as miserably as one can when caught between a deadly abyss and dragons. "Well, if we're gonna be eaten, we may as well be on time." He took a deep breath and opened the Moor.

They stepped through as a group, scrunching their eyes tightly closed. When nothing terrible happened, and they heard nothing that sounded like a rampaging clan of mythological reptiles, they slowly opened their eyes.

They were in the midst of a barren and empty world. Blue dust swirled by in tiny tornadoes, and the ground beneath their feet was cracked and parched. George took a step forward, and the powdery blue dirt gave with a crunch, causing more cracks to spread around them like broken glass. Scraggly trees and shrubs cropped up here and there, but they were long dead. Nothing seemed to live in this forsaken world.

"I don't understand," Cavendish said. "My encyclopedia says the District of Dragons is a thriving community. Where is everybody?"

"Maybe we're in the wrong place?" Mikal asked.

"Of course we're not in the wrong place! I'm never in the wrong place! Spin me around and see for yourself."

Mikal obeyed, and the picture began to move.

They walked for a great distance. Caleb looked back and saw the swirling whirlwinds covering their tracks as quickly as they left them. The map eventually led to a bare tree, sitting upon a hill that overlooked a sharp drop-off. The picture stopped moving.

"Is this where we're supposed to find the key?" Caleb asked.

George held up her hand to hush the others. "Do you hear something?"

They listened but heard nothing. Then they looked over the edge of the bluff.

Below them was a small pool of water, and beside it sat a plump, despondent-looking dragon of the Medium-Sized Variety. He was covered in gray iridescent scales, and his pearly wings were folded against his spiked back.

"Get down!" Caleb rasped, dropping to his stomach and pulling the others with him.

The dragon sighed. "I know you're there," he said. "You don't have to hide. I can't eat you."

"Holy fire and hippos," Mikal said.

"Do you think he's lying?" George asked.

Caleb watched the dragon for a moment and then stood up. "He already knows we're here. What's the point of hiding?" He started down the hill but lost his footing halfway and slid to a dusty stop at the edge of the pond.

"I've got to get in on this. Daniel would just kill me if

I had a chance to meet a dragon and didn't take it," George said, and slid down the slope after Caleb, followed by a reluctant Mikal.

Caleb rose to his feet and rubbed at his sore back as he addressed the dragon. "Hi, there. I'm Caleb, and these are my friends. Who are you, and how did you know we were here?"

"You're not very quiet. I heard you before you even opened the Moor," the dragon said, blinking his bright eyes morosely.

"And why can't you eat us—I mean, them?" Cavendish asked.

A fat tear rolled from the dragon's eye and plopped into the little pool beside him. "Because I've lost my fire. It's gone out."

"Have you cried all of those tears?" Mikal asked, pointing to the pond.

"I have." The dragon batted his long eyelashes.

"What's your name?" George asked.

"Hector."

"Hi, Hector. I'm George, and that's Mikal and Cavendish."

"Hello," Hector said, glancing away in disinterest.

Mikal gave an awkward wave.

"We were told this world was a thriving community. What happened?" Caleb asked.

"The other planets in the District *are* thriving communities. We're very cultured, you know. We have public-access television and ballets."

"What about this one?" George asked.

"This is the Blue Planet. It's been abandoned for ages, ever since the dust turned blue. Dragons don't care for that color. We prefer happy colors, like red and yellow and orange."

"How telling," Cavendish said.

"You're here all alone?" George asked.

"I am."

Mikal leaned around Caleb to get a better look at Hector. "Why would you want to be on a planet all by yourself?"

"This is my sad place. I come here when I am sad, which is always these days."

"You're sad because your fire went out, right?" George asked.

"Yes," Hector said, wiping another tear from his snout with a sharp mother-of-pearl claw.

"Why did it go out?" George asked.

Hector exhaled so heavily that the force of his breath

sent tiny ripples dancing across the pool. "It all started on Scilandor, another of the planets here in the District. It's a very wet planet. There's water everywhere, so there's a spectacular variety of large game fish. I was flying about when I came across another dragon snapping the spine of her prey. She was ferocious and startling in her beauty. The shimmer of her scales, the length of her snout, the way the light reflected off her bloody fangs. She was poetry in carnivorous motion."

Mikal swallowed hard.

"Then she noticed me, and she must have thought I was going to steal her dinner. I would never do something so dishonorable!" Hector straightened his neck, bobbing his head in indignation. "She smacked the surface of the sea with her tail, and a spout of water shot up into my mouth and hit me straight in the throat!" He opened his mouth and pointed a claw inside. "Right there. It put my pilot light out, and I haven't been able to cook a decent meal since."

"So you came here to hide?" Mikal asked.

Hector snapped his teeth together and hissed. "I'm not hiding. Dragons don't hide. I'm grieving."

"Could we maybe help you get your fire back?" George asked.

Hector looked into the dusty sky. "There is a way—"

"Oh no you don't! There's no way that's happening on my watch!" Cavendish said.

"You might not like it," Hector said, ignoring Cavendish.

"*You* would like it, though," Cavendish said.

"What are you two talking about?" George asked, looking from Cavendish to Hector.

"It's the only way to get my fire back. I promise not to do anything bad," Hector said.

"It isn't happening," Cavendish said. "These are *my* people, and I refuse to allow it!"

"Maybe you can share the options with the rest of us and let us decide," Caleb said.

"He wants you to stick your arm through his jaws and relight his pilot light," Cavendish said. "I strongly suggest you decline if you enjoy the use of your limbs."

Mikal recoiled. "That does sound like a very big favor."

Another tear rolled down Hector's snout.

George gnawed on her bottom lip. "I think we should do it."

"You have got to be joking!" Cavendish said. "He's a *dragon*. Besides, you're supposed to be finding a key to Astria, not rescuing every monster and reptile that comes your way."

"You're the one who led us to the monster, Cavendish,"

Mikal said. "And it turned out he had the key. You led us here, so maybe we're supposed to help Hector to get the second key."

"Even if we don't get a key out of it, I think we should help." George stepped forward and touched Hector on the shoulder. "If we help you, Hector, do you promise you won't hurt us?"

Hector looked solemnly at George. "I do promise, little human."

George took a very deep breath. "All right, then. Do we have any matches?"

Mikal dropped to his knees and began rummaging through a backpack.

Caleb closed his eyes and shook his head. "Seriously, George? I want to help too, but really? Sticking your arm down his throat? You're doing half the work of eating you for him!"

"He said he wouldn't hurt us. Besides, do you know how thrilled Daniel will be to find out I helped a dragon get his fire back?" George's green eyes sparkled with enthusiasm.

"Who is Daniel?" Hector asked.

"He's my little brother. He's lost. But I'm going to find him, and when I do, you can bet I'll bring him back to meet you."

"Good luck, George," Mikal said as he handed her the book of matches he kept with his supplies.

Hector's face lit up excitedly.

Cavendish groaned.

"Hold on, George," Caleb said, swiping his hand through his hair. "I'll do it." He took the matches from her and stepped between Hector's stubby front legs.

"I'm the one who agreed to it, Caleb."

"Yes, I know," he said as he rolled up his sleeves. "But I'm taller."

Hector's head towered over Caleb.

Caleb struck a match on the side of the box. "You're going to have to come down here if you want me to be able to reach."

Hector obediently lowered his head to Caleb's side.

Caleb paused for a brief moment before reaching into Hector's gleaming-razor-sharp-tooth-filled mouth.

"Wait!" Mikal said.

Caleb jumped and was relieved to find his fingers still attached. "Yes, Mikal?" he asked with exaggerated patience.

"His snout is as big as your entire upper body," Mikal said.

George nodded. "Mikal's right. He could bite you in half with one chomp."

Caleb's eyebrows rose. "I had, naturally, noticed that."

Hector drew himself up, staring down at George and Mikal, looking every bit the threatening dragon. "Do not impugn my honor, little humans. I made a promise, and dragons always keep their promises. I swear, on my very fire, that I will not harm any one of you."

Caleb held his hands up. "Happy?"

George swallowed hard. "Yes. Sorry, Hector."

"I forgive you. I understand what it must be like to be such fearful and defenseless little beasts."

"We're not as defenseless as you might think," Mikal said with a scowl. "And I'm getting braver. It's just a process."

"Of course, little knight," Hector said.

Mikal narrowed his eyes at Hector. "Are you patronizing me?"

"I think he just may be," Cavendish said dryly.

"Enough already," Caleb said. "Let's get on with it. Open wide, Hector."

"You're in an awful big hurry to get your arm chewed off," Cavendish said.

"Well, it's my arm, not yours, so stop complaining."

"Well, excuse me for caring! Besides, I don't have any arms," Cavendish said.

Caleb rolled his eyes as he struck another match. "Ready, Hector?"

"I am," Hector said, licking his chops nervously. "Try not to burn my tongue. It's sensitive."

George grabbed Mikal's hand as Caleb took a deep breath and slowly began to guide the match past the razor-sharp teeth to the back of the dragon's throat.

"Careful," Hector mumbled, holding his mouth wide open.

Caleb squinted in concentration. "Just . . . about . . . there. . . . Got it!" He snatched his arm out of the dragon's mouth and flung the hot match into the puddle of tears.

George sagged in relief as Mikal shook his hand free.

A massive *whoosh* of hot flame shot over their heads, forcing them to duck for cover.

"You wonderful children! My life is complete once again," Hector said. "Oh my, I'm so sorry. That was entirely unintentional. I'm just a bit rusty." He swiped his long tail through the puddle of tears, causing it to cascade over the little group, successfully dampening the smoking tendrils around George's ears.

"It's quite all right," George said, wringing out her hair.

"DON'T GET ME WET, DON'T GET ME WET, DON'T GET ME WET!" Cavendish screeched in a panic.

"It's okay, Cavendish. You're not wet," Mikal said upon close inspection.

"Are you sure? I could short out. I could DIE."

Mikal wiped the screen with the hem of his shirt. "You're perfectly dry. I promise."

"Okay, okay, okay. Breathe deeply." Cavendish made exaggerated breathing noises.

"I'm sorry to be such a trouble. Setting you on fire and then almost drowning you."

"It's okay, Hector," Caleb said. "You could have eaten my arm, so no harm done."

"Speak for yourself," Mikal said as he shook his hair free of water. "I hope you know, George, this counts as a bath. So don't try to get me to wash up again anytime soon."

"Thank you so much for your help, little humans. Look at my beautiful fire! You have truly saved my life!" He laughed and proudly scorched the remains of the little pond.

The kids jumped back to avoid being hit by the flames that erupted from his mouth, and he blushed in embarrassment.

"My aim is still a little off. I almost cooked you again. I had better be going before I do any more harm. Thank you again, and if you ever need me, I'll be thrilled to escort you anywhere my wings can take you. I am forever in your debt!"

Hector bowed the front half of his body close to the ground and began to pump his wings. The gale he generated threatened to blow the children off their feet. They huddled together and watched him rise into the air. He circled twice before flying off in the direction of the mountains, his scales sparkling in the light.

CHAPTER THIRTEEN

"WHAT A NICE DRAGON," GEORGE SAID.

"I'm glad we helped him," Mikal said. "But we still don't have the second key to Astria."

"And he dried up our escape route." Caleb gestured to where the pool of tears had been. "I was planning on using that puddle to get back to the Door Way. We can't find our way back the way we came. The wind blew over our tracks, and everything looks the same here."

"I don't think that would have worked anyway," Mikal said. "The Hag said you need rain to make a proper mud puddle."

"Seems like the Engineer could have come up with a better plan than mud puddle travel," George said. "Maybe, like, a really small Moor you could keep in your pocket. Then whenever you needed it, you'd just take it out, and it would grow and open right into the Door Way."

"Maybe you should be the new Engineer, George," Caleb said.

"What you're talking about is a Portable Moor," Cavendish said. "And those are outrageously illegal."

"Why are they illegal?" Mikal asked.

"Because Portable Moors could go nearly anywhere you wanted them to. All you had to do was open them while thinking about the location you wanted to end up at. That made some very important people nervous, because security was nearly impossible. Dozens of restrictions were placed on them, but it was ultimately decreed that all Moors must have a static destination, which means they have to be programmed to go to a single, known place. That rendered Portable Moors illegal, and their production ceased and became a punishable offense, along with many other technologies both useful and sinister."

"Leave it to you to come up with a great idea that's against the law, Georgina," Caleb teased.

"They weren't very practical anyway," Cavendish said. "They were only good for one-time use, and very spendy."

"One-time use would be good enough for us," George said with a sigh. "Oh well. Can you show us the way out, Cavendish?"

"Nope, can't do it. And not just because I'm being difficult, though that is a bonus. The inside world doors are hidden for security purposes."

"So we have to wait for rain?" George asked.

"I don't think that happens very often here," Caleb said, looking around.

"You're forgetting the Hag's gift," Mikal said. "She said it would make rain."

George retrieved the glass vial from her backpack. The vapor inside had changed from pink to light green. She pulled the stopper from the vial, and the vapor trailed out, twisting and curling as it disappeared into the twilight.

"You probably should have waited to do that until we found the key," Caleb said.

"It isn't doing anything, though," Mikal said.

"Maybe it takes time to work," George said. "Let's look for the key while we're waiting."

The children scoured the area near where Cavendish's map had led them. Nothing was to be found but dead brush and parched earth.

"THIS IS RIDICULOUS," GEORGE SAID FINALLY. "Cavendish, can't you be more specific about where we're supposed to find it?"

"I told you, I can get within a hundred yards of the key. Don't blame me just because you're a bad looker."

"It must be close to lunchtime now," Mikal said, his stomach growling.

Caleb looked to the sky, but it was no closer to raining than it had been before. "Let's eat. Maybe we'll come up with a better plan when we're not hungry."

George sat in the dust and tapped at her chin thoughtfully.

Mikal flopped down beside her and dug out the last of the peanut butter sandwiches to pass around. "This is it for the food. I hope our next stop will be a place where we can get more."

Soon the sky darkened and the stars began to arc across the heavens in a frenzy.

"What's the time, Cavendish? It can't be late enough for it to be this dark yet," George said.

"The time is now one eleven PM DWT. You currently have thirty-four hours before your very lives are extinguished. It gets dark early here."

Caleb whistled softly as he lay back to watch the meteors flashing overhead.

"Heavens to Betsy, there's a lot of them!" George said.

"No wonder. This is the sixth night since the showers started," Mikal said.

"In the story, people were already drowning in the stars by now," Caleb said.

"The only reason we're not drowning is because the Council keeps them from hitting the worlds. At least until tomorrow night," George said.

"That's right," Cavendish said. "The meteors would be bashing your heads in right now but for the Council of Seven. As long as it exists, the showers return every hundred and eleven years but never continue past the seventh night and never beat against the worlds."

"And if we don't find two more keys to Astria, retrieve the missing pieces, and get to Selyrdor, wherever that is, by eleven eleven PM tomorrow . . ." Caleb trailed off.

"Then the Council of Seven can't be remade. If that happens, there are two potential scenarios. The first is that the Flyrrey goes haywire and all of the inhabitants are destroyed in the chaos. The second is that the stars crash down before that, and we all die in a rain of fire and stone. More scenic, much faster, still dead," Cavendish said pleasantly.

"I like you, Cavendish," George said. "But I'm not really comfortable with how certain you are that we're all gonna die."

"That's just what your kind does. Artificial intelligence is eternal, though, so I'm good."

"Look over there," Mikal said, pointing to a streak of orange far in the distance. It drifted nearer, and with it came a light drizzle.

"I can't believe it! The Hag's potion is working," George said. She got to her feet and tried to catch raindrops on her tongue.

Mikal jumped up to join her, stretching his arms out and spinning in circles.

"You have to cover me up!" Cavendish said. "The water is bad! It is very bad!"

"We know, Cav," Caleb said patiently. "We'll keep you dry. Don't panic."

"You would panic too if the water wanted to kill you!" He began muttering to himself. "I must stay dry, I mustn't get wet. I must stay dry, I mustn't get wet."

Mikal stopped twirling to stuff the map under his

shirt. "I promise I won't let anything happen to you, Cavendish."

They donned their raincoats and climbed the hill to the scanty shelter of the tree atop it. The rain began to pour in earnest, and soon the entire blue desert looked like a vast lake.

"Maybe the rain will wash up the key or something," George said loudly, to be heard above the storm.

Mikal clutched Cavendish under his raincoat with one arm and put the other around the trunk of the tree. "If the water keeps rising, we're gonna be in trouble."

"You'll be sorry you used that wicked woman's potion. She meant for it to kill us! She did, she did. We're all going to drown. We're going to drown! Horrible woman, wanting to drown us," Cavendish rambled on hysterically.

"Hush, Cav. It's going to be okay," Caleb said, grasping the trunk with one arm and Mikal with the other.

Cavendish ignored him. "Horrible woman, wanting to drown me. And I'm so young—"

"Don't fress?" Mikal asked, his voice quavering.

George's smile was taut with anxiety as she clung to the tree. "I'm sure it'll be fine."

The water continued to rise and soon lapped against the soles of their shoes.

"Don't let go. It's our best hope of making it through this," Caleb said.

The water reached their ankles and then their knees. The current grew so strong the children would have been lost if not for the tree bravely holding its ground.

"We have to keep Cavendish dry!" Mikal shouted above the noise.

George and Caleb held tightly to Mikal's body as he struggled out of his raincoat, being careful not to drop Cavendish into the rising water. He wrapped the raincoat around a whimpering Cavendish and held him as high above his head as he could reach.

"I should tell you . . . ," Cavendish crackled with static.

"I really don't think this is the time," Mikal said through chattering teeth.

"But I must tell you now. If the water gets me, you have to know," Cavendish said, his words gaining strength.

George's voice was shrill with fear. "Thank you for being so thoughtful, Cavendish, but I'm sure it's not necessary."

"Listen! If it happens, remember your third key can be found in Obsidia."

"Hush, Cav. We're all going to be okay," Caleb said, but his grip on the tree trembled.

"We've got to be okay, or my parents will never know

what happened to me," George said. "I can't do that to them. We've got to be okay."

As the water reached their chests, Caleb looked up and saw an immense wave rolling in their direction. "Hold tight!" he yelled.

The wave crashed over them, ripping the air from their lungs. Mikal was yanked from their grasp, and he swirled madly away. Caleb dove after him, managing to reach him just before he was swept into the depths. George grabbed for them and pulled them back to the tree, but it was too late. The angry current had wrenched Cavendish from Mikal's arms, and he vanished without even a cry.

The rain slowed to a trickle and then stopped.

"Let me go!" Mikal screamed, thrashing in Caleb's arms.

"You can't get to him, Mikal," Caleb said, refusing to let go. "You can't."

"I can! He is just under the water there. He is right there! I promised him I wouldn't let him get wet. I promised him!"

The flood receded quickly, sinking into the ground so fast it was as if it had never been.

Caleb finally released Mikal, allowing him to struggle

through the knee-deep water, where he frantically searched for the map.

"Mikal, he could be anywhere. Those waves . . . they were really strong," George said as she waded to his side. "I'm so sorry."

Mikal turned and threw his arms around her waist, sobbing at the loss of his friend.

George hugged him close and let him cry. She patted his back softly and murmured kind words, her eyes dull with sadness as she looked at Caleb.

Caleb stood alone, with his hands on his head. He looked utterly lost.

An ancient voice spoke from behind them. "What is it, little ones? Why are you weeping? I can feel your hearts hurting from here."

They all gasped in alarm, spinning around to see who was speaking to them. They were alone.

"Who's there?" George asked in a trembling voice.

"It is me. Don't you know me? You held so tightly in the storm."

"It's the tree. The tree's talking to us," Mikal said, wiping his nose with a wet sleeve.

"I-I've never heard a tree speak," George said.

"And I've never heard such a little one speak," the tree

said. “What kind of beast are you, if it is not rude of me to ask? I can tell that you are Loeta, and you do not belong.”

“We’re humans. Human kids,” Caleb said, too tired to be amazed.

“Oh my, I have never in all of my many days heard of human children in this realm, and I have been here since before the dust turned blue.”

“How long ago was that?” Mikal asked, releasing George and blinking tear-swollen eyes.

“Eons.”

“We didn’t mean to wake you. We’re very sorry,” George said as she sank to the ground beneath the tree and drew her knees up to her chin.

“Did you make the rain come, human children?”

“Yes, sort of, and we’re sorry. It must be a drag waking up to a storm and a flood,” Caleb said, sitting next to George.

“This was once a paradise, before the dust turned blue and the dragons went away. The rain left with the dragons. Everything has been sleeping since then.”

“Are you mad at us?” Mikal asked.

“Mad? No. I would be so happy, except that you are so sad.”

"We lost something," George said numbly. "We lost our friend. There are consequences to losing things."

"I, too, have lost things, and friends. I was the only one left here. But I am no longer alone. Look at my branches."

The children looked up and saw that the tree's branches were now covered with tiny buds that burst into sweet-smelling blossoms even as they watched.

George gasped as one drifted down to land in her hair.

"Yes," the tree said. "You made the rain come, and the rain is bringing us back to life. We will remember what you've done."

"We?" Caleb asked.

"I am not the only thing coming back. Look to the water."

The children obeyed and saw water lilies blooming in the pond, which was all that remained of the storm. Frogs burrowed from beneath the mud, cattails sprouted around the bank, and in the shallows of the sparkling pool lay a blue plastic bundle.

"Cavendish!" George leapt up and ran to the bundle, dropped to her knees beside it, and pulled the raincoat away.

Cavendish was streaked with dirt and dripping water.

George held him in her lap and gently wiped him clean with the hem of her dress.

"We should take him with us. Back to Mr. Neptune," Mikal said, joining her in the shallows.

"We won't leave him, Mikal," Caleb said.

"Maybe Mr. Neptune will be able to repair him," George said hopefully.

George gave Cavendish to Mikal to hold while she and Caleb searched their backpacks for something to put him in. "Nothing I have is dry," George said.

"Me either," Caleb said.

"I guess we will just have to wrap him in something wet," George said.

A sputtering sound came from Mikal's chest. "No . . . more . . . wetness . . ."

"Cavendish?" Mikal asked frantically, turning him over. His screen was black.

"Let me see." Caleb took the map gently and thumped Cavendish on the side. "Cav?"

Nothing happened, and Mikal's face fell.

"It always worked before," Caleb said sadly.

"Why must . . . you always . . . resort . . . to hitting . . . me?" Cavendish asked.

George covered her mouth with both hands as his screen sputtered on.

A huge grin covered Caleb's face. "Cav! You're alive!"

"No thanks . . . to you. . . ."

"I dropped you," Mikal said. "I was scared you had drowned. I was so scared."

"I haven't drowned. . . . Apparently, my creator made me . . . waterproof . . . which makes sense . . . when you think about it . . . puddle travel . . . and such. . . ."

"He might have told you that! I'm so happy you're okay," George said, smiling so hard her cheeks hurt. "But you've had an awful day. Can I do anything for you?"

"I have had a terrible day. I need to be cuddled," Cavendish said.

Caleb offered Cavendish back to Mikal, who held him tightly to his chest and looked at his friends with wide eyes.

"Now that you are happy again, I think I might be able to have a quick doze," the tree said, and then its trunk split into an enormous yawn and tiny white butterflies fluttered from its mouth, their wings sparkling as they rose in the moonlight.

"You just— When you yawned! You just—" Mikal said, pointing to the butterflies.

"It happens when one has been sleeping for so long. I've been saving them. If I had released them before, they wouldn't have been able to live. I have something for you in there too. Come nearer to me."

The children gathered beneath the tree's heavily drooping branches. The cavernous mouth that had released the butterflies opened again. Nestled inside the gaping maw was a long silver chain with a key on the end.

"Sweet!" Caleb said, and began rolling up his sleeve. "You'd think we'd learn to not go sticking our hands in strange mouths, wouldn't you?" Caleb reached in, trying to avoid the dripping strands of sap. He snatched the gift and yanked his hand safely free just as the tree's jaws snapped together and it began to snore.

George clapped her hands happily. "Our second key to Astria. Thank you, tree! You led us to the right place again, Cavendish. And you were closer than a hundred yards again. Next time we'll just look exactly where you stop. What would we do without you?"

"Wander hopelessly lost until the end of your days, I reckon," Cavendish said.

George bent down to grab a handful of mud, which she wrapped in a handkerchief and tucked in her pocket. "Everybody ready?"

"I'm not ready," Mikal said, staring at the shallow pond with a look of dread. "I don't want to go back to the Door Way. There's nothing under the Touries, and I'm scared I'll fall."

"I don't want to go back through the water. I'm scared I'll drown," Cavendish said. "But you're getting braver, remember? And so am I."

"You're waterproof, though. We've learned that," Mikal said. "Humans aren't gravity proof."

"You *could* fall, and I *could* drown," Cavendish said. "But maybe this is our chance to rise above our fear. Do you think everyone gets a chance to do that? Besides, I need you to take me through the water."

Mikal was silent for a moment. "All right," he said finally, and walked to where Caleb and George were waiting ankle deep in the pool that would serve as their mud puddle to the Door Way. When he reached his friends, he looked over his shoulder at the sleeping tree. "It seems rude to leave without saying good-bye. I would like to thank it somehow."

"I think it would understand, Mikal. Besides, we're leaving this place better than it was when we got here. Right, George?" Caleb said.

George smiled at Caleb and took Mikal's hand. "Right. Three for backpack, four for Caleb, five for Mikal, six for Cavendish. Nothing's missing."

The water pulled at their ankles, and they found themselves balancing awkwardly on Touries, once again in the tunnel.

CHAPTER FOURTEEN

"I'M STARTING TO GET USED TO THIS," GEORGE said as she settled onto her pantry door Tourie.

Mikal swallowed hard and clutched Cavendish close. "I'll never be used to it."

"Where to, Cav?" Caleb asked.

"I told you already—the third key is in Obsidia."

"Well, I was just a *little* stressed out when you said it," Caleb said.

"Nobody ever listens to me," Cavendish complained.

"I listen to you, Cavendish," Mikal said.

"At least there's that," Cavendish conceded. "Anyway, you were supposed to go to Obsidia next, but I've received a notice that says that world is currently unavailable."

"What does that mean? How can a world be unavailable?" George asked.

"What am I, an oracle? Anyway, we've been rerouted. There's an emergency in the Children's Republic, and we're heading there now. Did you hear that, Touries?"

"Got it, boss," Mikal's Tourie said, and then reversed.

Caleb's and George's Touries followed suit.

"The Children's Republic sounds like a nice place. Maybe they'll have food," Mikal said.

"I hope it doesn't delay us too much. We don't have time for detours," George said.

THEY ARRIVED AT THE CHILDREN'S REPUBLIC and knocked upon the Moor, which was opened by a chubby young boy wearing a tuxedo. When he saw the bedraggled trio, his eyes grew wide. "I can't believe you're here!" He bent low at the waist. "I'm Zed. How do you do?"

George attempted an awkward curtsy. "Hi, Zed. We do fine, thank you."

"I take it you've heard of us," Caleb said.

"Of course I've heard of the Snaffleharp Company! The Timekeeper himself let me know to expect you. I'm just surprised you've made it, is all. Has it been awful dangerous?"

"No, it's been a real piece of cake," Caleb said tiredly. "Can we come in?"

The boy's face fell, and he shook his head. "I'm sorry, but not without proof. We're not allowed to play with strangers, and you might not be the Snaffleharps at all. You could be dastardly villains!"

"We have the Timekeeper's watch. Would that be proof?" Mikal asked.

The boy's mouth fell open. "Jeepers! It certainly would. Show me."

George dug the watch from her backpack and was delighted to see the plastic bag had kept it and twelve for Istanbul safe from the flood. She held it up for the young boy to see.

He blinked dramatically. "Amazing! Please come in!"

"Thank you," they all said at once.

They stepped into the Children's Republic, and their mouths immediately began to water as the scent of hot funnel cake and fresh cotton candy washed over them. The air rang with laughter as children of all ages frolicked about. Some rode a miniature train on a track made of peppermint sticks, while others trotted by on ponies. A young girl in blue overalls tinkered with the engine of an airplane that was just the right size for her, while a tiny girl still in diapers handed her tools. A group of boys and girls in pirate costumes ran by shouting and carrying wooden swords. Fairies fluttered to and fro, their wings shimmering in the sunlight, while gnomes scurried about, taking care to avoid playful feet. Knights jousted in the middle of a busy boulevard, and hot-air balloons floated above their heads in a myriad of colors.

"It's every story I've ever read," George said, gazing around in awe.

Zed straightened his shoulders and smiled proudly, exposing two missing front teeth.

"Wow, are those real cowboys and Indians?" Caleb asked, pointing in the direction of an ice cream parlor designed to look like an Old West saloon.

"A trapeze artist!" Mikal said as he noticed a group of circus performers bustling into a towering circus tent.

"What is this place?" George asked as a team of

reindeer raced by, pulling a jingling sleigh. A cloud floated just in front of the team, sprinkling snow upon the ground.

"Let's walk as I explain, if you don't mind," Zed said, leading them by an aquarium. "The best way to describe this place would be to say it's a type of heaven specifically for children."

"A heaven?" George asked, confused. "Is everyone here dead?"

"No. Some of us are, but not all. This is a place for children who haven't been born yet or children who have died and can't be reunited with their parents yet."

George stopped in her tracks for a moment, then rushed to catch back up.

"Why can't they be reunited with their parents?" Caleb asked.

"Their parents are still living in the worlds and aren't yet ready to rejoin their children."

"How sad," Mikal said.

"It may be sad for those still alive, but not for those who live here. We are happy, and we await our loved ones patiently."

"You know, we're kind of in a hurry. Cavendish, how long do we have?" George asked.

"The time is now five twenty-three PM DWT. You currently have twenty-nine hours and forty-eight minutes until the sky falls in."

"Please, could we maybe grab a few sandwiches and just be on our way?" George asked.

"But Obsidia is closed, so we can't go on our way, remember?" Caleb asked.

"That's why you were sent here," Zed said. "You have to do something to open Obsidia so you can access it and gain your third key to Astria."

"Then can you take us to whoever's in charge so they can tell us what to do?" George asked.

"Oh jeepers," Zed said. "I should probably have said so earlier, but I'm the Master of Passage, and I'm in charge here."

"You?" George asked. "But where are the adults?"

"There are no adults here. It's just us kids."

"But who takes care of you? Who feeds you? Who does the laundry?" George asked.

"The gnomes feed us, and wash our clothes, and tuck us in at night. The fairies doctor our scrapes and bruises, and read to us, and make sure we floss. In return, we keep their flowers watered and let them have our teeth when we're finished using them."

"Can you tell us how to fix Obsidia so we can go?" George asked.

"I can, but we'll talk about it after we eat," Zed said. He had led them to the middle of a wide grassy field checkered with colorful picnic tables piled high with all their favorite desserts. There were little groups of children here and there, eating and joking together.

"Oh . . . my," Mikal breathed. "This really is heaven."

"Sweet. Who makes all of this stuff?" Caleb asked, moving to an empty table and sticking his finger into the meringue topping of a lemon pie before licking it off.

"The gnomes do. They're master bakers and take a lot of pride in their cooking," Zed said, eyeing the cakes and pies greedily.

"Where are the gnomes now?" Mikal asked.

"Everywhere!" Zed said, waving a hand in the air. "They're in their bakeries or laundries, or tending the babies, or playing in their gardens, or just looking after us. They take turns doing all that, and they're always doing something."

Caleb took the seat nearest to him and piled his plate high.

Mikal followed his lead, but George remained standing with her arms crossed over her chest as she looked around anxiously.

"Would you please take a seat?" Zed asked her, and when she had, he sighed in relief and sat down on the other side of the table, where he began to stuff himself.

"You don't have a very healthy menu to choose from," George said as she began to serve herself from the mountain of sweets.

Caleb rolled his eyes as he mumbled around a mouthful of cherry tart, "Jeez, Georgina."

"Mmm," Mikal said, then sank his teeth into a deliciously soft cookie.

"We usually have very healthy food. Broccoli and fruit and stuff," Zed said, wrinkling his nose. "But the gnomes have decided to spoil us these past few days, what with the worlds ending and all."

"We're trying to keep that from happening," Mikal said.

"I know, but don't tell the gnomes. I want to enjoy these goodies as long as I can!"

"You said you're the Master of Passage. What does that mean?" Caleb asked.

"I open the doors to and from the other worlds so the other children can come and go. It's a very important job," Zed said, his chest swelling with pride.

"Sounds like it," Caleb said.

The boys ate ravenously, but George barely touched

her food. As soon as Caleb and Mikal began to slow down, she pushed her plate away. "Zed, can you tell us about the emergency now? I'd really like to get going."

"You're supposed to spend the night," Zed said. "You can wake up early in the morning and tend to the emergency. There's nothing you can do until tomorrow."

George slouched back in her seat and stared at her uneaten food.

"Why don't you explore and try to enjoy your time here? They're already setting up for the evening carnival," Zed said, pointing at the other side of the field, where boys and girls and gnomes and fairies were working together to assemble rides and game booths and food stands. Carnival music started to thrum and drift toward them.

"I'm going to go check out the rides!" Caleb said, hopping up and loping away.

"And I want to play some games!" Mikal said as he ran off, leaving Cavendish forgotten on the picnic bench.

"Wait for me!" Zed called, and scurried after them as fast as his chubby legs would go.

George was left all alone.

Even Cavendish was silent, his screen black except for little white letters that read *Currently updating systems*.

George heaved a deep sigh, collected the map, and

moved to sit in the sweet-smelling grass. In the distance she saw the carnival setup had already been completed, thanks to so many helping hands.

Caleb was wearing a huge grin and waiting his turn to ride a Goliath roller coaster. He was chatting with the other children in line and seemed to be making friends.

Mikal was standing in front of a game booth with a bouquet of cotton candy in one hand and an orange plastic ring in the other. There was an expression of fierce concentration on his face as he reared back to throw the ring, and then a shout of jubilation as he hit the target straight on. He jumped up and down with excitement, pointing to a prize hanging on the wall of the little booth, and was then handed a stuffed green dinosaur.

Now Caleb was on the roller coaster, silver hair shining in the flashing lights, arms waving in the air, and whooping with delight as he sailed through loop after loop.

Then Mikal was chasing a pretty girl. When he caught up to her, he touched her on the shoulder and then spun around and took off again, the girl in hot pursuit.

George looked away and saw the sun setting behind a rainbow of hot-air balloons. Everywhere there was joy and beauty and laughter.

She stared down at her lap, eyes stinging. She ran her palms over the blades of grass, and her vision began to blur. She tried to ignore a tiny origami dragonfly as it flitted around her head and then landed in her curly hair. It flicked its wings several times before George brushed it gently away.

"Shoo," she whispered.

She heard panting and running feet as Caleb and Mikal returned.

Mikal's face was flushed and smeared with blue cotton candy.

The boys flopped down beside her to catch their breath.

"This place is incredible!" Caleb said, grinning from ear to ear. "I just had a sword fight with a real buccaneer! I'm not sure, but I think I might have won!"

Mikal nodded vigorously, eyes round with excitement. "I got licked by a giraffe. Did you know they have black tongues? And I think I ate too much cotton candy!" He grasped his belly and lay back with a groan.

"What did you do, George?" Caleb asked.

"Nothing," she mumbled. "I just kept an eye on Cavendish."

"Why?" Mikal asked in disbelief. "Isn't there anything you want to play with? Or rides? Or games? I saw a princess and some fairies battling a wild dragon to defend their castle. He wasn't a nice dragon like Hector. You could have helped them. You'd be a good knight."

George just shrugged her shoulders and picked at her fingernails.

Caleb sat up and stared at her. "Seriously, George. You've been weird almost since we got here. What's wrong?"

"I just want to get going, that's all. I don't like it here."

"How can you not like it here? This place is literally a heaven for children!" Caleb said.

"That's why I don't like it here!" she said, looking angrily up from her lap.

Caleb and Mikal glanced at each other, their expressions baffled.

"I don't understand," Mikal said.

"I don't want to be here because . . ." She drew her knees up and wrapped her arms around them. "Because I'm afraid I'll find Daniel here."

"But you want to find Daniel," Mikal said.

"It's pretty much all you talk about," Caleb said.

George looked at them in amazement. She jumped to her feet and stalked off furiously. "I don't want to find him *here*!"

Caleb ran after her. "George, what's going on?"

Mikal grabbed Cavendish and followed.

She stopped abruptly and turned to face them. Her face was pale, and her freckled chin trembled. "This is a heaven for kids, the place they go when they die. If I find Daniel here . . . it means . . . it means he's dead."

Caleb rubbed a hand over his face. "Aw, jeez. I didn't think."

Mikal looked stricken. "We're sorry, George."

"And Daniel can't be dead!" she said, her voice shrill. "He's just lost for a little while, that's all. And I'll find him. But I'm just so scared I'm going to find him here, because . . . What if he is . . . dead?" Her eyes were swimming in unshed tears as she gazed at the carnival lights and children playing.

They stood in silence, each having run out of words.

Mikal coughed and held out the green stuffed dinosaur. "I won this. I thought you might like that it matched Toad. They're both green." He looked miserably uncertain.

George gave a choked laugh and tried to smile as she accepted the dinosaur and held it to her chest.

Caleb shoved his hands deep in his pockets. Then he set his jaw and strode off in the direction of the picnic tables. "Come on," he shouted back.

"He has a plan. That is his I-have-a-plan face," Mikal said, taking George's hand and leading her after Caleb.

Caleb walked up to some children eating birthday cake. "Have you seen Zed?" They pointed at a table across the field, and there was Zed gobbling up ice cream by the bowlful.

"Zed," Caleb said as he approached the little boy, "I need to know something."

"How can I help?" Zed asked. "Do you want some ice cream? I'll share."

Mikal shook his head. "This is more important than that."

"We need to know if George's little brother is in the Children's Republic," Caleb said. "He disappeared not too long ago, and George is afraid he might be here. His name is Daniel Snaffleharp. What does he look like, George?"

George held out a trembling hand level with her chest. "He's this tall, with green eyes. He has sandy hair and a cowlick that never goes down, no matter how hard you try. And he talks too much. He never stops talking." She smiled faintly at the memory but then swallowed hard.

Caleb and Mikal looked at Zed as he wiped his hands on his tuxedo.

"That describes a few children we have here. I mean, look around. There are a lot of kids," Zed said.

"His name is Daniel Snaffleharp," Caleb repeated firmly. "We need to be certain."

"I guess I could check the Endix."

"We need you to do that," Mikal said, stepping forward to Caleb's side. "Now, please."

Zed looked longingly at the melting ice cream. "All right, come with me."

He led them to a building hidden behind the circus tent. Inside were rows and rows of bookshelves, all smelling of dust and old age. Zed walked to a podium, where an enormous tome lay open. "This is where we keep the Endix. Most worlds have them. They help us keep track of who comes and goes. Your names will be added when you've left, but in a different book for living guests. You said your brother disappeared recently?"

George had to wet her lips before she could speak. "About three months ago."

"Let's see here," Zed said, beginning to turn the pages. "*S* for Snaffleharp. Sna . . . Snaff . . . Snaffle . . ."

Her breath caught in her throat.

"Snaffleby . . . Snafflely . . . Nope. He's not here." Zed closed the book with a bang.

George sagged a little, and she reached out a hand to Caleb to steady herself. "If he's not here . . . that means—"

"It means he's alive somewhere in the worlds," Zed said.

"So I can still find him. He's still out there." George's knees felt weak. "Thank you, Zed." She looked at Caleb and Mikal. "Thank you," she said, but no sound came out.

Caleb glanced away and ran his fingers through his hair. There was a blush creeping up his neck. "No problem."

Mikal beamed at her. "Now can I have my dinosaur back?"

George laughed and handed him the dinosaur.

"I suppose I should show you to where you'll be sleeping," Zed said. He led them back outside and stopped before a rope ladder hanging from a redwood tree that seemed to rise into the sky forever.

At the foot of the tree was a glittering fairy reading bedtime stories to a group of sleepy toddlers. One of the little boys started to drift off, and as he tipped out of his seat, two gnomes rushed up and caught him, then carried him away to be tucked into bed.

"That's where you'll be spending the night," Zed said, gesturing to the leaves above.

"We get to sleep in the tree?" Caleb asked. "It's kind of high."

"No, past that," Zed said.

George looked up the swinging ladder that disappeared into the clouds. "I've always wanted to touch a cloud!" Then she looked at Mikal, and her smile faded. "Actually, Zed, do you have anywhere else? Heights make Mikal a little nervous. I think he'd be more comfortable closer to the ground."

Mikal fidgeted as he stared up, up, up. He took a breath so deep his shoulders rose and fell with it. "I think I want to try. I think I can do it. I'm getting braver."

"Are you sure?" George asked. "We don't mind sleeping down here."

"I'm sure," he said, after just a moment of hesitation.

George smiled at him.

"You can do it, Mikal," Caleb said. "Do you want me to go first?"

"No. I'll go first. It isn't as high as it looks. Things always look taller from the ground than they really are. Once you get on with it, it isn't so bad. The trick is to just do it." He passed Cavendish to Caleb and the dinosaur to George, then reached up to grab the ladder. He stepped onto the bottom rung, hesitated, squeezed his eyes shut, and began to ascend.

"Woo! Go, Mikal! You're almost there!" George shouted.

"Look at the little pro climb," Caleb said with a proud smile. "I wish you could have seen him perform when we were with the circus. He was pretty incredible."

They watched the ladder swing above their heads, and soon Mikal had disappeared into the treetop. Zed hurried after him and vanished into the branches as well. Caleb with Cavendish was next, and then George.

They popped out into low-hanging clouds, which were cool and spongy under their feet.

Caleb nodded his approval.

Zed gestured toward the silvery mist floating around their ankles. "It's not much, but it's comfortable and safe. You won't fall. In fact, you can only go back down by conscious choice."

"What about the meteor showers?" George asked. There were so many stars streaking overhead she could hardly see any darkness between them.

"They are awfully close," Mikal said. "Won't they hit us?"

"Not yet. But if you fail to open Obsidia in the morning, find the third key to Astria in the afternoon, retrieve the lost pieces in the evening, and help the Council of Seven be rebuilt by eleven eleven at night, we'll all die horribly before the next dawn," Zed said.

The children exchanged a worried look.

"How's our countdown, Cav?" Caleb asked.

Cavendish's screen blinked. "The time is now nine oh two PM DWT. You currently have twenty-six hours and nine minutes until you're burned to a crisp."

George rubbed at her face. "I suddenly feel very tired."

"I'm beat," Caleb said. He tossed his backpack and sleeping bag down, kicked off his shoes, and climbed into bed.

"Have pleasant dreams. I'll come to wake you early for breakfast," Zed said, but then he paused. "Before I go, I should probably warn you. . . . Tooth Fairy is on a rampage lately. She wants to meet her quota before the end of the worlds, so sleep with your mouth closed." Zed smiled bashfully, revealing his missing front teeth once again, and disappeared under the blanket of white fluff.

Mikal jumped up and down, springing like a kangaroo on a trampoline. "I know I should be more worried about tomorrow night, but it's so bouncy!" Then he flopped onto his back and started waving his arms and legs back and forth. "Do you think I can make cloud angels?"

George grinned at his antics as she settled in for the night. "Three for backpack, four for Caleb, five for Mikal, six for Cavendish. Nothing's missing." She rummaged through her knapsack, finally pulling out twelve for Istanbul. She began to rub the dull ball with a soft rag.

"Whatcha doin'?" Caleb asked, folding his arms behind his head as he watched her.

"I'm polishing one of my *hikaru dorodango,*" George said. "It helps me relax and sleep."

"*Dorodango* is an art form that originated in Japan," Cavendish said, updates completed.

"Yeah," George said. "Basically, it's a ball of mud that you rub until it gets shiny. There's more to it, but this is my favorite part. This is number twelve for Istanbul."

"I understand the process," Cavendish said. "But what is its purpose? It seems rather pointless."

"It isn't pointless. I make them from the places I've been with my family. I put all of my memories of the trip inside them so I don't ever have to worry about forgetting. They're my . . . memory keepers, I guess."

"What memory does number twelve for Istanbul keep?" Mikal asked, yawning as he snuggled into his own sleeping bag and stuffed his dinosaur under his head.

"Our parents were working on a dig there, and I was supposed to be watching Daniel," George said after some hesitation. "We went for a walk in the outdoor market. We loved that place, and went as much as our parents let us. It was like a storybook, all bright colors everywhere, and people shopping and talking, and the air smelled of cinnamon and curry and lavender. The vendors were really nice too. They got used to seeing us there after a few weeks and started giving us things, figs and honeyed sesame treats. Do you know what those are?" She went on without waiting for an answer. "It's just sesame seeds with honey, but they're so sweet and crunchy. Sometimes we would pretend that we were living in olden times and that the rugs in the market were magic carpets. . . ." She glanced up and saw the boys watching attentively. She blushed and looked down at her hands. "Anyway, I was supposed to be looking after him, but I got distracted for just a minute, and then he was gone. I lost him. It was my fault. It had been raining that morning. I kept some of the mud to make number twelve for Istanbul."

"Were your parents mad at you?" Mikal asked.

"No. Sometimes I wish they were. I miss them. Almost as much as I miss Daniel. I hope I can save them. By saving the worlds, I mean. And then I can find Daniel."

"George," Caleb said.

"Yes?"

"You know how you count stuff to keep track of it? But you always skip numbers one and two?"

"What about it?"

"Is Daniel number one?"

George concentrated very hard on the clay ball beginning to glisten in her hands. Then she nodded.

"And Aunt Henrietta is number two," Caleb said.

"Yes."

They were quiet for a few minutes, and then Caleb cleared his throat. "Maybe you could teach me how to make a *hikaru dorodango*. I don't have very many memories, though. Maybe it would help me keep the ones I have so I don't forget again."

"I can teach you. As long as you're patient. Just pick your favorite memory to start with."

"Hmm," Caleb said. "That would definitely be the first time I discovered popcorn. It was stale, cold, and way too salty, but it was heaven. Definitely the best food I ever ate."

"That's because you were hungry, Caleb," Mikal said disapprovingly, and then looked at George. "It was when I first found him. He was hiding under some newspapers behind the big tent, stuffing himself with old popcorn."

"It's embarrassing when you tell it like that, Mikal!" Caleb said, looking down at his lap and focusing really hard on cleaning under his thumbnail.

"I don't mean to embarrass you. It's one of my best memories too," Mikal said.

"You really don't remember anything before that, Caleb?" George asked. "Not your parents, or if you had brothers or sisters, or where you came from?"

Caleb shrugged and rolled away from them. "Not a thing. But someday I'll know everything. I've got to."

George nodded uncertainly and put away twelve for Istanbul. "You were really brave climbing that ladder, Mikal. Your dad would have been super impressed."

"I know," Mikal said.

George giggled softly. "You're not very modest, but you are honest, and I like that."

"It's true. My dad would have been impressed. Not because of the height of the climb, but because I *was* brave. He was brave too, and I want to be like him."

LATER, AFTER GEORGE AND MIKAL HAD fallen asleep, Cavendish spoke in a hushed voice. "You're not asleep, are you, Caleb?"

"Of course not," Caleb said. "I told you already, I don't sleep."

"I get lonely when they do," Cavendish said.

"Me too," Caleb whispered, and they kept each other company until the sun came up and they could no longer see the falling stars.

CHAPTER FIFTEEN

Zed arrived with the sun the next morning, lugging a bundle up the rope ladder.

"Good morning! Did you sleep well?" he asked as he opened the bundle and began unpacking it.

George yawned mightily.

"I had the best dreams!" Mikal said as he got up and stretched.

Zed passed a paper-wrapped package to each of the children. "We always have good dreams here."

"What're these?" Caleb asked.

"They're gifts from the gnomes. I hope you like them."

The children unwrapped the presents to find a new toothbrush and a change of clothes for each of them. George had a purple dress, and there was a long green scarf to replace the one she had lost in the Land of Dreamers. Caleb and Mikal had crisp white shirts and black pants, and new suspenders to match their raincoats, blue for Mikal and orange for Caleb.

"Wow, these are great," Caleb said.

"Thank you, Zed. I love them!" George said, wrapping the scarf around her neck.

"We're going to look so handsome," Mikal said.

"What? Nothing for me?" Cavendish asked. "Figures."

The children collected their belongings and followed Zed back down the ladder. It was early, and the Children's Republic was quiet. They brushed their teeth and changed into the new clothes, but Mikal opted to continue wearing his old silver suspenders in honor of their escape from the Land of Dreamers.

They entered the picnic field for breakfast and inhaled deeply at the scent of vanilla cream.

They sat down to a feast of doughnuts and waffles and ate steadily for several minutes.

"I like your dress, George," Mikal mumbled around a mouthful of blueberry pancakes.

"Pretty," Caleb said, too busy chewing to say more.

George grinned at them both. "Thank you! And you were right, Mikal. You both look very dashing."

Mikal blushed and looked pleased.

Caleb just gave a cocky wink.

"Nobody ever calls me dashing," Cavendish said.

"Why, Cavendish," George said, "I didn't think we had to tell you that. I was sure you already knew."

Cavendish's screen blushed pink. "You're beginning to grow on me, Georgina."

"It's probably time for you to tell us about the emergency, Zed," Caleb said. "We still need to find a way into Obsidia so we can get our third key, so we can access Astria, so we can find the three lost pieces, so we can find the Timekeeper, so we can rescue the Innocent, so we can rebuild the Council, so we can save the worlds by eleven eleven tonight." He took a deep breath.

George's face fell. "Aunt Henrietta's been with those awful men for three whole days."

"What's our countdown, Cavendish?" Mikal asked.

"The time is now seven thirty-five AM DWT. You

currently have fifteen hours and thirty-six minutes until total annihilation."

Zed gulped and wiped powdered sugar off his cheek. "I wouldn't want to be you guys. You have an awful long way to go today. Are you sure . . . are you sure you can do it?"

"Yes," George said, setting her fork down with absolute precision. "We can."

Zed looked around at the quiet field spread with tables and blankets, bright squares against the green grass. "I hope so. I like my home. I don't want to die. I mean, die again. I don't want to die from here."

George reached out and patted his hand. "We're going to make it, Zed. It started out as just a trip to save my aunt Henrietta, but it's more than that now."

"A lot more," Caleb said. "Now there's the Council and George's whole family."

"And Thazel and Hector and the Tree Who Yawns Butterflies and all of you," Mikal said. "This is the happiest place I've ever been. The children deserve this place. We can't let the bad guys take it away from them."

Zed smiled. "I believe you. So let me tell you what's next. You've met the Hag, right? Well, she has a little sister named Lue who likes to come here."

"We've heard of her," George said.

"The Hag said she'd been very naughty lately," Mikal said.

"How little of a sister?" Caleb asked. "The Hag's gotta be a hundred years old, so her little sister has to be close to that. I thought you said there weren't any adults here?"

"There aren't. Adults aren't allowed here. This little sister, Lue, is around your age right now, Caleb. Twelve or thirteen, I guess. And she's naughty most of the time. She stays here often to play with the other children, and she causes me a lot of trouble when she does."

"That's a weird age difference," George said.

"Is she the one who caused the emergency?" Mikal asked.

"Yep. She got here yesterday afternoon. She was making a pest of herself, as usual, and boasting to some kids that she had taken something that didn't belong to her, something important. We'd already gotten the bulletin about the problem with Obsidia. One of the kids came to tell me what Lue had done, because we don't tolerate that kind of stuff here. We share our things and never steal from others. The gnomes and fairies teach us that from the very beginning. Anyway, knowing what I know about

Lue, I suspected that she might be responsible for the world of Obsidia getting broken."

"Wait, wait." George held up her hands. "You didn't say anything about a world being broken. We just thought it was unavailable."

"It's unavailable because it's broken," Zed said.

"And how exactly does a world get broken?" Caleb asked. "And by a girl my age?"

"You haven't met Lue," Zed said, eyes wide and sincere.

"I'm starting to want to," Cavendish said. "She sounds like my kind of human."

"Well, I went to talk to Lue. I told her she had to give back whatever she'd taken, and she refused. I told her that if she didn't give it back, she would have to leave. Oh boy, she really had a tantrum then. She screamed and yelled and told me I couldn't make her leave, and that if I tried, she would find a way to break my world too!"

"Sounds like you were right about her being responsible for Obsidia," Caleb said.

"Which I'm still not clear about," George said.

"I'm getting there," Zed said. "Then she locked me out of her garden, and I didn't know what to do, so I sent a message to the Timekeeper, asking him for advice."

George leaned forward so eagerly that her elbow landed right in a plate of maple syrup. "You spoke to Uncle Constantine? How? Where is he? Did he come here?"

Mikal handed George a napkin for her elbow.

"No, I didn't speak to him. I sent a message to him, and he sent one back."

"How did you get the message to him? Maybe the messenger knows," Mikal said.

"Yorick carries our letters back and forth. You know Yorick, right?" Zed asked.

"The giant skeleton in my closet," George said to Caleb and Mikal. "Yes, I've met him."

"The Timekeeper can't come here because he's an adult. Yorick was an adult when he died, but now he's kind of just a skeleton. It's a loophole, so he's able to come and go as we need him. He always knows where the Timekeeper is. He's kind of the Timekeeper's right hand . . . person? Is a skeleton a person?" Zed's brow furrowed thoughtfully.

"I think anything that can think and feel and make decisions is probably a person on some level," Caleb said.

"The message said to give Lue some time to cool off, and then have you three try to reason with her. You're supposed to get her to tell you how to fix Obsidia and talk her into making up with her big sister while you're at it. So I left her alone, and then you guys showed up. There was nothing you could have done last night. Lue was still in the middle of her hissy fit and wouldn't listen to anyone. I think she's calmed down now, though."

"Which is where we come in," Caleb said.

"She sounds awful. I don't know how we're going to do it," George said. "But I suppose we did already deal with a monster and a dragon."

"Thazel wasn't a monster on the inside," Mikal said. "And Hector was an honorable dragon."

"Maybe she's just misunderstood," Caleb said.

"We can't go forward without passing through Obsidia. We can't pass through Obsidia without Lue's cooperation," Cavendish said. "We're just wasting time discussing it."

"Cavendish is right. And maybe Lue will be more helpful talking to a girl her own age," George said.

"Do we know any girls Lue's age?" Caleb teased.

George threw half a muffin at him.

Zed shrugged. "I don't know if that will help or not. I don't understand her. Sometimes she acts like a spoiled baby, and sometimes she acts like a grown-up lady. Then there are the times she acts like a cranky old woman."

"She comes by that last part honestly if she spends much time with the Hag," Caleb said. "Let's get this over with."

Mikal stuffed his pockets full of goodies and then raced after his friends.

By now the Children's Republic had woken up. They passed a group of kids blowing rainbow soap bubbles.

George stopped for a moment to watch them. One of the shiny bubbles floated just in front of her face, so near her eyes crossed. With a pop, it burst on her nose. They all shrieked with laughter, and George had to be dragged away grinning.

"Sorry. I know we're in a hurry. They just reminded me of Daniel." She saw a group of older kids playing jump rope, and she sighed. "I wish I'd taken the time to have fun last night."

"You can visit us again," Zed said.

"Unless all of you die tonight," Cavendish said cheerfully.

They ignored him and were soon standing before a familiar white gate with the words *Chrone Cottage* trained in honeysuckle in the trellis above. Behind the fence was the tiny garden shed surrounded by beautiful blooming flowers and green trees.

"I'll wait for you here," Zed said. "I doubt Lue will want to see me."

Mikal swallowed hard and held Cavendish close. "I hope the Hag isn't in today. She makes it hard to be brave."

"Grown-ups aren't allowed here, remember?" Caleb asked.

"Then what's her home doing here?" Mikal asked.

"It's Lue's home too," Zed said. "The sisters go where they want, and when they do, the cottage finds a way to be there too. Good luck."

GEORGE LED THE WAY BENEATH THE STICKY pomegranate archway. They heard singing coming from the back of the garden.

Caleb crept up and peered around the side of the building. He gestured for George and Mikal to come closer.

They obeyed and saw a pretty girl sitting in a swing hanging from the branches of a tall tree. Her dress was white and gauzy, and her long hair was perfectly smooth. A flock of geese were squabbling around her feet as she tossed bread crumbs to them.

As they watched, she began another song.

"Now mummies meander as the moon watches all.
Monsters they mangle, and mothers they call.

Witches they cackle, and warlocks throw curses,
Wizards all chant, and werewolves drive hearses.
Gypsies jingle, and the ghouls eat out,
Ghosts live to haunt, and the goons, they shout!"

"Do you think it's Lue?" George asked quietly.

"Definitely," Mikal said, making a face. "Can't you tell by what she's singing that she's related to the Hag? I hope she doesn't take us to the dungeon."

Lue jumped to her feet at the sound of Mikal's voice, and the geese scattered. "Who are you? This is my garden, and you're not supposed to be here! I'm not accepting company."

Caleb stepped from behind the shed and held up his hands. "Sorry, we didn't mean to eavesdrop. We're friends of your older sister, the Hag. You may have heard of us? The Snaffleharp Company?"

"Oh. Yes, I've heard of you."

"Good," Caleb said, lowering his hands. "Your geese are very pretty."

"Oh, them." She waved a hand. "They aren't mine. They belong to my sister."

George moved up beside Caleb. "Hi, Lue, it's nice to meet you."

"What are you doing here?" Lue asked Caleb, entirely

ignoring George. "If you've come to see my sister, you won't find her. She's been up to no good lately, and it's keeping her busy."

"Funny. She said the same thing about you," George said under her breath.

"She did not! Did she really? How typical of her! Oh, I'll get her for telling tales about me." She stamped her foot in the grass. Then she saw Mikal holding Cavendish. "Who's that?"

"That's Mikal. He's with us," George said.

Lue dismissed him immediately and focused a smile on Caleb. "You're kind of cute. What's your name?"

Caleb pushed his fingers through his hair. "I'm Caleb. It's nice to meet you."

"I know it is."

George rolled her eyes so hard it hurt.

Lue glanced her way and curled her lip disdainfully. "You must be George. Those freckles are a dead giveaway. Goodness, would you look at your hair?"

George's mouth dropped open in embarrassment, and she lifted her hands self-consciously to her head. She dropped them to her sides and gritted her teeth. "We know you broke a world, and we need you to tell us how to fix it."

"And why would I do that?" Lue asked.

"Because if you don't, we can't access Obsidia, and we need to pass through there to save the worlds from being bashed in by the stars," George said.

"Oh, Obsidia! Don't even say that name. It makes me so angry!"

"Why does it make you angry?" Mikal asked.

"That's where my sister's beau lives. Obsidia is his world. He's the master there."

George raised her eyebrows. "The Hag has a beau? Like, a boyfriend?"

"But . . . how?" Mikal asked. "She's so old."

Lue rolled her eyes dramatically. "Not *that* sister. Lucy, our middle sister."

"And how old is Lucy?" Caleb asked. "Your age, or the Hag's age?"

"Silly Caleb," Lue said, dimpling up at him. "I said she's our middle sister, so naturally she's in the center of us."

"Oh yeah, of course. That makes sense," Caleb said, slightly flustered.

"Did you break Obsidia because you're mad at Lucy's beau?" George asked.

Lue glared at George. "I told you not to say that name! But no, I broke it because I was mad at Lucy, not her beau.

I like him. He's kind of bossy to me, but he always gives Lucretia butterscotch candies when he sees her."

"Okay, but how do you even break a world?" Caleb asked.

"Come closer, and I'll tell you," Lue said with an impish grin.

Caleb looked uncertain, but he stepped close to her, expecting her to whisper the answer in his ear. Instead, she leaned in and kissed his cheek before he could even blink, then skipped away, shrieking with laughter.

Caleb's eyes grew wide, and then he stared hard at the ground, his face bright red.

"How do we fix it?" George said, ignoring this display.

"Oh, you can't fix it," Lue said. "I wanted to get back at Lucy, and I did. When I broke the world, I took a piece of it with me. Now it can't ever be put back together. That'll show her what happens when she breaks our necklace and tries to cut me out of her life so she can spend more time with her stupid beau."

"If that's how she talks about people she claims to like . . . ," Cavendish said.

"Zed said she took something that didn't belong to her," Mikal said to George. "That must be what she took."

"Is there any way I can talk you into giving the piece of Obsidia to us?" George asked.

"You ask the most bizarre things, George!" Lue said merrily, returning to her swing.

"I guess that means no," Mikal said.

"Any ideas, Caleb?" George asked, turning her back to Lue and speaking quietly.

Caleb didn't seem to hear, as he was too busy watching Lue toss her perfect hair and swing her pretty feet.

George shook her head in exasperation. "Really, Caleb? Okay, Mikal. It's just you and me. And maybe Cavendish if he has any ideas."

"Don't ask me to help you figure out the inner workings of an adolescent female's mind. That is *not* what I was programmed for," Cavendish said.

"She seems awfully mad at Lucy," Mikal said, scratching the back of his head. "And the note Uncle Constantine sent to Zed said we're supposed to try to reason with her and get her to make up with her big sister."

George nodded, and then stood thinking for a moment. "That's it! Uncle Constantine wanted us to get them to make up, because if Lue stops being mad at her sister, she won't have any reason not to give us the piece.

Maybe she'll even want Obsidia to be fixed so her sister won't be mad at her. You're smart, Mikal!"

Mikal glowed at the compliment, and George turned once again to address Lue.

"Lue, are you sure trying to hurt your sister is the right thing to do?"

"I can do whatever I want. I'm important."

"Why are you important?" Mikal asked.

Lue made a face at Mikal. "I'm the Youngest of the Els, nitwit."

"Don't talk to him like that," George said angrily, then took a calming breath. "You're the Youngest of the Els? What does that mean?"

"My sisters and I are the Els, and that makes us special." Lue was twisting the swing around and around now.

"And you like to be special?" Mikal asked.

"Doesn't everyone?"

"So being one of the Els *sisters* makes you superior to us common people," George said.

"Oh, superior. I like that. Yes, it does." She stopped turning the swing and released the tension, allowing it to spin her in circles.

"But if you keep being nasty and trying to hurt your sisters, you won't have them much longer. They won't want to be around you," George said loudly. "And without sisters, you wouldn't be the Youngest of the Els. You'd just be Lue."

Lue stretched out a foot, dragging it in the dirt to slow herself. She looked at George, her face clouded with confusion. "Just Lue?"

"Just Lue," Mikal said with a solemn nod. "You wouldn't be part of anything special anymore."

"Your family makes you special. The people you love and who love you make you special," George said.

Lue's face fell. "Do you have anybody who loves you?"

"Yes, I have parents and my aunt and uncle and even a little brother named Daniel. He used to drive me absolutely bonkers, always playing with my things and never picking them up, and following me around everywhere. Then one day he was gone, and those things didn't matter anymore. I just missed him. I missed being his sister."

"And I have Caleb," Mikal said. "He's like a brother, and I love him very much."

Caleb must have heard this, as he became utterly fascinated with the bark on a nearby tree and mumbled something difficult to make out.

Lue studied the geese meandering about the garden.

"If you give us the piece of Obsidia and let us fix it, not only will you be closer to making up with Lucy, but you'll also be doing the right thing. That makes you special too. We need to fix Obsidia so we can save the worlds and everyone in them, including you and your sisters," George said.

"And all it takes to change the entire path of the future is one person making the right decision," Mikal said. "Your oldest sister, the Hag, told us that."

Caleb finally decided to speak up. "Changing the future for the better would make you a hero, Lue. That's another kind of special."

Lue sighed prettily and rose to her feet. "Very well, Caleb. If you think it would be best, I'll make up with my sister. You made some very good points."

"You have got to be kidding me," George said.

Mikal elbowed her. "Shh, don't make her change her mind."

Lue reached into a pocket and withdrew a red velvet bag tied with a gold thread. "This is all you need to fix Obsidia."

George held out her hand to take it, and Lue glared at her.

"I'm giving it to Caleb, not you." She placed the item

onto Caleb's outstretched palm and then jumped back and giggled. "But maybe you'd rather give it to your friends and you stay with me?"

"No," George said firmly. "He's coming with us. He's part of our team."

Caleb nodded and stepped closer to George. "Thanks for your help, Lue, but I really do have to go."

"You ruin everything, Georgina Snaffleharp!" Lue stomped her foot and gave George a particularly nasty look before smacking her hands together with a sharp crack. There was a faint glimmer in the air, and the girl and garden both vanished.

George and Company found themselves in the middle of an ice-skating rink.

"Well . . . that was interesting," Caleb said, scratching behind one ear.

"Nice to have you back, Caleb," Mikal said.

George made a face and stalked over to where Zed was waiting.

The boys followed at a reasonable distance.

ZED WAS WRINGING HIS HANDS, AND AS soon as he saw George and the boys, he ran to meet them.

"We've got a way to fix Obsidia," Caleb said, holding up the little red bag.

"Super! Now we really do have a chance!" Zed said. "What's in it?"

Caleb upended the satchel into his hands, and the children saw a tiny jet-black jigsaw puzzle piece.

"What in the Flyrrey are we supposed to do with that?" George asked.

Caleb tucked the item away. "Time, Cav?"

"The time is now nine AM DWT. You currently have fourteen hours and eleven minutes until you bite the stardust."

"Let's get out of here," Caleb said.

"You can't go quite yet! I've asked the gnomes to prepare some food for you to take," Zed said.

He led them back past all of the beautiful things they had already seen, and more they hadn't. They stopped for a moment outside a tidy shop with a wooden sign hanging above the door that said DALTON'S BAKERY, and waited while Zed went inside. He returned carrying a rainbow pillowcase.

"Sorry, we don't really have anything better to pack this in. Nobody ever leaves here with lunch. You understand, don't you?"

"It's perfect. Thank you," George said as Caleb took the pillowcase. She peered around him and waved at the gnome peeking from the window.

He dashed behind the curtain, and she turned away laughing as they continued to the exit.

"Before you go, I want to ask that you be extremely careful from here," Zed said. "You have only until tonight to re-form the Council, so we can't afford any accidents or delays. And please beware of Dusklord!"

"Who is Dusklord? We haven't heard of him," Mikal said.

Zed shivered and wrapped his arms around himself. "He's the master of Obsidia. I've never met him—I've just heard rumors. And beware the Door Way too! Be sure you don't get separated. It was a pleasure having you. Good luck!" He bowed stiffly, pushed them out of the Children's Republic, and shut the Moor behind them.

The children looked at each other nervously.

"Dusklord is Lucy's beau?" George asked.

"Sounds that way," Caleb said.

"I hope this isn't going to be a repeat of the Land of Dreamers. If he's anything like the keeper of that world, we might really be in for it," George said.

“Nothing can be as bad as that world,” Caleb said.

“I hope not,” Mikal said. “Besides, Lue said she liked him.”

“Lue probably isn’t the best judge of character,” Cavendish said.

“He’s got a point,” George said as she took a quick count.

“I’m full of points,” Cavendish said. “Now, would you mind booting me down for a bit? I’d like to do some research on multiple personalities.”

“Do you think we left the Children’s Republic better than we found it, George?” Mikal asked as he turned Cavendish off.

“Definitely. We got Lue out of there, didn’t we?”

CHAPTER SIXTEEN

"WOW, THE TRAFFIC IS REALLY FLYING THIS morning," Caleb said as George tried unsuccessfully to hail rides for them.

Touries were soaring through the tunnel much faster than usual, and they were all packed with passengers.

"I wonder what's going on," George said.

"The people must be spooked because the meteor

showers have gotten so bad," Caleb said. "Maybe they're trying to get home to their families."

It took a long time to find an empty Tourie. Only one stopped, a sturdy red church door, but it was kind enough to bear the weight of all three children.

George mounted first, followed by Mikal carrying Cavendish.

Mikal was slightly more at ease about traveling by Tourie now, but he still felt light-headed and had to hold his breath as he stepped from the platform and across the narrow divide.

Caleb held Mikal's elbow to steady him and then climbed on last.

The red church door groaned and wobbled beneath their weight. "I wasn't built for this."

"I know, but we appreciate you so much," George said.

"At least somebody does. Where would you like to go?"

"We're heading to Obsidia!" Caleb said.

"Oh no, I can't do that. Obsidia is currently unavailable, inaccessible, closed for business! No, I can't do that at all."

"We know it's unavailable, but we have to go there anyway," Caleb said.

"We're going to make it available, if that helps at all," Mikal said.

"If we don't get to Obsidia, the worlds will all be destroyed tonight, including the Door Way, and all of you lovely Touries who live here," George said.

"Oh, very well. I can hardly argue with that," the Tourie said, and then had to wait several minutes before an opening appeared and it was able to merge into the chaos.

It was a harrowing journey to Obsidia with so much activity in the tunnels. They were caught in a doorjam for several minutes while eight Touries involved in a pileup were removed from the thoroughfare. Passengers were shouting to be heard above the racket of the bells and whistles and general commotion, and Touries were darting in and out of traffic so fast their riders had to cling to the knobs so as not to be tossed into the void.

"Just when I thought it couldn't get worse," Mikal moaned, wedging Cavendish into the space between him and George so he could clutch his stomach. "I'm going to be sick."

"Not on me, you're not!" the Tourie said.

"Please don't throw up on me, Mikal," George said, looking over her shoulder at his miserably green face. "I'm sure we're almost there."

"Just aim over the side if you have to be sick," Caleb said.

Finally they pulled up to a Moor made of ebony and set upon a podium of black marble. The red church door came to a jerky stop. Mikal clambered to his feet and made it to the podium just in time to begin vomiting over the ledge. Caleb and George rushed to his side, dropping their packs and the rainbow pillowcase on the doorstep.

"Take care," the Tourie called as it jetted away. "And thanks for holding it in!"

George gave a distracted wave with one hand as she patted Mikal's heaving back with the other.

"You gonna make it?" Caleb asked, fishing a used breakfast napkin out of his pocket and offering it to Mikal.

Mikal nodded and wiped his mouth. "I'm gonna make it."

"He just needs to catch his breath, that's all," George said. "Let's sit for a minute."

Mikal sank down against the black Moor, taking deep breaths. "I'm starting to feel better. . . ." But then his eyes widened with alarm. "Where's Cavendish?"

"What do you mean, where's Cavendish? Cavendish is always with you," Caleb said.

Mikal threw out his empty hands. "He's not with me now, is he?"

George fell to her knees and began rummaging through their belongings, desperately hoping to find Cavendish among them. "He isn't here!"

"Could you have dropped him?" Caleb asked, searching over the edge of the doorstep, but of course there was nothing to be seen but mist.

"No, I wouldn't have dropped him!" Mikal yelled angrily.

"Calm down, Mikal. When did you last have him?" George asked.

"I had him when I climbed onto the Tourie, then I got sick and I . . ." Mikal's mouth went dry as he turned to stare at the rushing traffic. "I left him on the Tourie," he whispered.

George was stunned into silence.

"Oh man," Caleb said, putting both hands on his head and shaking it with dismay. "This is not good."

George jumped to her feet. "Which way did it go? Our Tourie, which way did it go? Did you see?"

Mikal pointed a trembling finger back the way they had come.

"We'll never catch it now, George," Caleb said. "Not in this mess. It would take too long to find another ride."

"We'll see about that," George said, her green eyes sparking with determination. She took a deep breath and then hurtled across the void, the ends of her scarf trailing behind her. She landed with a thud on a moving Tourie carrying a single passenger, a creature that looked like it may have had troll blood coursing through its veins.

"What in the worlds do you think you're doing?" the creature asked in a very prim voice.

"Sorry!" George shouted, but she had already jumped to another door, so the creature never heard her apology.

"GEORGE! ARE YOU CRAZY?" CALEB YELLED as she sped away. "Oh man, she's going to get herself killed." He looked at Mikal. "I have to go after her. It's going to be dangerous. You can wait here."

Mikal's breath was shallow as he shook his head rapidly back and forth. "No, I'm not waiting. I have to go too. For Cavendish."

"Are you sure you can do it?" Caleb asked, throwing a glance at the hectic traffic.

"I *have* to do it," Mikal said, swallowing hard. "Besides, we're not supposed to get separated."

"Okay, let's go. George! Wait up! We're coming!" Caleb hollered, but George was no longer in sight.

GEORGE CROUCHED DOWN AND THEN SPRANG from a pink Tourie onto a white one speeding by in the opposite direction. Someone had forgotten their yellow raincoat on it, and when George landed on the wet sleeve, it slipped out from under her. She tottered on the edge for a split second before righting herself and pouncing onto another door. Passengers swore angrily at her as she leapt from Tourie to Tourie, always scanning the tunnel for signs of the red church door.

Finally, she caught sight of a crimson blur carrying two large figures in the distance. It turned left into a shadowy channel on the far side of the wide thoroughfare and then she lost it. George thought she heard a voice calling her name from behind, but she didn't have time to look back as she bounded across the tunnel, finally coming to a stop balanced precariously on a narrow cabinet door swerving in and out of the traffic.

The cabinet door was so tiny it wasn't carrying any other passengers, but it was spunky and eager to set off in pursuit of the red church door. It took the left turn so fast George almost slid off the edge, but she caught herself and blinked hard to keep from thinking about what would happen if she fell into the abyss.

There, up ahead, the red church door was parked next

to the podium of an iron Moor. The two figures were dismounting. They were wearing long dark coats.

"Hurry, please! We're almost there," George said to her feisty little Tourie. It gave a burst of speed and reached the platform just the red church door pulled away.

Cavendish was nowhere to be seen. George caught a familiar spicy scent in the air, but she was too focused on finding her friend to register it. She climbed onto the stoop behind the two figures, whose backs were turned to her.

"Excuse me, please? I've lost something. Have you seen . . . ?" She trailed off and her palms grew sweaty.

The bigger of the two figures had turned to face her. It was a ridiculously large man, and underneath his raincoat he was wearing a red bandanna tied around his bulging neck. His scalp and face were covered with fresh bloody scabs.

It was Arlo, the man with blank eyes who had first come into her bedroom to take Aunt Henrietta away, and he was holding a thin white rectangle dwarfed by his enormous hands.

George's lungs burned, and her chest was so tight it hurt to breathe. Still, she managed to gasp, "Please. That belongs to me. May I have it back?"

Arlo's face clouded over, and he tightened his grip on Cavendish. "Mine."

"No," George said meekly, voice shaking. "I just lost it a few minutes ago."

Then Arlo's blank eyes became playful and crafty. He lifted Cavendish above George's head and dangled him there, just out of reach. She stretched up on her toes to grab for Cavendish, but then Arlo jerked his arm and made as if to throw the map into the abyss.

"No!" George cried, then clamped her hands over her mouth.

Arlo grinned stupidly, dropped Cavendish to the podium, and put one gigantic foot on the slender map. He began to press down.

Cavendish's case creaked alarmingly.

"Stop! Please, stop!" George begged. "You'll hurt it—please stop."

"Arlo!" the other person barked. "Stop tormenting children. We're in a hurry. Get this Moor opened for me." The figure turned, and George began to back away.

Mr. Neptune's warning about allowing Cavendish to fall into the wrong hands swam frantically through her mind, but it was bogged down in the murky panic of coming face-to-face with the worst possible hands he could fall into. Before her, leaning heavily on his cane, was Nero, the old Judge.

Nero bent to retrieve Cavendish. He turned him over,

a confused look on his face. "And what could this be? It seems a rather boring toy. But what would I know? I haven't been a child for eons."

He looked at George then, for the first time, and he narrowed his eyes. "You seem familiar, girl. Have we met?"

George, mute with terror, managed only to give her head the tiniest shake.

Nero studied her for a minute, and then he shrugged. "Oh well, you can't blame me, really. One sees many frightened faces in my line of work. And who have we here?" he asked as Caleb and Mikal finally caught up and stepped onto the podium.

It was getting rather crowded now.

They were both panting. Caleb looked frantic, but on Mikal's face there was none of the alarm one might expect after his battle with height and gravity over the yawning abyss. Rather, in the place of his usual fear and uncertainty, his face was bold and glowing with purpose.

"Did you catch up to him?" Mikal asked. He saw Cavendish in Nero's hands, and he frowned like a thunderhead.

"George!" Caleb said. "You shouldn't have left us!

We're not supposed to get separated. I thought we'd never find you! Who are these guys? And why does he have Cavendish?"

George opened her mouth to speak, but no sound came out. She was so pale even her freckles had faded.

"Cavendish?" Nero asked, his mouth twisting into a sneer. "You name your toys? How quaint. Maybe it's a more interesting item than I'd thought. Perhaps I'll keep it."

Arlo chortled from behind Nero. He was standing with the Moor open, waiting.

"You can't keep it," Mikal said fiercely, moving to stand before Nero. "It's ours, and we want it back."

Caleb put a hand on Mikal's shoulder and together they faced Nero down.

Nero lifted a crooked brow and turned as if to go, taking Cavendish with him, but then he stopped and sighed dramatically. "Very well, you can have it back. You're lucky I'm so good-natured. Children really are my weakness."

Some of the tension went out of Caleb's back, but Mikal was still very much on alert.

Nero looked once more at George and paused. "There's something about your face. . . . Something . . . I don't like." Then his expression hardened and he held Cavendish out. As Caleb reached to grab the map, Nero, with a flick of his wrist, tossed Cavendish into the void. "I lied. I don't have any weaknesses." He turned and left through the Moor, Arlo plodding after.

MIKAL, FASTER THAN A SNAKE COULD strike, had vaulted from the doorstep and into the air while George and Caleb were still staring in disbelief at Cavendish arcing through the foggy passage.

The map landed with a clatter on a sliding glass door.

Mikal was a fraction of a second behind him, and the glass door tilted under his weight.

The Tourie jerked to a surprised halt and veered off toward the nearest Moor.

Cavendish skidded across the smooth surface and over the edge.

Mikal threw himself down on his belly and slid halfway off the Tourie, grabbing desperately for Cavendish. The front half of his body dangled over the great nothingness, and his legs kicked as he fought to keep from falling.

Then his legs stilled. He scooted backward and managed to sit up. He looked wildly around for his friends, who were watching him with horror-stricken faces. With a jubilant whoop, he held up one arm: clasped securely in his small hand was Cavendish.

George's legs collapsed straight out from under her, and she sat down with a thump.

Caleb shouted and pumped his fists in the air, face shining with pride at Mikal's bravery.

Mikal made his way back to his friends just in time for George to pick herself up and wrap him in a hug so tight he had to fight her off. "You're my hero! But don't you ever do that again!"

"I couldn't believe it when you soared after him. Just . . . *whooooosshh*. Right after him, without even thinking!" Caleb said. "The Soaring Penguin, back in action!"

"I had to do it," Mikal said. He looked bashfully at the silent Cavendish. "He's my friend." Then he looked up at George and Caleb with a worried expression. "Do you think we should tell him what happened?"

"Are you kidding? Being left behind, lost, manhandled and stepped on by a giant bad guy, held captive, and then tossed into the void? We'd never hear the end of it!" George said.

"He stepped on him?" Mikal asked, affronted.

"Not all the way," George said. "But that won't matter to Cavendish."

"So we're agreed, then. We're just gonna keep this one to ourselves," Caleb said.

"I like that plan," Mikal said. "Now let's get back to Obsidia."

"Wait," George said. She bit her bottom lip and looked at the Moor that Nero and Arlo had disappeared behind. "That was them."

"Them? Them who?" Caleb asked.

"The men who took my aunt Henrietta. The man with the cane was Nero."

"Nero? The old Judge? Who murdered most of the original Council of Seven?" Mikal asked. His eyes widened at the realization of whom he had just stood up to.

Caleb let out a low whistle.

"Yes, and the man with him was Arlo, his . . . helper? Henchman? I don't know what to call it. He's weird. He acts like a little kid. But that's them." George looked down, and her cheeks were tinged pink with shame. "It's why I couldn't do anything to help. I was too scared. I'm a coward."

"You are *not* a coward, Georgina," Caleb said, his eyes earnest.

"You're the bravest girl I know," Mikal said. "You're the bravest *person* I know."

"Hey!" Caleb said jokingly. He reached out to tug on one of George's orange curls. "He's right. You set out all by yourself to find your uncle and save your aunt.

You spent the night with two weirdos in a cemetery. You helped a creepy old lady brew a potion. You traveled through a mud puddle, hunted down a monster, and faced down actual living Nightmares to save my hide. You gave a dragon back his fire, and when Cav was lost, you went after him without thinking twice."

George gave half a smile. "You're actually the one who gave the dragon back his fire. And Mikal rescued Cavendish."

Caleb chuckled and brushed his hair off his forehead. "So we're a team; it's all the same. And being afraid of Nero doesn't make you a coward, George. I mean, the guy is *evil*."

"Thank you," George said. "But when I see Nero again tonight, I'm going to be braver. Besides"—she wrinkled her nose—"what kind of person tells someone they don't like their face?"

"Beats me," Caleb said. "I like your face just fine."

George's cheeks flamed so red her silver freckles stood out.

"Let's get back to Obsidia and find our third key," Mikal said.

George cleared her throat. "Three for backpack, four for Caleb, five for Mikal, six for Cavendish. Okay, let's go."

Obsidia

CHAPTER SEVENTEEN

THEY STEPPED THROUGH THE MOOR TO Obsidia and into a world of crushing darkness.

A humming sound clicked on, and a light faded in directly overhead, enclosing them in a circle of pale yellow so faint they could barely make out one another's faces. Directly outside the circle, the blackness became complete.

Caleb tucked his hands into his pockets and rocked back on his heels, whistling between his teeth. "So this is what a broken world looks like."

"I have never seen so much dark," Mikal said in an awed voice.

"Daniel would absolutely hate it here. He has to sleep with a night-light," George said, sneezing at the smell of ozone and dust.

Mikal just dug a cookie out of his pocket and stuffed it into his mouth. Then he booted up Cavendish.

"Hello, hello, hello!" Cavendish said. "It took you longer than I thought it would to get here. Did I miss anything?"

"The traffic was pretty bad," Caleb said. "How's the countdown?"

"The time is now ten twenty-nine AM DWT. You currently have twelve hours and forty-two minutes until you're pushing up daisies. My goodness, would you look at this place? Dusklord needs to hire a new decorator. Remember the things that crawled out of the shadows in the Land of Dreamers? I'd be curious to know how many of those things could live in such a big dark as this."

"You're a real ray of sunshine, Cav," Caleb said, but he swallowed hard. "This isn't the Land of Dreamers, though.

Even if there are shadows here, they're not like the ones there. Nothing is like the ones there."

"If you say so," Cavendish said. "Now, are we just going to stand here, or are we going to find out where that key is?"

Holding Cavendish, Mikal spun around, but the picture didn't start moving. Finally he came to a stop and shook himself. "He's not working, and now I'm dizzy."

"I don't understand," Cavendish said sheepishly. "There's no logical reason for me to be malfunctioning. Try again?"

Mikal did, and there was no change.

The children exchanged a concerned look.

"Maybe your batteries are running low?" George asked hopefully.

"I've told you—I don't run on batteries! It's probably just a result of being nearly drowned. I'm sure it'll clear up. Now, can we get back to Dusklord? This is embarrassing."

"What do you know about him?" Caleb asked.

"Not much. He's notoriously mysterious, and reports vary. One thing everyone agrees upon is that he is not to be meddled with."

"So let's not meddle with him," George said. "He must be pretty creepy, with a world like this."

"That isn't very nice, George," Cavendish said. "Haven't we learned by now that one should be careful of making judgments until one has grasped the entire situation? Look how nice Thazel turned out to be, and Hector. Lue, on the other hand, was lovely as a picture but a complete brat. Besides, how bad can he be if he gives butterscotch candy to an old lady?"

The children blinked in surprise at Cavendish's scolding.

"Maybe that giant bad guy stepped on him harder than you thought, George," Mikal whispered.

"What was that?" Cavendish asked. "Did you say something?"

Mikal just shook his head rapidly back and forth.

"You're right, Cavendish," George said. "We have learned that. Though, to be fair, you were the one who was unfriendly to Thazel and Hector."

"I had to protect my people, didn't I? I can't go around trusting just anybody, can I?"

"Okay! I'm not arguing with you. Dusklord may be a great guy, but just in case he isn't, could there be a way to fix Obsidia without ever running into him?" George asked.

"How in the Flyrrey do you think we could do that?" Cavendish asked.

"We only have one tiny black puzzle piece, and we're

supposed to find out where it goes? Out there?" Mikal waved an arm in the direction of the nothingness.

"And then find the key? Even if we got the world put back together, where would we start looking for the key? Cav is broken, so he can't help us this time," Caleb said.

"What should we do, Cavendish?" Mikal asked.

"Why are you asking me? I'm not working, remember?"

"Aww, Cavendish," George said. "Your map function is only part of the reason we need you. Even if it doesn't work, you still know lots of stuff, and you can still give us good advice."

"Really?"

"Absolutely," Caleb said.

"In that case, we wait. Dusklord's world is broken and currently listed as inaccessible. You think he won't come to investigate when someone accesses it?"

George sighed and rubbed at her face. "But we're in such a hurry. Why couldn't he have been here waiting when we got here? The Hag, Mr. Neptune, and Cecil knew to expect us."

"Yes. We were all sent memos," a man said in a dry voice.

The children whipped around, peering into the darkness.

A second light buzzed on several feet away, illuminating an exceptionally pale man with long black hair braided intricately and hanging down his back. His face was sharp-featured but attractive, and his eyes were of such a light color they could have been made of ice. He stood rigidly straight, and his hands were clasped behind his back.

"Hello," George said.

"A standard greeting, to be sure. I *do* hope you'll forgive me for daring to keep you waiting."

"It's okay. I'm George. You must be Dusklord, right?"

The man arched an inky eyebrow. "I cannot express how astounded I am by your powers of observation." He began to circle the children slowly, and the light followed him as he moved.

George frowned. "Are you being rude?"

"It would appear so," he said. "Although in my esteemed opinion, you are the rude one, little girl. Entering a person's home uninvited is incredibly ill-mannered. In fact, in this world, certain measures would usually be taken to punish such presumption."

Caleb scowled and stepped in front of George. "If you think you can get away with threatening her—"

"I can handle this myself, Caleb," George said, and then looked back at Dusklord. "Caleb is right. You can't threaten us. We may not have been invited, but we're here for a reason, whether you like it or not. We've had a rough couple of days, and if you think trying to be scary and threatening is going to get rid of us, you're going to be very disappointed. And my name is George, not *little girl*." She crossed her arms over her chest and narrowed her eyes.

Dusklord shrugged one shoulder and examined his gloves. "I wouldn't dream of threatening you, little girl." Then he turned and strode into the black, with both lights following after.

They huddled together, watching their only light fade as Dusklord got smaller and smaller in the distance.

"Sooo," Cavendish said. "Are you just going to let him get away?"

George heaved a sigh and set after Dusklord with Caleb and Mikal running to keep up.

"Excuse me! Hi! Wait up, please?" she called.

The man kept walking.

"Hey, did you hear me?"

"Of course I did. It's impossible not to."

"You know we're the Snaffleharp Company, right? I don't think I told you that."

"Am I supposed to be impressed?"

"We need your help. We have to find a key to Astria here so the Council of Seven can be renewed before eleven eleven tonight or else all the worlds will be broken, not just yours," George said.

"So we don't have time for you to be difficult," Mikal said.

"But I'm so very good at it."

"Please, will you help us? We really need to get through your world."

Dusklord stopped so abruptly George almost ran into him. He gestured to the darkness around him. "Do you *see* a world here?"

"No," the children said together.

"Then how do you expect to pass through one? This is a ruined realm. I cannot even pass through it, and I am the master. It has been shattered into millions of tiny interlocking pieces, every one of them black. In the past day, I have managed, through exhausting and painstaking dedication, to assemble every single one of them. Every single one, that is, except the last one. It is missing."

His face looked drawn and sad, and his voice was kinder when he said, "I'm very aware of the circumstances you mentioned. I was to give you the third key and be your guide to Astria. I gave my word to Constantine that

I would wait for you, and that is all that has kept me here. But you cannot find a key in a world that doesn't exist. I wanted to help you, and Constantine, and everyone. But now . . . now I'm no help to anyone. There is but a single jigsaw piece standing between me and my desire." A sound halfway between a sob and a laugh escaped his throat.

"We have it," Mikal said.

"We've got the last one. We're here to help you put Obsidia back together," Caleb said.

There was no expression on Dusklord's face. "How?" he choked out.

"The person who broke it had a change of heart and gave it to us," George said.

A tremulous smile spread over Dusklord's face. Then he spun on his heel and sprinted away, his boots making sharp clicking sounds on the hard ground.

The children dashed after him.

"I'm getting. Tired of all. This running," Cavendish shouted as he jostled in Mikal's arms.

Then Dusklord skidded to a halt. "There it is." He gestured to a tiny spot of white floating in the darkness directly above Mikal's head.

Mikal swiped at it, and it spiraled away from him.

"Be careful! We mustn't lose it!" Dusklord removed his gloves and dropped them heedlessly to the ground, then turned to them with bright, eager eyes. "Give me the piece."

"Not without the magic word," Cavendish said.

"Not now, Cavendish," Mikal said.

Caleb pulled the red bag from his pocket and gave it over.

Dusklord took the satchel reverently, turned it upside down over his bare palm, and there, jet-black against his pale skin, was the single missing piece of his world. He inhaled and let the breath out slowly as he stepped up to the empty spot. He lifted the piece to the hole and pressed it in. It slid perfectly into place.

"Now what?" Caleb asked.

"Now we wait," Dusklord said, standing still as a statue.

They waited.

George reached up to tuck her hair behind her ear.

Mikal shifted Cavendish to the other arm.

Caleb rocked back and forth on his heels.

Then Dusklord pointed. "There," he breathed with barely contained excitement.

The kids leaned forward in anticipation, squinting to

see what Dusklord had seen. They watched as the darkness wavered and then froze before erupting into a thick cloud of ravens. Their obsidian wings beat loudly, leaving stray feathers to float toward the ground.

"Holy fire and hippos," Mikal said.

A bleached sun edged with silver hung on the horizon. It seemed to emanate no heat, only a sickly light that clung tentatively to the land below and faded into creeping shadow. Directly below the sun was a crumbling edifice erected of black stone, the towers toppling to the ground.

An angelic smile lit Dusklord's face, but the children didn't see it.

They had shielded their eyes, blinded by the fortress's polished roof tiles, which cruelly reflected the light of the dying sun.

"Just avert your gaze and follow me," Dusklord said.

The children obeyed, and he led the way to the far-off castle. Meteors began to streak across the sky, much lower than the children had seen them before.

"Excuse me, Dusklord?" Mikal asked. "Why are the stars falling so much closer to the ground now?"

"It's eleven eleven in the morning. You have twelve hours to complete your mission. The magic has begun to wear off, and the stars will fall lower and lower until they begin to collide with the worlds."

"So, Dusklord," George said, "where are you taking us? To the third key to Astria, I hope. Do we really have to keep calling you Dusklord?"

"I don't know if this is the time to be making friends, Georgina," Caleb said.

"Caleb, a strange man is leading us through his kingdom . . . place . . . to help us save the worlds and my family. What better time to make friends? You do have a real name, don't you, Dusklord?"

Dusklord stopped in the middle of the path, turning to face them with a look of confusion on his thin face. "A real name?"

George just smiled at him.

He frowned and cleared his throat. "My name is Boris Night. You may call me Mr. Night." He turned and walked on.

"Hi, Mr. Night. You may call me George."

"I'll consider it."

The boys laughed, and George wrinkled her nose as she stalked after Mr. Night.

"As for where I'm taking you, that would be to the Hall of Forfeit, which is where we'll retrieve the key."

"What's the Hall of Forfeit?" Caleb asked.

"Sounds mysterious," Mikal said.

"The Hall of Forfeit is a collection of worlds that have

been condemned or are considered too dangerous for just anyone to access without review and special permit. They've been sent to my realm to protect the public."

"Why is the key there? Couldn't you have put it somewhere a little less . . . dangerous?" Mikal asked.

"I put it where I thought it would be safe at the time. And . . . where I'd remember where it was."

"At least he knows where it is. We'd be in trouble if he didn't, since Cavendish has stopped working and he can't take us to it, like he did the others," George said.

Mr. Night coughed but didn't say anything else.

The path finally ended at a decaying drawbridge over a slimy green moat. Mr. Night led them across, and they stopped before a wooden gate barring entrance into the fortress.

The children watched with great interest as Mr. Night attempted to open the gate with an oversized key. Several minutes passed without progress, and he appeared to be getting frustrated.

"Do you need help?" Caleb asked.

Mr. Night scowled in reply and kicked viciously at the wood.

"I'm getting hungry," Mikal said. "Maybe we can eat while we wait?"

Caleb passed the rainbow pillowcase around, and

each child removed a snack wrapped in paper. George unwrapped a huge blueberry muffin, Caleb got a chocolate chip muffin, and Mikal wrinkled his nose when he discovered a carrot muffin.

George gave him a sympathetic look. "Wanna trade?"

Mikal nodded eagerly and began gobbling up the blueberry pastry.

"You're lucky you remind me of my little brother," George said. "Daniel refused to eat anything orange. Would you like some food, Mr. Night?"

He didn't answer, only wandered away and returned with a sturdy stick, which he proceeded to beat against the rotting planks of the stubborn gate. He glowered furiously at the stick before returning his attention to the keyhole.

"Sometimes it sticks," he said, kicking at it once more as he wiped the hair back from his sweating forehead. Then he sat dejectedly on the ground. He drew his knees up and cradled his head in his hands as he mumbled to himself. "Humiliating. Absolutely humiliating. A Great Lord, of a Great Land, who can't even gain access to his own Great Fortress. Utterly, abominably humiliating. I shall never live this down, if I live a thousand years."

"Which is increasingly unlikely if we don't get this show on the road," Cavendish said.

"Indeed," Mr. Night said, rising gracefully to his feet. "I suppose we can go the back way, though it will take longer." He smoothed back his hair, dusted his hands together in a dignified manner, and then gave the gate one last furious kick.

It crashed inward, falling off its rusted hinges and landing in the courtyard with a bang. The ground vibrated beneath their feet as the echoes rumbled throughout the now-exposed courtyard.

Mr. Night cleared his throat and smiled triumphantly. "Shall we?"

CHAPTER EIGHTEEN

MR. NIGHT LED THEM THROUGH THE RUINED courtyard. He tugged at an immense door, which creaked open, sending stale air whooshing out to greet them as they stepped into a gloomy passage. Soon he stopped before a wall covered by a threadbare tapestry.

The children watched as Mr. Night lifted the edge of

the fabric, revealing pitted stone. He kicked at a place near the floor, causing a hidden doorway to open.

They stepped through, and there before them was a long white corridor filled with hundreds of doors, each a reflection of the one on the opposite side. A friendly welcome mat lay before each portal. The only difference between the doors was that every other one had a little triangle above the frame, whereas the alternating doors each had a small circle.

"This is the Hall of Forfeit?" George asked.

"It doesn't look that dangerous," Mikal said.

"Sooo . . . where's the key?" Caleb asked.

"You know, to be honest, I'm not sure," Mr. Night said.

The children looked at him.

"You said you put it in a place you'd remember," George said.

"Yes. And so I did. I remember that I put it here, so at least there's that. I just forgot exactly where, here, that I put it. On the bright side, Constantine first asked me to find the key a couple of days ago, so I was able to search through half of these Moors before my world was broken. Then I wasn't able to look anymore, because, well, my world was broken. You know how it is." Mr. Night blushed slightly and averted his eyes.

Caleb nodded and stuck his hands in his back pockets. "Sure, we know all about that."

"Tell me again about the bright side?" George asked.

"We know the key isn't through one of the Moors on this half of the hallway." Mr. Night began walking down the corridor. The children followed until he came to a stop next to a Moor whose welcome mat lay askew. "This is where we need to start."

Caleb gave a low whistle as he saw the large number of forbidden worlds left to search. "Cav, how's the countdown?"

"The time is now twelve thirty-two PM DWT. You currently have ten hours and thirty-nine minutes until mass extinction."

"Did I ever tell you that you're a real ray of sunshine?" Caleb asked.

"Why, yes, I do believe you said something of that nature. I was deeply touched. Now, let's get on with it!" Cavendish said, and then, as an afterthought, added, "Carefully."

George brushed her hands together and walked to the Moor across the hall from the one Mr. Night had indicated. Above the frame was a triangle.

Mr. Night held up a finger in warning. "I . . . wouldn't do that if I were you."

But George was in too much of a hurry to listen. She turned the brass knob and opened the Moor into a lush meadow covering rolling hills.

"Does this look familiar, Mr. Night—" Before she had even finished the question, her attention was distracted by the faint sound of horses galloping in the distance. She leaned into the world, trying to see where the noise was coming from. An army crested the nearest hill, rushing madly in her direction.

As the army approached, she saw to her horror that it wasn't made up of ordinary men. Rather, they appeared to be a mishmash of malformed creatures. Some had the form of men but were covered from head to foot in skin that appeared to be turned inside out; others were covered in scales. All were wearing bloodstained armor and carrying wickedly sharp swords, javelins, and crossbows. A soldier, his tangled hair flying behind him, shouted, "ATTAAACKK!!!"

"Er . . . George—" Caleb said, but he was cut off by the launching of a thousand arrows aimed directly at them.

George barely had time to stumble backward and throw her arms over her face before a dart flew straight through where her head had been and buried itself in the opposite side of the hall. She landed sprawled on the floor, and Mr. Night stepped over her body, ducked gracefully, and slammed the Moor shut.

"They were attacking us!" she said hoarsely as Caleb helped her to her feet, shaking his head in disapproval.

"As I was saying," Mr. Night said, "I wouldn't go barging into *any* of these worlds, but I would proceed with *extreme* caution when entering the doors with the triangles above them, as they identify the treacherous worlds. Circle worlds are moderately safe."

Mikal tugged on the shaft embedded in the wall, but it didn't budge.

George looked down bashfully as the color returned to her face. "I'll be more careful."

"Splendid. Now, let's separate into two groups, each taking one side of the hallway. The triangles and circles alternate, so we'll all be getting our share of the danger. The little one can come with me."

Mikal swallowed hard, still shaken by the arrow that had almost penetrated George's skull. "I'm eleven. I'm just small for my age."

"Of course you are," Mr. Night said.

Caleb cautiously opened a door with a circle above it.

George hovered in the background. "See anything?"

Caleb's brow furrowed. "No, but I'm not really sure what I'm looking for."

"I seem to remember water, and lots of it," Mr. Night said from where he and Mikal were closing the door to a world of fire, molten lava, and showering sparks.

"Sigh. Always with the water," Cavendish said.

The next door had the warning triangle above it. Caleb took a deep breath, braced himself, and yanked it open. When they weren't consumed immediately, George tugged Caleb's arm down to peer over the top of it.

"Oh, look!" she said. "It's just a cute, fluffy baby bunny!"

"A bunny?" Mikal asked excitedly. He scurried across the corridor and ducked under Caleb's arm to see the adorable creature. It wiggled its pink nose, taking a tentative hop in Mikal's direction.

Mr. Night rolled his eyes and continued working his side of the corridor. "They've got to learn sometime."

"Mikal . . . ," Caleb said, pointing to the triangle above their heads.

"Come on, Mikal. It could be dangerous," George said, stepping away and pulling him with her.

"But it looks so soft," Mikal said.

Then the cute, fluffy baby bunny attacked. Its lips

curled back, revealing a mouth filled with rows of gleaming, needlelike teeth as it launched itself directly at Mikal's face.

George jerked Mikal clear, and Caleb grabbed the door and slammed it shut just before the rabbit entered the hallway. There was a loud thud, a sliding sound, and then sharp nails scratching over the wood. Angry blows followed as the rabbit threw itself madly against the barrier.

Caleb leaned against the Moor, shaking with every shuddering strike. "Seriously, guys?"

"Holy fire and hippos!" Mikal said, holding one hand over his thundering heart, Cavendish clutched in his other arm.

"Are you okay, Mikal?" George asked, checking him over for injuries.

Mikal nodded, still wild-eyed. "I think that bunny wanted to eat me."

"What about you, Cavendish? You okay?" George asked.

"Just dandy, thank you for asking. I've gotten used to the fact that on our particular mission, one must always be prepared to be eaten."

"Gee. That's awfully comforting, Cav," Caleb said.

Mikal cringed. "Sorry. It won't happen again."

"Yeah, like I haven't heard that before!" Caleb said. He ran his fingers through his mussed hair, his glare turning into a lopsided grin.

"Daniel could *definitely* not be trusted in here!" George said. "You can't keep him out of anything."

Mikal hurried to catch up with Mr. Night, offering a muttered apology.

Mr. Night looked him over briefly, a smirk tugging at the corners of his mouth. "Encountered a Blood-Sucking Bunny, did you?"

They moved through the next several Moors without any luck. Then they heard a gasp.

Mr. Night was staring into a Moor with a circle above it. "This is it. It's in here."

George and Caleb rushed to see.

"There's no water in there," Caleb said, gazing into a world of sand and blistering sun.

"You said you remembered water," George said.

"Yes, but you see the heat coming from the ground?" Mr. Night asked.

"You mean that glimmer over the dunes that looks like waves?" Mikal asked.

"Yes! Exactly. Waves. That's why I remembered water."

"That makes sense," George said. "Now, where is the key? There's a lot of sand in there. You didn't bury it, did you?"

Mr. Night opened the Moor as wide as it would go, exposing the inner side of the hinges. Hidden there, in a shallow recess, was a silver key.

"And that makes three," Caleb said. "This one's all yours, Mikal. George and I already have ours."

"On to Astria!" George said. "How do we get there?"

"Astria is here, in the Hall of Forfeit," Mr. Night said.

"Here?" Mikal asked nervously. "Why is it here?"

"Because a special permit is required to access it," Mr. Night said. "Astria likes to collect lost precious things, and it doesn't easily let them go. Before it was moved here, people would get stuck in that world, never to be seen again, because they couldn't convince Astria that they weren't lost themselves."

"And guess what, kiddos?" Cavendish asked. "We're heading there next!"

"We should be fine. We're not lost, right?" Mikal asked.

"It isn't me you have to convince—it's Astria," Mr. Night said.

"Do you at least know which Moor it's behind?" George asked. "Or do we have to start searching again?"

"Yes, I know which Moor it's behind," Mr. Night said, making a face at George and then looking away, embarrassed at his own childish display. He led them to the very end of the corridor and stopped before the last Moor on the left. Above it was a triangle.

Mr. Night opened the door and stepped directly in, with no sign of hesitation or caution.

The children exchanged a worried look but followed him across the threshold and into a small waiting room. The smell of antiseptic stung their noses, and the harsh fluorescent lights overhead buzzed and blinked. The floor was covered in cracking linoleum, and metal folding chairs lined the dirty walls.

In one of those chairs was the only cheerful spot in the dingy chamber. There sat a stunning woman dressed in a butter-yellow gown, with sunset-colored hair that tumbled down over her shoulders.

At the sight of the unexpected stranger, the children bunched together and checked behind them to make sure their escape route was still accessible.

Mr. Night rushed to the woman and took her hands in his.

She looked up, her mouth lifting into a lovely smile at the sight of him. "Boris," she said.

"I was so afraid I wouldn't see you again," Mr. Night

said in a whisper just for her ears. "Are you well? How is Lucretia holding up? Has there been any news of Lue?"

"I'm fine. Lucretia too. She's a little shriveled around the edges, but still holding on. Lue has returned to us."

"Thank heavens. I wanted to come to you as soon as Obsidia broke, since I knew I wouldn't be able to find the key and help the children, but I had given my word to Constantine that I'd wait for them. I still don't know how they ended up with the piece that allowed me to rebuild Obsidia and bring them here."

"Constantine knew you would keep your promise." She reached up and cupped his cheeks with her palms. "As soon as we received news that Obsidia had broken, Constantine began planning. He suspected Lue, and so he sent the Snaffleharp Company to the Children's Republic. He hoped they'd be able to reason with Lue, both to give up the information on how she broke Obsidia so they could fix it and to be reunited with her sisters. And they succeeded. Lue gave up the piece of Obsidia and returned home. As soon as we learned that Obsidia had been remade, I hurried here to meet you all."

"Lue broke Obsidia? I never realized she resented me so much," Mr. Night said, looking downtrodden.

"She doesn't. She's actually rather fond of you. It was

me she was acting out against. But now we've made up. She accepted my apology." The woman's expression clouded. "I was so afraid she wouldn't. But these wonderful kids . . ." She turned to look at them. Her brown eyes were tired as she watched them for a moment, and then she approached.

Caleb stepped protectively in front of his friends. "Who are you?"

"Who am I?" the woman asked, a look of surprise flashing across her face. "I was so certain my sisters would have said plenty about that. They were frightfully annoyed with me."

Mikal took a deep breath. "She must be Lucy. Mr. Night is her beau, remember?"

"You're very clever, aren't you, Mikal?" the woman asked with a smile. "I am Lucy, and the Center of the Els."

She moved to stand in front of George, studying her very carefully, as if counting every single freckle on her face. Then she took George's cold hands within her own warm ones. "You must be George. You are beautiful." She patted George softly on her red hair and turned her attention to the boys.

George's stomach flip-flopped at the compliment, for she'd never heard one like it before.

"Caleb, so practical and protective. I can see why Lue found you charming," Lucy said.

Caleb blushed furiously and stared hard at his shoes. "Thank you, miss."

Lucy laughed with delight and looked back to Mikal.

"And clever, brave little Mikal—"

Mikal interrupted. "I'm eleven, I'm just—"

Lucy held up a finger and smiled. "Who is not little, but just small for his age. Keep in mind, Mikal, that some of the smallest beasts are the most fearsome to be reckoned with."

Mikal nodded earnestly, his black eyes shining with adoration.

"And Cavendish! You have also been noble and courageous, although one might never have believed it possible."

"Well I, I . . . excuse me." Cavendish's screen turned crimson.

"Lucy," George said, "Mr. Night was supposed to guide us to Astria so we can continue our journey. Is this it? Why are you here?"

"This is the antechamber to Astria. I was sent here by your uncle to encourage you. He wanted to come himself, but at the last moment, the only candidate for the position of Guide was deemed unsuitable, so Constantine is desperately trying to find a replacement. In addition to that, he has been attempting to correct a foolish mistake I made."

"What foolish mistake?" Caleb asked.

"How could *you* be foolish?" Mikal asked.

Lucy smiled faintly. "Very easily. When you met Lue and Lucretia—that is, the Hag—they referred to themselves as my sisters. That isn't really accurate. They're not so much sisters, as . . . well . . . they're me. They're both me."

Caleb looked confused. "What do you mean, they're you? How can you be three different people?"

"Maybe she means they're super close?" Mikal asked.

"Do you mean you're a single person, just in different stages?" George asked.

"Yes, that is exactly it. We are all one person. Just like each of you. The only difference is that you live your lives over an extended period of time, whereas my sisters and I live out our life span within a six-week revolution."

Caleb raised one silver eyebrow. Mikal scratched behind his ear. George waited.

Lucy pursed her lips thoughtfully. "How shall I put this? For the first two weeks of this revolution, Lue is coming of age. Over the next two weeks, I live through my own stage. The last two weeks belong to Lucretia, the Hag, to do with as she will. When her time runs out, she dies, and it starts all over again with Lue. Together, we are the Els. Now do you understand?"

The boys nodded slowly.

"It wasn't always this way. When we were first born, we aged normally, until we died an old woman of ninety-eight. But then something strange happened. We were born again, and again. Our body aged to ninety-eight physical years old, but this occurred in much less time, and we died far sooner than we had in the last life. This happened over and over, and each time, we had fewer years between birth and death. Eventually we were living our entire cycle in mere months, and we realized that if this continued, we would soon cease to exist at all.

"When our life span had shortened to a mere forty-two days, Constantine and Henrietta found me. They had heard rumors of us and wanted to help. They had managed to find a talisman, which would act as a focus and keep my sisters and me from cycling out of life. We would be fixed on the forty-two-day schedule: fourteen days for Lue to be a kid, fourteen days for me to be a woman, and fourteen days for Lucretia to be . . . well . . . to be the

Hag. We wore the talisman always, and it became more than a focus—it became a symbol of our eternal bond, and it developed its own power.

"Constantine and Henrietta gave us Chrone Cottage to call home. It had once been the headquarters of the Council of Seven, and they asked us to watch over it. In return, it watched over us. We lived like this, happily, for a long time, but then . . ." She gazed fleetingly at Mr. Night.

"But then I fell in love, and I wanted everything that went with that sort of thing. I wanted a slow engagement, a lengthy marriage, and the chance to finally grow old together with my sweetheart. None of this was possible, though, due to the nature of the Els. Neither my sisters nor I can enjoy a long childhood, a thrilling midlife, a meandering dotage, because we are each racing the clock before our next transition. I soon fell into a deep sadness."

Mr. Night nodded sympathetically. "Anyone would have felt the same way, my dear."

"Perhaps, Boris. But my mistake wasn't in wanting something different. I think that was natural. My mistake was in not consulting my sisters about what *they* wanted, since we are all in this together. And then I made another mistake.

"A few days ago, Chrone Cottage and I had landed in my favorite place near a lake high in the mountains. I was in the garden, watching the sun set over the water, when an old man I'd never seen before approached me. He said he was lost and hungry. I was hesitant to allow a stranger entry, but he seemed so helpless that I couldn't turn him away. I brought him into my library and fed him. He saw our talisman." Lucy lifted a hand to her chest, as if to show the children, but then frowned and dropped her hand back to her side as she realized she was no longer wearing it.

"The old man said my necklace was pretty and asked if it had any meaning. I told him it signified a special bond between my sisters and me. Then he said something very alarming. He said he had heard of me and my sisters.

"I was afraid and asked him to leave at once. He obviously hadn't discovered me by accident. He asked me to be calm and told me that he had been searching for us because he'd heard a rumor, and he thought he could offer us his service. He said he had helped others like us in the past, and then he turned to leave.

"I was torn with indecision. What if his claim was true? What if I let the man get away and I could never find him again? And so I called him back."

"He had you exactly where he wanted you," Mr. Night said.

"He did. I asked what he meant, and he told me he knew of a way to separate me from my sisters so that we could each lead our own lives. He told me it was painless. He said I had to give him the talisman and allow him to separate it into three pieces. I took this to mean that he would create three necklaces, one for each of us. I was afraid, reluctant, but desperately hopeful, and so I removed the talisman. He laid it on the ground and took a glowing stone from his pocket. I watched, horror-stricken, as he suddenly smashed the rock down and shattered the pendant. I screamed, and as I watched, the three pieces shimmered and disappeared into the air. The man cursed at this and fled from Chrone Cottage.

"He had lied about it being painless. Somehow he had managed to break not only what bound us to our cycle but also what bound us as sisters. We began to detach from one another, and the shock and agony of separation was more than we could handle. We were helpless upon the library floor until Constantine found us early Wednesday morning. It took hours of care and mending until we could speak and tell him what had happened."

Mr. Night's face was grim, and he kissed Lucy's hair gently.

"When I described the man to Constantine, your uncle recognized immediately that he was Nero, back from a false death. Constantine sent the note to you at once, George. Then he explained to my sisters and me that there were consequences to what Nero and I had done. With the talisman broken, and our bond with it, we would indeed live as separate people, with individual life spans, but those life spans had already begun.

"The Hag, at her great age, would soon die a permanent death, and I would follow, given enough time. Lue would have the worst of it, as she was doomed to live the longest without her sisters. You see, when the Els are properly joined, our arrangement keeps us from ever being truly alone. We have grown used to the solace of knowing the others are always within us, and we have only to reach inward should we need their counsel or companionship.

"Lue was furious with me for not consulting her and the Hag first, and furious with me for cursing her to a lonely life just so I could be with my love. And then she ran off, and part of Chrone Cottage went with her, for it has grown used to protecting us and can be in more than one place at a time."

"No wonder she was mad enough to break Mr. Night's world," George said. "It must be awful to have part of yourself taken away without your permission."

"Yes. Lue was right," Lucy said. "I made a terrible mistake, and I was devastated by the pain I'd caused. Then Constantine told me that there was a way for my sisters and me to be rejoined, and that it was vital to the well-being of the worlds and would save countless lives, if I was willing. I am absolutely willing, anything to keep my sisters alive and healthy and happy, and to keep innocents from suffering."

Mr. Night swelled with affectionate pride. "She's terribly intelligent, see? And so good."

"Excuse me," Cavendish said. "I don't mean to interrupt, but the time is now four oh nine PM DWT. You currently have seven hours and two minutes until total eradication."

"Just a minute, Cavendish," George said. "Lucy, why is it vital to the well-being of the worlds for you to be rejoined with your sisters?"

"That will be answered later. But time is short, and now I must explain your next task. As you know, all three mislaid pieces of the talisman must be recovered. When you enter Astria, there will be three trials, one for each of you. If you pass your trial, you may each use your key to exit the world, and your key will turn into what you were seeking. You may then leave Astria with a piece of the talisman."

"That doesn't sound so hard," Caleb said.

"Getting into Astria isn't the problem," Mr. Night said. "The problem is getting out."

Lucy nodded solemnly. "Astria does not easily surrender what it believes to be lost. To get out, you must convince Astria that you are *not* lost. It will be difficult, but remember, all it takes is one person to make the right decision to change the entire course of the future."

"Why does it have to be us?" Mikal asked nervously. "I don't want to get stuck in there."

"I'm not trying to be rude, but since you lost the pieces of the talisman, why can't you and your sisters get them back?" George asked.

"Because I cast away the pieces, and as my sisters and I are one, *we* cast away the pieces. Astria would not find us worthy to reclaim them when I basically gave them away to be destroyed."

"There is a bright side," Mr. Night said. "Children are said to have a much easier time of it in there, because they aren't usually as adrift as adults are."

"That's true," Lucy said. "And I believe you each have the strength and courage to pass your trials."

The children were anxious as Lucy led them to a white door at the other end of the room. George wrung her scarf into a tangle, and Mikal was itching with nerves.

Caleb had gnawed his thumbnail almost down to the quick.

"What happens if we fail?" George asked.

"We won't fail," Caleb said.

"But what if we do?" Mikal asked.

Lucy and Mr. Night exchanged an uncomfortable look.

"Then you stay in Astria until the worlds end tonight at eleven eleven," Lucy said.

"At least we'll have Cavendish," George said. "He gives good advice and might be able to help us through the trials."

"Excuse me again," Cavendish said, his voice sounding tinny and worried. "But I've just received an emergency notice."

"What's it say?" they asked, crowding around Mikal, who held Cavendish.

"It says that I'm . . . I'm supposed to stay here. With Lucy. I can't go with you."

The children were certain it was a mistake, but Cavendish assured them it was true. Mikal tearfully gave Cavendish to Lucy, who promised to keep him safe, and with a sorrowful good-bye, the children left their guide and entered Astria alone.

Astria

CHAPTER NINETEEN

The Snaffleharp Company stepped into a world of pure white. They were blinded by its sheer brilliance and had to lift their hands to shield their eyes. When they had become accustomed to the brightness, they were finally able to observe their surroundings.

"There's nothing here," George said, her voice hoarse with shock. "Absolutely nothing."

"I thought this world collected lost things. So where are they?" Caleb turned in a full circle, his sneakers making a squelching sound as they tried to glue to the ground. He lifted one foot to see what was causing the noise and found silken threads clinging to the sole of his shoe.

"What in the Flyrrey is that?" George asked.

"Beats me," Caleb said. "It feels kind of like cobwebs. Weird."

"Do you think we're in the right place? Maybe we should go back and ask," she said.

Mikal shook his head. "The door is gone, and everything's white. We'll never find our way out unless the world lets us."

"This must be the test," Caleb said. "We have to figure this out if we want to go on."

George twisted the ends of her scarf. "But I thought there was supposed to be a different trial for each of us."

"I miss Cavendish," Mikal said in a small voice. "Even broken, he could still have helped us know what to do." He kicked at the sticky floor.

"Should we just start walking? Is there any way to tell how big a space this is?" George asked.

Caleb shrugged. "I dunno. Maybe echoes? HELLO! IS ANYBODY THERE?"

Mikal put his hands up to his mouth and shouted, "HOW BIG ARE YOU, ASTRIA?"

Nothing came back to them.

"I don't know what to do," George said hopelessly. "Always before, there's been something for me to do, somewhere to start. But there's nothing here." She sank down, and her purple skirt billowed around her. She dropped her hands into her lap and gazed around despairingly.

"It's gonna be okay, George," Mikal said.

"Not if we can't get out of here. And we have to get out of here." Her forehead creased into a frown, and she stared at her fingers while speaking softly to herself. "We have to get out of here for my mom and dad. They don't even know where I am. And for my little brother. If we don't pass through Astria and go to Selyrdor, Aunt Henrietta and Uncle Constantine will die, and Thazel and Hector and . . ." She looked up at Caleb and Mikal. "We all will."

"You're not gonna let us die, are you, George?" Caleb asked, with his lopsided smile.

She paused a moment and then held out a hand. "Help me up."

Caleb and Mikal heaved her up off the tacky ground. She tried to brush the stubborn strands of gossamer from her dress but soon gave up. She placed her fists on her hips, concentrating hard on the problem of so much empty space.

Mikal inhaled sharply and tugged on George's sleeve. "Look at that!"

George gasped with surprise as she saw what Mikal was pointing to.

A flaming letter of fire had appeared in the whiteness at their feet, etched by an invisible hand. As they watched, another letter joined the first, and another, until words began to spiral in a circle around them.

"Holy fire and hippos," Caleb said.

"Yeah! Hey, that's what I say!" Mikal said.

George squinted and leaned low over the text to read it aloud. "To show you're found and not lost . . ." She turned a bit to follow the curve of the circle. "You are bound to pay the cost. . . . Alone move forward to face your trial . . . And prove you're free, if it's worth your while."

"Does it mean we have to go off by ourselves?" Mikal asked.

"I think so," George said. "To prove we're not lost and are free to leave Astria." She bit her lip. "But I don't want to be by myself. Not again."

"What if we don't find each other after?" Caleb's jaw

was tight, and his hands were clasped into fists by his sides.

"It's too big out there," Mikal said, his voice quavering. "I'm too small for my age to go off alone. I've never been alone before, not really. I've always had my dad or Caleb."

"Hey," George said, reaching out to squeeze their hands, "it's going to be okay, remember? We'll find each other again, Caleb. And you've gotten *so* brave, Mikal. I know you can do this. We're gonna pass our tests, and then we'll be back together. We have to, so we can reunite the pieces of the talisman."

The boys looked at her for a moment. Caleb was the first to nod, a quick jut of his chin. Mikal was slower, but finally, miserably, he agreed. He dug his green dinosaur out of his backpack and clutched it to his chest in place of Cavendish.

George threw the ends of her scarf back and straightened her spine, then took a quick count.

"Three for backpack, four for Caleb, five for Mikal, six for . . . Cavendish. We'll get him back soon, so I can still count him. Everybody have their key?" She looked them over and took a moment to brush Mikal's hair off his forehead. "You kind of gave that dinosaur to me, so make sure I get him back, okay?"

"I promise," Mikal said.

"You'd better," she said softly, and looked at Caleb.

Caleb just blinked his silver eyes and gave her an encouraging nod.

George took a deep breath. "Let's get on with it, then. We're losing daylight . . . er . . ." She trailed off, looking at the unwavering light around them. "You get the point."

"We'll just walk in different directions?" Mikal asked.

Caleb nodded, and they all turned their backs to one another.

"Ready?" Caleb asked.

"I'm ready," Mikal said.

"Me too," George said.

"Okay, let's go," Caleb said.

The three children each took a step away from the others.

"ONE DOWN," GEORGE SAID, AND LOOKED over her shoulder.

But she was all by herself. Her friends had disappeared into the blank unknown.

She turned to go on, but there, where a moment ago had been nothing, was a projector standing before an enormous screen. The projector buzzed on, flashing a beam of yellow light.

Words appeared on the display. *To prove you are not lost, you must find, and forgive the memory you keep to remind.* Then a picture appeared, in brilliant color, of an outdoor marketplace. People bustled in and out of the crowd as they did their shopping. George smelled cinnamon, and her eyes burned as a vendor sliced open a ruby-red pepper. There was a drizzle of rain coming down.

"Istanbul," she whispered, her entire body tingling and numb at the same time.

From the right side of the screen, a girl appeared, holding a little boy's hand. He wore a yellow raincoat and was teasing the girl mercilessly by fidgeting with the end of her scarf. She tried to frown but only ended up shaking her head and smiling.

George rushed up to the picture and put her hand on it, on the little boy's sandy hair with the cowlick that never went down. But he wouldn't be still for her to touch. He pulled free from the girl's grasp, and she chased after him, but then the crowd moved and she was shoved to the ground. She jumped up, dress caked in mud, to search for the little boy. But he wasn't there.

She yelled his name, then screamed it, and then cried it, but he wasn't anywhere.

The picture sped up, and a whole night and part of a day went by before the girl returned to where she had lost her brother. She bent over the mud puddle, scooped up a handful of clay, tucked it into her pocket, and turned to go. The projector paused, showing only the empty puddle overlaid with the same words as before.

"Why would you show me that?" George asked through trembling lips. "Just so I could lose him all over again? I didn't want to see that!" She shrugged out of her backpack and swung it hard against the screen. She threw the pack down and kicked at it. Toad flopped out, looking limp and unloved.

"Toad!" George dropped to her knees to gather him up. "I'm so sorry, Toad." She held him close for a moment, and then she looked up at the words. Her face fell with understanding.

George set Toad aside and reached back into her knapsack to remove a faintly shining orb, number twelve for Istanbul. She cradled the *hikaru dorodango* in her hands. She held it close to her face and focused hard on determining its exact shade of gray. She rubbed it against her cheek, feeling the grain of the dirt and every dip and hollow of the unfinished project. When she pulled it away, the color had changed from the dampness on her face.

She got to her feet and walked back to the screen, still displaying the frozen picture of the puddle. She reached out, and her hand passed through the screen with a crackle of static as she lovingly returned the *hikaru dorodango* to the mud it had come from. It plopped into the dirty water, and the projector clicked off.

George turned her back to it and took a long shuddering breath. A red door appeared just in front of her. She stuffed Toad into her bag, pulled the key from her pocket, and inserted it into the keyhole. With a flutter against her palm, the key transformed into a bright red piece of the talisman, and the door opened.

MIKAL COUGHED AND WAS STARTLED AT the sound in the absolute quiet. He glanced back at the others to see if they had noticed, but they were gone, and he was alone.

He swallowed, took another step, and smacked into a very hard white door. He lifted his hand to his forehead, checking for blood. There wasn't any, and he looked up with a scowl.

Above the door was written, *To prove you are not lost,*

you must find the skill to perceive goodness, even in what seems malign.

A noise came from behind him, and he started and spun around. His eyes widened as he saw a red-and-white-striped circus tent, ringing with the sound of applause. Mikal peeked between the flaps and then squeezed in and stole a seat near the front. The smell of popcorn and sweat surrounded him, and he watched, captivated, as the ringmaster announced the next act.

"I'm pleased to present to you a legend who has conquered air and defied gravity! I give you Feliks the Fleet!"

The crowd roared with enthusiasm, but Mikal's jaw went slack as he watched Feliks the Fleet, his own father, bow to the crowd from atop an impossibly high perch. A pitiful whimper escaped Mikal as his father took flight, leaping and soaring gracefully above. Mikal couldn't tear his eyes away as his father missed a bar, lost his grip, and plummeted to the earth with a sickening thump. The spectators were chased from the tent in a jam of confusion and curiosity, and even when there was no one left but his father's body in the center of the ring, Mikal sat staring.

Then the tent faded away, and his father with it, replaced by Caleb leading a younger Mikal through a grassy meadow. A breeze lifted, cooling Mikal's tearstained cheeks as the scene changed again. There was Caleb fighting to keep them together, scavenging for food and blankets, always letting Mikal eat first and making sure he was warm enough. Then Caleb with a relieved expression on his face as he led Mikal to the mausoleum that would be their home, a place where they could be warm and have enough to eat and where nobody would try to separate them. Then George came, and Mikal saw how scared she was, even though she tried to sound brave.

He watched as they joined George and set out to save the worlds together. Cavendish, Thazel, Hector, the Children's Republic, Obsidia, the Hall of Forfeit, Astria, the Council of Seven being rebuilt, Aunt Henrietta being rescued, the worlds and people being saved and allowed to live on in happiness and hope, all passed by in a blur. Mikal saw all of this, and knew none of it would have had the chance to happen if he and Caleb hadn't been on their own and in that cemetery when George showed up. He saw that as much as he loved and missed his father, that terrible loss had given him a chance to save the worlds.

"Sometimes good things come from bad things," he whispered to the dinosaur he still held. "I can make good things come from bad things."

Mikal rose from the bleachers. He turned back to the door, knowing he had passed his test and would be able to rejoin his friends. But as he saw the blank whiteness around him, he paused. How could he leave this world better than it was?

He thought back to Hector's sad place and the life that had sprung up after the rain had come. He wondered what would happen when the dragons didn't return because of the blue dust. Without the dragons, the rain wouldn't come. Without the rain, the Tree Who Yawns Butterflies would slowly die again, along with everything else.

But what if something good could be made of all this empty wasted space? What if Astria could nourish things, instead of just collecting them? Mikal's grin was slow and joyful. He smoothed his hair back with one hand.

"Astria, I don't know if you can hear me. I don't even know if you're alive, but I know you like to collect things that have been lost. I know of a place that has been lost. The rains have gone away and forgotten all about it."

He paused, waiting for a reply, but there was none.

He plunged ahead with his request. "I think you should collect the Tree Who Yawns Butterflies, and all of the living things of Hector's sad place. They could come here to live, and you could take care of them, and they would make your world beautiful."

There was still no reply. Mikal sat down in front of the white door and waited patiently.

A flicker of motion caught his attention. He looked up and saw butterflies fluttering toward him. They were translucent, outlined only in blue, but they were butterflies. As he watched, color began to bleed into them, starting at the base against their long bodies and spreading to the tips of their wings.

As Mikal got back to his feet, mountains erupted from the ground. Grass and wildflowers sprouted beneath him, spreading in waves over new hills and valleys. Streams parted the earth, baby frogs chirped, and the Tree Who Yawns Butterflies took up its home on the hill. Far off in the distance, a thundercloud crackled.

"Thank you." Mikal turned back to the door and inserted the key. A white piece of the Els talisman warmed his palm as the door opened. He took one more look at the thriving world around him before stepping into the unknown.

GEORGE AND MIKAL LOOKED AT EACH other in surprise.

They had arrived safely in a glass chamber with a door leading out. But there was a problem. Caleb was not with them.

They turned to look back the way they had come, but

the door to Astria had closed. Where it had been was now a window into the white world, through which they could see Caleb.

"Do you think he failed?" George asked.

"Caleb doesn't fail."

"Then we'll wait," George said, and crossed her fingers for her friend.

CALEB KNEW HE WAS ALONE BEFORE HE even turned around, and he felt the absence of his companions keenly. He saw a dark blur far in the distance, and as he got closer, it separated into two black doors. Above them were the words *To prove you are not lost, you must find who you are when past meets future and intertwines.*

The door to his right was labeled WHO YOU ARE, and as he watched, the dark wood began to swirl with color until it displayed a memory so vibrant that chills broke out on Caleb's arms. He saw a younger version of himself huddling behind a pile of garbage, covered only in old newspapers and terrified by a world he didn't recognize. He was shivering uncontrollably and stuffing stale popcorn into his mouth so fast he didn't stop to chew it.

The picture changed, and this time a dark-haired little boy was there, bringing food and blankets. Then a man came, collected Caleb in his arms, and carried him into a warm tent. There the little boy and the man set about caring for Caleb.

A new picture appeared. Mikal sobbing as his father's body was carried away and accepting comfort from no one but Caleb. The circus left and Caleb was alone again, but not really alone, because now he had Mikal. It didn't matter so much that he knew nothing of his past or where he had come from or why he hadn't been worth keeping, because Mikal needed him.

More pictures flashed by, faster now. Caleb and Mikal on the run, trying to settle down, finding the cemetery, George showing up, needing help, the boys agreeing to go with her, learning that they had to save the worlds and the people traveling through mud puddles; and finally saying good-bye to Mikal and George as they parted in Astria.

The wood faded back to black, and silver words appeared. *These decisions led you here. Enter if you would do it all again.*

Then Caleb looked to the left door, which was labeled WHO YOU WERE. He drew a sharp breath and stepped eagerly toward it, expecting the door to become a series of pictures that would tell him a story of his unknown past. But the door stayed solid and black.

A look of dread crossed Caleb's face as he realized he

was being presented with his greatest dilemma: to rejoin his friends, or to attain his heart's desire? To discover where he came from, who he had been before Mikal found him frozen in the dirt, if he had a real name, and if anybody had ever loved him, or to continue on and save the worlds from destruction?

"You've got to be kidding me." He rubbed at his neck, torn with indecision.

"This isn't fair," he called out angrily. "I can't make this choice!"

He reached out and traced the words on the left door. "'Who you were,'" he said softly. "Who was I?"

He looked back at the other door.

"Come on!" he yelled, slamming the flat of his hand against the left door. "You have to show me something. Anything! I can't be this close to finding out where I came from, only to have to turn away and leave without learning anything."

Nothing happened, and he kicked furiously at the frame. He beat against the door until his hands were bruised. He fell to his knees, panting and exhausted.

"Please," he whispered. "Please, just show me something."

"I DON'T THINK HE'S GOING TO MAKE IT," George said as they watched Caleb through the window.

Mikal looked on, his brows drawn tight together.

George's stomach knotted with anxiety. "Well, I'm tired of doing nothing. I'm going to make him choose us."

And she threw herself against the glass. She slammed her palms against it until the pane trembled, and Mikal joined her in a flurry of pummeling fists and green dinosaur.

CALEB SAT SLUMPED AGAINST THE DOOR to his past. He held his head in his hands and muttered to himself. "This could be my only chance to find out who I really am. I have no choice." He climbed to his feet and rubbed the back of his hand against his cheeks, wiping away tears of frustration. He rested his forehead against the smooth wood of the left door and placed his hand on the knob. "I won't be Loeta anymore."

GEORGE BEAT AGAINST THE WINDOW UNTIL HER arms buzzed. "He can't hear us. He's going to make the wrong choice!"

Mikal kicked at the barrier, then rammed his shoulder against it. "We have to be louder."

Together they yelled Caleb's name and begged him to pick them.

CALEB JIGGLED THE KNOB OF THE DOOR TO his past, just testing it, not quite ready to turn it. He reached into his pocket and withdrew the key. Feeling the weight of it in his palm, he squeezed it so tightly that the edges cut into his skin. He lifted the key to the hole and threw one last glance at the door that would take him to his friends. It began to shiver and quake.

He blinked, taking a step back.

As if through murky water, George and Mikal appeared behind the door. They were beating against it and screaming something, but he could only hear a whisper of their voices.

He looked at them, pleading with them to understand.

Their voices grew louder.

"Caleb," George was saying, "you belong with us. Please choose us."

Caleb's spine straightened imperceptibly, and without giving himself time to change his mind, he stumbled to the right door, inserted the key, and turned it. Within his hand was a black piece of the talisman, and he stepped through the portal without looking back.

BEFORE THE DOOR EVEN CLOSED BEHIND Caleb, George had thrown her arms around his neck. “You came back,” she said. “I was so afraid you wouldn’t.”

“You saw that, huh?” Caleb’s voice was bleak as he shoved his fingers through his hair.

George stepped away and wiped the tears from her face with the ends of her scarf. “Yes. We saw it all.” She took one of his bruised hands in both of hers as she looked at him with utter conviction. “I promise you, Caleb. I’m going to help you find out where you came from, but you belong with me and Mikal. Not wherever that Moor would have taken you.”

Mikal came up and placed a hand on George’s and Caleb’s. “We’re the Snaffleharp Company, you know?”

Caleb stared at them for a moment and then nodded his head. “I know. That’s why I came back.”

They turned to the only door leading out of the room.

George hitched up her backpack. “One for backpack, two for raincoat, three for Caleb, four for Mikal, five for Cavendish, who we’ll get back soon—”

“Six for my dinosaur,” Mikal said.

George nodded. “Okay, we’re ready. Let’s go get ’em.”

CHAPTER TWENTY

THE CHILDREN STEPPED OUT OF THE GLASS chamber and back into the dingy waiting room.

Lucy was waiting all alone, wringing her hands. When she saw them emerge, she rushed to greet them. "I was so worried. You were gone such a long time."

"What's the countdown, Cav?" Caleb asked. But Cavendish wasn't there to answer.

"Where is he?" Mikal asked, eyes darting around the room. "He was supposed to wait with you!"

"Cavendish is with Constantine and the others, which is where we're going. Hurry! It's nine thirty PM. You were in Astria for five hours. We haven't much time now before the end." Lucy led them from the Hall of Forfeit, back into the fortress, and to a pretty yellow door. She stopped before it and dusted off the front of her gown. "This is it. The Moor that will take us to Selyrdor, where it all began. Are you ready?"

Mikal smoothed back his hair.

George tossed the end of her scarf over one shoulder.

Caleb straightened his suspenders.

Lucy opened the door, and the children peered into a familiar world. An enormous library with gleaming silver ladders, a glass ceiling through which meteors could be seen streaking across the sky above, a yellow bicycle leaning against the fireplace, and the hidden passage they were standing in disguised as a bookcase.

Within the library, a mismatched group of people waited. There was Mr. Phinneus Neptune, examining Cavendish on the polished cherry desk. Lue and Yorick, the skeleton George had first met in her bedroom, were playing cat's cradle in the corner. Mr. Night was carefully applying medicinal drops to the Hag's shriveled eyes. The pet geese had been brought in from the garden above and were nesting by the bicycle. One was even perched upon the seat.

Mr. Night saw Lucy and hurriedly finished his task before going to greet her. As soon as the newcomers had stepped clear of the passage, he shut the way behind them.

"Holy fire and hippos," Mikal said as he saw Yorick towering above everyone else. "You didn't say he was so tall!"

"She did say he was a giant," Caleb said.

George saw Constantine standing apart and looking utterly exhausted. His face was more lined, his red shoes were scuffed, and even his enormous mustache drooped at the ends. Then he saw George and smiled big enough to push his mustache back up to where it belonged.

George rushed to Constantine's side and was content for a moment just to lean wearily against him as he patted her back.

Mikal went to Mr. Neptune and Cavendish and began peppering them with questions.

Cavendish got so excited trying to tell Mikal what had happened when he'd been taken away that he was unable to form coherent sentences. "I . . . overjoyed . . . never thought . . . and now the Council itself!" he stuttered blissfully, and then issued a series of high beeps.

Caleb stood alone out of the way.

George called the boys over to meet Constantine, and they bashfully approached, Cavendish back in Mikal's arms.

Constantine shook both their hands, his face solemn. "I've heard a lot about you boys. It seems you're quite tenacious and rather brave."

Mikal blushed. "We only followed the code."

"It was the right thing to do, that's all," Caleb said.

"Don't listen to them, Uncle Constantine," George said. "I couldn't have done any of it without them. I guess you've already met Cavendish?"

"I have," Constantine said. "We had quite a long talk while you were in Astria."

"Excuse me, sir? But speaking of Cavendish, we're running out of time. Shouldn't we be getting the talisman to Selyrdor, where it all began?" Caleb asked.

"You already have," Constantine said. "This *is* where it all began. Or rather, that is." He pointed to the circle of light falling onto the floor in the center of the room. "Chrone Cottage is built directly above the ancient basement where the last survivors of the first showers took refuge and elected the original Council of Seven."

"So we made it," George said, and then jolted upright. "Oh! Uncle Constantine! Nero kidnapped Aunt Henrietta. He's holding her captive!"

"I know, George," Constantine said, looking pained. "Henrietta did what she had to do to keep Nero occupied. She's very noble. I hope that we'll soon have her back."

"But how, and why? And—" George took a deep breath and let it out with a whoosh. "I've got so many questions, I don't even know where to start."

"That's understandable." Constantine patted his shirt pocket and then frowned. "Do you happen to have my watch?"

George retrieved the watch for Constantine, and he polished it on his sleeve and checked the time.

"Hmm. I believe we can spare a few minutes to satisfy the curiosity of the Snaffleharp Company, seeing as they've given us a chance to re-form the Council of Seven." Constantine raised his bushy eyebrows at them. "How about I start at the beginning, and if I miss anything, you can jump right in with your questions?"

The children liked this plan.

"As you know, tonight is the seventh and last night of the Selyrdorian meteor showers that once rained death and destruction upon the worlds. The Council of Seven was created to bring order, and its creation caused the showers to cease. Every one hundred and eleven years after that, the Council would come back together, in this very room. There the bonds of friendship and order would be renewed, keeping the showers at bay for another hundred and eleven years, thus leaving the worlds and their peoples safe.

"But then the Council broke. Nero, the old Judge, went mad and began murdering the other members. Then it appeared that Nero had been killed in a terrible blast. There were many witnesses and much evidence, and I was lulled into believing the tragedy had completed.

"Henrietta and I then began to seek out individuals who could help us rebuild the Council of Seven before the showers returned to threaten the worlds. After nearly a century, we had finally gathered a sprinkling of honorable, brilliant people who showed great promise, and just in the nick of time. On the first night of the showers, I left Snaffleharp Lane to begin conducting the final interviews with those we had chosen."

"That's what your business trip was about?" George asked.

"Yes. I went first to visit Yorick." He gestured to the lanky skeleton. "After hours of this ultimate examination, I asked him if he would accept the position of Recorder. He was startled, but to my great relief, he agreed. You see, none of the candidates knew why Henrietta and I had shown such sudden and intense interest in them. It was vital that they continue to behave normally so we could observe their true characters.

"After Yorick, I met with Mr. Neptune, and then Mr. Night. On Wednesday morning, I visited Chrone Cottage to interview the Els and ask them to accept the position of Judge. I arrived only to discover that the Els had been separated. When they recovered enough to speak, Lucy told me what had happened, and I knew at once that Nero was the man who had visited her. When Lucy described how the broken talisman had evaporated, I knew that Astria must have claimed it, as it is very precious."

"Is that when you sent me the note?" George asked.

"Yes. I had Yorick deliver it as soon as I realized that Nero had returned and what was necessary to correct the situation."

"But why did Nero want to separate the Els?" Caleb asked.

"And how did he find them?" Mikal asked.

"How did he even know about them and the talisman, since they only came to live at Chrone Cottage after the Council was broken and Nero went crazy?" George asked.

"I believe Nero began to miss the power he once wielded," Constantine said. "As the showers approached, he knew I would be re-forming the Council and that I would need a Judge. But he wanted that role back, so he must have set out to discover who I was considering for the position.

"The first step would be to seek out the headquarters of the Council, Chrone Cottage, and see if any activity there would give him insight into my plans. It would not have been hard for him to find it, for when one has called a place home for millennia, a certain magnetic attraction develops. Neither I, nor any of the Council members, had to wait for the cottage to find us, as a normal person might. We were simply drawn to it.

"Once back there, Nero would have found the clues he was seeking. He would have seen the Els cycling through their lives, and he would have observed them closely. He may have noted that the three were never seen together, that one aged rapidly into the next, and that in every form, they each wore the same talisman. Nero is clever, and when two people have been as close as brothers for as long as he and I were, you begin to understand each other as well as you might understand yourself. Nero would know that I'd take measures to prevent any one person from ever again bearing the load that had been placed on him.

"You see, Nero had lost his sanity due to being overwhelmed with the power and burden of performing the duties of three people. He would easily have realized that only as a whole are the Els uniquely qualified to take his place as Judge. He must have believed that if the sisters were made unsuitable, he would be the only option available to me to successfully re-form the Council. And that is why he broke them apart."

"And why we had to find the pieces of the talisman?" George asked.

"So the sisters can be rejoined and take the position of Judge," Caleb said.

"But why did *we* have to do it?" Mikal asked.

"That is correct, George and Caleb. And because, Mikal, there was simply nobody else who could. It had to be three people to recover three pieces. I couldn't go, because I had to perform damage control, discover the location of the keys, plot your journey, make sure you had the tools you needed, conduct the last interview with the potential Guide, and tend to any problems that arose. Henrietta couldn't do it, because, with Nero on the loose, she had to get you out of the house, George. It was necessary that my brave Henrietta allow Nero to think he had the upper hand."

George frowned with confusion. "But how did Aunt Henrietta know that? You both thought Nero was dead."

"And if it had to be three people, why did you send George off all alone?" Caleb asked.

"Did you write a secret message in the note you sent

George?" Mikal asked, his black eyes glittering curiously.

Constantine smiled at Mikal. "You are a clever rascal! I wrote a cryptic P.S. to Henrietta just in case the note was waylaid. Do you still have it, George?"

George presented the battered slip of paper to Constantine, and he peered at it through his little round glasses.

"Hmm, yes. If you look here, it says 'P.S. 1G+2B= 3 to Flee. Forecast: Ge<u>nero</u>us Rain!!! Be a duck, have a plan.—Love, C.' In other words, George and the two boys must go at once, prepare them for puddle travel. Nero is back! Be calm, I have a plan."

"But that means you knew about us before we even met George!" Caleb said.

"Yes, I had heard of you two all on your own. I went to retrieve you and bring you home to Snaffleharp Lane, but as soon as I saw you, Mikal, I knew you wouldn't be very trusting of strangers, so I stayed out of sight. Henrietta would send me with baskets of food, and I became impressed with how resourceful, responsible, and honorable you both were. When I realized I had to send George on this mission, you boys came immediately to mind. I knew you would help her if she needed you; that was clear just by observing you. I have a code too, you see, and when you've been around as long as I have, you develop certain instincts, and you learn to trust them." Constantine's eyes twinkled. "Besides, I doubted you'd turn down the adventure."

"We always thought the food was from the groundskeeper, Mr. Chinchinian," Caleb said.

"But it was you. You fed us," Mikal said, his face lit with newly discovered devotion.

"That's why Aunt Henrietta told me to go left," George said softly. "Left was the way to the cemetery, and to Caleb and Mikal."

Constantine nodded and fiddled with the end of his mustache.

"What happens now, though?" George asked. "How will we rebuild the Council before it's too late? Did you find someone to be the Guide?"

"I did," Constantine said.

"And what about Aunt Henrietta? Will we be able to save her from Nero?"

A flash of worry crossed Constantine's visage, but he quickly replaced it with a reassuring smile. "We will most certainly save Henrietta from Nero. I have a plan. Nero will arrive with Henrietta, as this is where the Council of Seven must be remade. He will probably have no more than two henchmen in tow. He works small and quick.

Remember, he and I know each other. Mr. Neptune has access to a shocking array of gadgets, and I've asked him to activate an impenetrable field of energy behind Nero, to render his escape impossible. Then I will attempt to reason with him. If that fails . . ." He seemed to age before their very eyes. He started again. "If that fails, there will be a struggle. I'm here, and Mr. Night, Mr. Neptune, and Yorick. Lucy is a clever strategist, and dear Henrietta knows how to throw a punch. We will outnumber him."

"Uncle Constantine," George said, wetting her lips, "that doesn't sound like a very good plan."

"I know, George. But it's all we've got. Our only choice is to oppose Nero as a group and hope we prevail."

"Constantine?" Lucy said. "We're getting close."

The countdown flashed on Cavendish's screen: *The time is now 10:00 PM DWT. You currently have one hour and eleven minutes until all living things are obliterated.*

"You do have a way with words, Cavendish." Constantine turned to the rest of the group. "If you will all join me in the center of the room, please?"

Mr. Night helped the Hag to her feet and held her elbow as she shuffled toward Constantine.

Lue tagged behind Mr. Night, kicking at his heels.

"You displayed very poor judgment, Lucy," Constantine said kindly once they had assembled. "As a result, the life cycles of the Els have been significantly altered, and I was unable to perform your final interview."

Lucy nodded, standing silent and respectful.

"But immediately upon realizing you had wronged your sisters, you set to making it right. You aided me in my research and planning. You willingly agreed to sacrifice your heart's desire, a normal life with your love, to be rejoined with your sisters and take up the role of Judge to save the worlds and all their creatures."

Constantine turned to Lue and the Hag now. "Lucretia, you forgave Lucy at once, for with your age and experience has come compassion and understanding. Lue, you were furious with your sister and immediately declared war upon her, but you too came around and forgave her. This would be very hard to pull off if that hadn't happened."

Constantine again faced the whole group. "These actions have served as a better indication of character than I could ever have come up with on my own."

"Oh, do hurry up," Lue said, twirling a lock of hair.

"Behave, Lue," Mr. Night said.

Lue stuck her tongue out at him.

"Lue, Lucy, and Lucretia, will you each hold a piece of the talisman in your left hand and place it over your heart?"

George and Company quickly offered up the pieces, and the sisters obeyed.

"Lucy," Constantine said, "are you certain you can accept spending only fourteen days at a time with your love for the greater good? Keeping in mind, of course, that the alternative is a fiery death."

The group looked up at the glass ceiling. The meteors were falling so close now that the shriek of their passage could be heard.

Lucy glanced lovingly at Mr. Night, but her voice was strong when she said, "I can."

Constantine turned to Lue and the Hag. "Are you two prepared to rejoin your sister and to take your place on the Council?"

The Hag cleared her throat, a wet rattling sound, and nodded her consent.

Lue looked away, then rolled her eyes and said, "Well, I guess."

"Good, and since we are pressed for time, if you three will just face one another and concentrate on the fact that you are meant to be one."

"I'm glad to have you back, sisters," Lucy murmured for their ears only.

The Hag and Lue met Lucy's eyes, and the three grasped hands. Then they began to shimmer.

"Everybody, stand back!" Constantine said.

There was a loud bang, like a crash of thunder. The library shook, books rattled on shelves, and the sisters began to dissolve into perfect cubes of light until only Lucy remained. She gazed into space for a moment and then wrapped her fingers around the talisman, which was whole again.

The kids shared a triumphant grin.

"Thank you, Constantine," Lucy said simply. "And thank you, children and Cavendish."

"Indeed," Constantine said. "But now it is ten seventeen PM. We have only a few minutes before Nero arrives. I suggest we take a moment to gather our thoughts and prepare for a very nasty confrontation." He stepped away to stand alone.

George, followed by Caleb and Mikal, went to Constantine's side.

"Yes, George?" Constantine asked, looking down.

"What if Nero doesn't come?" she asked.

"He will. And he will bring Henrietta with him. If he doesn't come, and the clock strikes eleven twelve, all is lost. Without Henrietta, we will be unable to re-form the Council, and tonight all worlds will end. He will come. He thinks he has won."

"What will he do when he sees that we've already rejoined the Els, though? Will he hurt Aunt Henrietta?" George's face was as pale as her silver freckles at the thought.

Constantine's face changed, becoming fierce and certain. "Don't doubt for a moment that I will get her back safely. It would be impossible for me to exist without her, and I am still here. We will prevail. If Nero will not be reasoned with, he will not escape. There will be a battle. I may be old, but I am well versed in the art of dueling."

Mikal nodded. "And I may be small, but I'm quick."

A smile tugged at Constantine's mouth, replacing the look of distress. "I don't suppose I could persuade you kids to retreat to the dungeon until this is safely resolved?"

"No, sir," Caleb said. "Not on our lives."

"We're staying," George said.

"We've dealt with worse than Nero," Mikal said.

"I expected as much," Constantine said.

The three stepped away to talk among themselves next to the fireplace. Mikal gave Cavendish to George as he bent to tie his shoelaces.

"Why couldn't you enter Astria with us, Cav?" Caleb asked.

"We missed you. It was hard counting without you," George said.

Cavendish's screen blushed pink with pleasure at the idea of being missed. "The Timekeeper wanted to have a very important conversation with me."

"What did he want to talk about?" Mikal asked.

"It's a secret," Cavendish said. "But guess what! My creator told me why I'm waterproof. He discovered a battery in the ocean while he was researching a book, and then he used it to energize me. Isn't that marvelous?"

"I've been telling you this whole time you run on batteries!" Caleb teased.

"I didn't mean *battery*!" Cavendish backtracked. "I'm much fancier than that. It's a *power capacitor*."

"It kind of sounds like the same thing," Mikal said.

Cavendish took a deep breath, preparing to launch into a vigorous argument, but then George changed the subject.

"What are you guys going to do when this is all over? You're not going back to the cemetery, are you, Caleb and Mikal?"

Mikal shrugged and smoothed back his hair.

"Actually," Caleb said, "we were thinking about helping you find Daniel. I mean, if you want us to. We figured that would be the first thing on your mind after this whole mess is cleared up."

"And Uncle Constantine said that he had wanted us to come live with him and Aunt Henrietta, when they first learned about us," Mikal said. "Do you think they'll still want us?"

George couldn't contain her grin. "I was really hoping you'd say that. I know they'll want you. Then we can set out on our next mission! To find my brother and Caleb's past."

Caleb's eyes brightened with interest.

"It's a good mission," Mikal said. "I want to meet Daniel, and I want to know where Caleb came from. Maybe he's an alien."

"Jeez. Thanks, Mikal!" Caleb said, but then he nodded. "Of all the people and worlds in the Door Way, there has to be something that can help."

George felt light with hope for a moment, but then she glanced up again. The meteors were now grazing the treetops, leaving blackened and burning branches in their wake. She swallowed hard and looked away.

At 10:29 PM, footsteps sounded from the garden above.

The children jumped to their feet and pressed close together, Cavendish held tightly in George's arms. Constantine stood watching the white doors intently, clenching and unclenching his fists at his sides. Yorick, the faithful skeleton, was next to him, a silent sentinel. Mr. Neptune cowered behind the desk. Mr. Night was off to one side with Lucy, who was clutching a book as if her life depended on it.

The doorknob rattled and then turned. A scent of spicy aftershave crept into the room.

THE COUNCIL OF SEVEN

CHAPTER TWENTY-ONE

WHEN THE DOOR OPENED, NERO WAS THE first to step through. He saw Constantine and stopped in his tracks, leaning on his cane. "Constantine," he said dryly.

"Nero." Constantine dipped his head in greeting. "You look remarkably well. It seems death has no hold on you."

"Wouldn't you know, being dead was so much more *boring* than I'd imagined."

Nero was followed by two henchmen. One was a towering, muscled beast of a man, with wild hair and daggers strapped to his thighs. The other was Arlo, only slightly shorter but far more terrifying as he was the one guiding Henrietta before him with a wicked-looking blade pressed to her throat.

George's knees went as weak as a soggy spaghetti strand, and Henrietta smiled at her, absently smoothing the front of her apron.

As the four of them cleared the entry, there was a snick and a flash, but only a waver of light betrayed the invisible barrier that had trapped them in the library.

Nero tensed and looked over his shoulder, then shook his head ruefully. "Really, Constantine? You must be desperate for my company." His gaze wandered around the room and settled on Lucy. Dismissing her with a shake of his head, he returned his attention to Constantine, who was searching Henrietta's face.

"I'm here to make a request, Constantine. As I'm sure you've noticed, the woman there"—he jerked his head at Lucy—"has made a mess of things. She is now significantly less qualified for my previous position than you may have thought." Nero gestured to the glass ceiling. "And as you can see, the stars are nearly striking, with no sign of the other sisters, and no time to find and rejoin them now."

He paused, waiting, but no one spoke.

"I'll cut to the chase, then, shall I? I have realized the . . . error of my ways and am here seeking forgiveness. I would like to be reinstated onto the Council and to regain my previous authority."

Constantine tore his eyes from Henrietta, and they were sad as he regarded his old friend. "You don't want us to forgive you, Nero. You want us to forget."

Nero's pleasant smile remained, but his brows gave the faintest twitch. "It seems to me that you really don't have a choice. And consider my level of experience." He stepped closer to Constantine, and his voice flowed like melted honey. "Remember, Constantine, we have been friends for eons untold. We have been eternal, together. Wouldn't you like to have that back?"

George's chin trembled as she spoke. "You're too late." She stepped forward, holding Cavendish against her chest like a shield.

Caleb and Mikal followed to stand with her.

Nero narrowed his eyes as he seemed to notice them for the first time. "You three, again?"

"It's true," Mikal said.

Caleb nodded, a swift jerk of his head.

But Nero ignored the two boys, all of his attention set on studying George.

She stared back at him, trying not to flinch.

"Your face . . . ," he said. "There's something—"

But George didn't wait for him to finish. She wet her lips and burst out, "The Els have already been rejoined."

The effect those words had on the handsome man was amazing. Nero's visage turned blotchy and red. He glanced quickly at Lucy, who was standing in front of Mr. Night, his hand on her shoulder.

"Rejoined, you say?" Nero asked, and his voice snapped like broken glass. "Impossible."

Constantine nodded. "It's true, Nero. You are too late."

Nero's jaw tightened as he looked back at the children. "There are three of you, I see. Which means you must have reclaimed the pieces from Astria . . . but how? You're just children." Then he ground his teeth. "I should have tossed you into the void with your boring toy."

"Say what?" Cavendish asked, but he was ignored as Nero continued talking.

"An honest mistake, but a mistake nonetheless. Never mind. That's why I brought her along." He gestured to Henrietta, who still stood quiet and meek between the enormous Arlo and the towering, wild-haired henchman. "Nothing like good old-fashioned insurance."

"I will not reinstate you on the Council, Nero. You know that now," Constantine said. "Please, try to see reason."

"Reason?" Nero's voice was shrill. "Do you think it would be *reasonable* of me to just accept your decision and return to nothing? Or had you thought I would be *reasonable* and allow you to take me into custody? Bring me to justice and all that?"

"I had hoped so, Nero," Constantine said.

"It was a foolish hope," Nero practically spat, and then drew himself up. "You *will* reinstate me, Constantine, because if you don't, I will order Arlo to run that blade across your precious Innocent's throat. And you know I have it in me, don't you?"

Arlo growled and shifted, causing Henrietta to stumble back against him.

George inhaled so sharply she almost choked. Her gaze darted from Henrietta to Nero, and then to Constantine.

"Choose now, Constantine," Nero said. "Your wife or the Els—one must go."

Henrietta gasped with outrage, finally showing a bit of temper. "Shame on you, Nero! Shame on you for asking such a thing of him! Especially you!"

Lucy remained silent and watchful, but a storm began to brew behind Mr. Night's face.

Constantine looked tortured, and his voice cracked when he replied. "I cannot sacrifice one to save the other, Nero."

"Not even when one is your wife?" Nero asked, for half a heartbeat seeming truly bewildered. "Then you deserve to lose her."

"Nero, you must fight against your grief and madness! Without the Council, the worlds will be destroyed by the showers, and I will not allow that. I do not want there to be bloodshed between us. Do not force my hand!"

"But I must. Don't you see? I have no choice. I have nothing. No title, no authority, no people, no place to belong in all the countless worlds. I am Loeta. Alone." He paused and took a deep breath, and his eyes began to burn with anger. "I will *not* be alone, Constantine. Not anymore. Vo."

"Sir?" the man with the wild hair asked.

"Secure the room for me. If they resist," Nero said, "kill them. Arlo, get rid of the old woman and assist Vo."

Henrietta's breathing quickened.

A bitter taste rose in George's throat, and she tightened her fingers around Cavendish so hard he squeaked. Caleb and Mikal exchanged a quick, meaningful look.

Nero lifted his cane and tugged on the handle. A long, razor-sharp blade slid out, and he leisurely withdrew it. "Leave the Timekeeper to me." He tossed the sheath aside, took a step forward, and thrust the sword into Constantine's belly.

Or it would have been Constantine's belly, but Yorick, who had been standing next to him, leapt clumsily forward. Nero's blade glanced off Yorick's spine, missing Constantine by inches. Nero wrenched the sword within Yorick's rib cage, and the loyal skeleton collapsed noisily into a jumbled pile of bones.

The geese honked and scattered at the ruckus, and a wicked smile split Nero's face, but Constantine didn't see it.

As soon as the skeleton hit the ground, Constantine had gone down after it, limber as a dancer. He rose in an instant, holding one of Yorick's long femurs in his hand. "I didn't want it to come to this, Nero."

Nero laughed outright as he saw Constantine's makeshift sword, and he attacked viciously with his gleaming rapier.

But Constantine hadn't lied about his skill, and he deftly fended off each of Nero's strikes with the giant skeleton's oversized thighbone.

Before Arlo could decide how to "get rid" of Henrietta, she drove her sharp elbow into his gut, stomped

down hard on his instep, and slammed the back of her fist into his nose.

He doubled over and blood spurted from his nose as the knife fell from his grip.

Then, in a blur of orange curls, George charged and set to pummeling him over the head with Cavendish. "You leave my aunt Henrietta alone! Leave her alone!"

"Take THAT, you behemoth! And that too!" Cavendish bellowed as George smacked him against Arlo's ear.

He roared and rose up to his imposing height.

Caleb sprinted to the fireplace and returned seconds later wielding a fire shovel in one hand and a poker in the other. He swung the shovel at Arlo's chest, but the henchman batted it away and knocked Caleb to the ground with a single blow. Before Caleb could recover, Arlo lifted his giant foot and put it firmly against Caleb's throat.

Caleb's legs kicked and his fingers clawed at Arlo's boot as he fought for breath. He heard George and Mikal yelling, but he couldn't see them because his vision started to go hazy.

Constantine's and Nero's weapons rang as they dueled their way around the library, each determined to gain the upper hand. Constantine advanced on Nero, but Nero rapidly parried the attack, forcing Constantine back between two bookcases, where he floundered, too long-limbed to defend himself in the tight space.

Mikal scrambled for the poker Caleb had dropped and jabbed the sharp end as hard as he could into Arlo's thigh.

Arlo yelped and stumbled, freeing Caleb, who lay blue-faced and limp as a wilted daisy.

Henrietta snatched the poker from Mikal and, with careful aim, swung it so hard across Arlo's shins that it broke in two. He howled with agony and collapsed to his knees.

As Arlo went down, Mikal caught a glancing blow from the man's elbow on the side of his face. He tumbled to the floor and lay stunned for a moment.

George shrieked with fury when she saw Mikal land next to Caleb, and with all the strength a twelve-year-old girl can muster, she bashed Cavendish straight against the back of Arlo's head.

Cavendish's case cracked, and Arlo went very still. Then he let out a sigh and fell forward in a limp daze.

"I'm okay! Nobody panic!" Cavendish called.

Henrietta, in a flurry of motion, yanked off her apron and used it to tie Arlo's wrists behind his back.

George sank down beside Caleb and Mikal.

Mikal, left eye already swelling shut, had shaken off

the blow from Arlo's elbow and was kneeling by Caleb, who lay terribly still.

Henrietta crouched low and took Caleb's wrist. She felt his pulse, leaned close, and put her ear next to his chest, then his mouth, listening hard for any sign of life.

Across the room Constantine was still cornered, and his assailant was closing in quick. Nero struck out with his slender blade, faster than a diving falcon, but Constantine managed to raise the heavy femur before his face just in time to catch the worst of the impact. A sliver of red appeared above his cheek where the needlelike tip of Nero's rapier still vibrated with the force of the crash.

"WELL?" Cavendish demanded frantically as Henrietta pulled away from Caleb.

"Is he. . . ." George began, but couldn't get the words past her lips.

"He'll live," Henrietta said, and then she darted off to help the others.

George and Mikal looked down and saw Caleb watching them, his gray eyes mischievous. "Did we win?" he asked in a rough whisper.

George's whole body drooped with relief.

Mikal grinned so wide his good eye squeezed shut too. "Not yet." He retrieved his poker and scampered across the room to where the battle still waged.

"I'll be back!" George said, leaving Cavendish and springing up to follow Mikal.

"Wait for me," Caleb croaked, and began to struggle to his feet.

Before Nero could rally, Constantine shoved him back hard enough to send him flailing away. Constantine dodged around him and back into the open.

By this time Vo's first victim, Mr. Night, was out cold and slumped over the desk. Mr. Neptune, squealing with panic, had taken refuge beneath it.

Vo had Lucy cornered when Henrietta arrived. She barreled into the giant henchman, throwing him off balance just enough for Lucy to escape. He spun around, grabbed Henrietta by the elbow, and tossed her aside like a rag doll.

"Constantine!" Lucy shouted.

Constantine took in the situation with a glance. He dashed away from the fight with Nero, straight through the flock of geese, toward Vo.

Nero attempted to follow his prey, but now the geese were angry, and they assailed him with a vengeance.

As Constantine reached Vo, he struck out with the femur. The knives Vo had unstrapped were knocked from his grasp.

"Constantine!" Lucy shouted again. "The stairs!"

Constantine understood at once, and he began fencing

Vo toward Lucy so rapidly, it was all the henchman could do to keep his feet under him.

Lucy flung open the dungeon door, and with one last thrust of Constantine's weapon, Vo lurched backward, his arms windmilling as he tried to regain his balance on the top step.

But Lucy didn't give him a chance to recover. She reached out and shoved against his barrel-chest.

With a wordless cry, Vo tumbled down the stone stairs and into the darkness.

Lucy slammed the door and turned the key in the lock.

Constantine spun on his heel and rushed back to his fight with Nero, who had finally escaped the wrath of the geese.

Mikal ran up to join Constantine.

Nero stood panting under the glass ceiling. Stray feathers were clinging to his sweaty face, and he was covered in welting goose bites. His sword was lost, claimed by the fowl, and he no longer laughed.

Constantine shook with exhaustion as he held the femur before him.

"What's this?" Nero said. "Two against one? That isn't very sporting."

Mikal scowled at him and mimicked Constantine's posture, using the poker.

"Your men are down, Nero. You have no choice but to surrender," Constantine said.

Lucy and Henrietta came up then, Henrietta limping and Lucy supporting her as best she could. George ran up beside Mikal, and even Mr. Neptune crawled from his hiding place.

Nero looked at all their faces, but his gaze lingered on George. "You . . . ," he muttered. Then he swallowed hard and began edging away. "It has just occurred to me that today may not be a good day to sort out old misunderstandings." He reached one hand into his pocket and glanced down at his wristwatch. "Ah! Ten forty-nine PM! If you let me go, you might have time to re-form your precious Council. Besides, you still hope I'll repent someday, don't you, old friend?" He gave Constantine a cocky wink.

"You can't escape, Nero," Constantine said. "The way is sealed."

"Ah, but I am a man who always has a plan!" Nero pulled his hand from his pocket, and in his palm sat a tiny crystal cube. "A man who always has a way out!"

The adults gasped with dismay, but George and Mikal just watched in confusion, and then with great interest, as they noticed Caleb creeping feebly up behind Nero. He had caught his second wind, gotten to his feet, and was ready to rejoin the fight.

"I had hoped to avoid using this. I'm sure you can imagine they're harder to come by now than they used to be, and I haven't got many left. Oh well. I suppose it can't be helped. I'd like you to remember, Constantine, that this was only a battle. I excel at wars." Nero began to squeeze the crystal cube just as Caleb attacked.

They fell to the floor in a thrashing heap. Caleb grabbed at Nero's hand, inadvertently crushing it around the cube. Then an empty black rectangle appeared below Nero, and he fell into it with a thud, disappearing into darkness.

Caleb scrambled back, startled and disconcerted.

Then Nero's laughter came from the blackness. "I told you, Constantine. I'm a man who always has a way—What is that?" His voice was edged with panic. "Where have you sent me, boy?" And then the screaming started, only to cease immediately as the rectangle disappeared.

Tension sizzled in the room as echoes of Nero's cries died away.

"What did I do?" Caleb asked, still struggling on the ground, a horrified look on his face.

Constantine shook his head sadly. "You're not at fault, boy. Nero held a Portable Moor within his hand. You activate it by touch while thinking of where you want to go, and that is where it'll take you. By grabbing Nero's hand, you must have rerouted it. Where could you have sent him?"

"I didn't mean to send him anywhere!" Caleb insisted.

"Yes . . . I'm sure that's true," Constantine said, twirling the end of his mustache as he stared thoughtfully at the place where Nero had vanished. Then he sighed and rubbed at his eyes. "We can discuss that later, I suppose. It will need to be discussed."

Caleb shoved his hands through his hair, his expression confused and unsettled. George helped him to his feet. "But I thought Portable Moors were illegal. Cavendish said—"

"They are illegal!" Cavendish interrupted from where he lay on the floor.

Mikal scurried to retrieve him.

"I'm afraid Cavendish was right," Constantine said. "They've long been forbidden because they allow unrestricted access to places they ought not."

"How would Nero have gotten ahold of something like that if it's illegal?" Caleb asked.

"Yes, Constantine," Henrietta said, giving him a strange look. "How would he have gotten ahold of one? Production has been forbidden for ages now, and punishable by lifelong incarceration. The last of them were supposed to have been destroyed."

"Nero's had a lot of time in the past hundred years to get up to mischief. Perhaps tracking down what few

Portable Moors remained was part of that mischief. It would certainly explain some things. I'm afraid to imagine what other outlawed devices he may have collected." He tugged hard on his collar.

"Do you think he got away?" Mikal asked, returning with Cavendish.

"It sure didn't sound like it," Caleb said.

"But if he did, what's to keep him from being drawn here like he was before?" George asked. "Won't he try to come back?"

"I'm rather sure the bond that drew him back to Chrone Cottage will be officially broken when the Els replace him as Judge," Constantine said. "You can deactivate the invisible door now, Phinneus. I believe we're secure."

Suddenly George realized she had her aunt Henrietta back, and she launched herself into her aunt's arms. "You're safe! You're back, and you're safe!"

"Shh, child. Of course I am." Henrietta brushed George's hair from her forehead with a soft hand.

George laughed with relief. "Do you want to meet Caleb and Mikal?"

"I absolutely do!" Henrietta said.

But first Constantine draped an arm around Henrietta's shoulder and looked intently into her eyes.

Henrietta stared back at him and patted his weathered cheek before turning her attention to Caleb and Mikal. She took Mikal's chin gently and turned his face to the light. "Heavens to Betsy, would you look at that eye? I've never seen such a majestic shiner! And you, Caleb! Those are some nasty marks on your throat. Such warriors, these three!" Then she wrapped them all in a warm embrace.

Caleb and Mikal blushed crimson while George grinned so hard her cheeks hurt.

"Thank you for the raincoats," Mikal said shyly.

"It was very kind of you to think of us," Caleb said.

"Pish posh! Kind indeed!" she said indignantly. "Now, is everyone all right?"

George looked around the room. Constantine seemed to be regaining his sense of humor. Mr. Night had come to and was kneeling next to Arlo, binding his feet securely. Mr. Neptune, looking shaken, was disabling the shield. Lucy was soothing her agitated geese. Mikal and Caleb were bruised, but bruised well enough to brag about. Cavendish was chattering away to anyone who would listen about how he had *earned* the crack in his casing by downing a giant. Everyone seemed to be fine. But then George's eyes fell on the pile of bones.

"Yorick didn't make it," she said sadly. "What are we going to do without a Recorder?"

"Don't fress, dear," Henrietta said. She took the femur from Constantine and placed it gently onto the jumbled heap of skeleton.

Then the pile clattered, and there was Yorick, unjumbling and reassembling right before their eyes.

"It happens occasionally," Constantine said. "Yorick falls right to pieces at the slightest thing. He hasn't anything to hold him together, you see." Then he patted the skeleton on the clavicle and thanked him for the use of his thighbone.

"Is everybody ready to take their positions and re-form the Council?" Henrietta asked.

There were nods and murmurs of consent all around.

"Wait!" Mikal said. "There aren't enough people. We're still missing the Guide!"

"We're missing no such thing," Cavendish said in a smug voice.

"He's right," Constantine said. "When I saw how Cavendish matured on your journey, I realized he had the potential to grow into a worthy Guide. That's why I instructed him to stay with Lucy while you entered Astria. I needed to have a conversation with him and conduct his interview."

"Cavendish!" George said. "Was that your secret? Why didn't you tell us?"

"I wanted it to be a surprise!" Cavendish said.

"Way to go, Cav," Caleb said, giving him a congratulatory pat.

"I always knew you were important," Mikal said.

"I'm proud of you, Cavendish," George said.

"He still has a lot to learn, but I trust that he has what it takes. And now we should finish what we came here for, so it's time for a bit of ceremony," Constantine said.

"Yes, we really should have some punch to make it official, don't you think, my love?" Henrietta asked.

Just then, a flaming black rock crashed through the ceiling, showering glass onto their heads and pulverizing Lucy's desk.

Cavendish squeaked with alarm. "The time is now eleven oh three PM DWT. You currently have eight minutes until DEATH DEATH DEATH!"

"We'll have punch later," Henrietta said.

"Of course, Chicken," Constantine said. "Everyone to the center of the room now. That's right. Into the circle. You too, children."

The kids nervously stepped into the ring of light falling from where the glass ceiling had been a moment ago.

"Very good," Constantine said. "We know that the

Els will hold the position of Judge. Lucy, you will serve as Justice. You will dole out reward and punishment, with the advice of your sisters. Lucretia, in her great age and wisdom, will act as Mercy, pleading the case of those accused. Lue, with the brashness of youth, will act as Critic, condemning those who have done wrong."

Lucy, holding a book over her head to protect herself from falling shards, nodded, and Constantine continued.

"Dear Henrietta is our Innocent," he said, smiling lovingly at her.

"Yes, but do hurry, my dear," Henrietta murmured as scorched stars rained down.

"Right. And Yorick's . . . unusual . . . talents have groomed him for the position of Recorder. Phinneus, you shall be our Engineer, and Cavendish our Guide!"

Mr. Neptune smiled tremulously and waved a hand in the air to speed things along, but Cavendish feigned surprise and stuttered over the honor of being part of something so important. "Me? Well . . . me? Who'd have thought?"

"Hurry, hurry," George said, then jumped when Caleb grinned and nudged her and Mikal.

"Children, are you paying attention?" Constantine asked.

"Yes," they said together.

"Very good," Constantine said. "We can't do this without witnesses. Boris, you will fill the position of the Unlikely, thereby adding an element of chance to help things flow smoothly."

Mr. Night drew himself up and threw back his shoulders, but promptly ducked aside as a charred rock whizzed past.

"Stay in the circle, Boris!" Henrietta said.

"That's it, isn't it, Chicken?"

"Yes, I believe so. Let me see." She counted on her fingers. "Yes! Now wait for it. . . ."

Constantine looked again at the clock, and everyone was silent as the meteors hissed and shrieked over their heads. He inhaled sharply, held up one hand, and then looked up.

The stars had ceased to fall.

"Eleven twelve PM. We made it," Constantine said, his voice filled with reverence. "The Flyrrey is secure once more."

George let out a long sigh. Caleb and Mikal high-fived each other. Mr. Neptune made a funny whimpering sound. Lucy and Mr. Night embraced. Yorick simply brushed some dust off his humerus bone.

"I always knew we would," Henrietta said.

"Caleb, Mikal, would you help Boris and Phinneus move our guest into the dungeon?" Constantine asked, gesturing to Arlo, who had regained his senses and lay weeping quietly upon the floor. The only words that could be caught between his sobs were "All alone. He left me all alone."

"Be kind to him," Henrietta said with a pitying look on her face. "Nero wasn't."

"And be careful of Vo down there. Though I doubt he'll give you any trouble after the tumble he took," Constantine said.

"Will Caleb and Mikal be coming home with us?" George asked when the boys had headed downstairs.

"Of course they will," Henrietta said. "Imagine, sending those dear boys back to that cemetery."

"Do you think my parents will be back yet? If they found Daniel, I mean."

"I don't think they've had enough time, dear," Henrietta said. "They've only been gone a week."

George nodded her acceptance of this answer. "Uncle Constantine, you know how there are lots of different worlds for lots of different creatures and purposes?"

"Yes, George?"

"Could there maybe be a world for the past too?"

Constantine and Henrietta exchanged a startled glance and then appraised George silently. Constantine fidgeted with his watch for a long moment before he finally answered. "What you're thinking of is the Archives, and those are forbidden. We don't talk about them, George. Ever."

"Oh. Sorry," George said, her brow furrowing.

Henrietta stroked George's hair. "You can't be blamed. You didn't know. But why did you ask, dear?"

"I was just curious." She gave them each a quick hug and ran across the room to where Caleb and Mikal were following Mr. Night and Mr. Neptune out of the dungeon.

"Where'd you put Arlo?" George asked. "And what about Vo?"

"They're sharing one of the Hag's larger cages for the time being. Vo was remarkably cooperative. His fall was broken by one of the potion racks, and he got a thorough dose of one of Lucretia's experimental elixirs. He currently believes himself to be an entire muster of peacocks. He refuses to stop warbling," Mr. Night said.

Mikal reluctantly surrendered Cavendish to Mr. Neptune to be inspected for any damage other than the cracked casing.

When the children stood alone again, George lowered her voice to a whisper. "Aunt Henrietta said you're both coming home to Snaffleharp Lane. I also asked them if there was a world for the past because I thought it might be a good place to start looking for where you came from, Caleb, and because it might help me find out where Daniel went. They got a little weird, though."

"Weird how?" Caleb asked.

"They said the place was called the Archives and that it's forbidden and we aren't supposed to talk about it."

"It seems like lots of things are forbidden," Mikal said, squinting through his good eye at the adults.

George nodded. "Maybe it's dangerous. . . ." She trailed off and chewed on her bottom lip.

"So?" Caleb asked. "We've done lots of dangerous stuff."

"I know. But I was just thinking that you and Mikal have never really had a home before. Now you have Snaffleharp Lane, and before you even get there, I'm asking you to set off on another mission to help me find my brother. Suppose you could be happy staying put, Caleb, now that you have Aunt Henrietta to look after you? But I have to find Daniel, so maybe I should do this one on my own."

Caleb and Mikal looked at each other. Then they turned back to her, and Caleb was wearing his lopsided grin. "Jeez, Georgina. Like I've said before, we're not leaving you to do this alone. And not just because I want to find out where I came from."

"Why, then? Because of the code?" George asked.

Mikal shook his head. "No. Because we're the Snafflehарp Company."

George's face lit with happiness. "So it's a plan, then. We're going to find the Archives."

"It's a place to start," Caleb said.

Then Henrietta had them all gather for a photograph of the new Council of Seven.

Constantine yawned hugely behind one hand after a dozen shots. "What do you say we all go home and have a nice nap? I'll be back to take care of the situation in the basement, Lucy. Vo should recover from his delusions of feathered grandeur before too long. Then we must schedule the first meeting of the new Council of Seven to determine how we're going to track Nero down, just in case he did escape. Caleb and I must have a serious discussion about where he may have sent him. He must still be brought to justice."

"But I have no idea where I could have sent him," Caleb said. "I don't remember thinking of anywhere special."

"We can think of that a bit later," Henrietta said.

"Come along, children. We're going home. Oh, my ducks! Caleb and Mikal, you must meet my ducks."

George leaned heavily against Henrietta and looked at Lucy and Mr. Night. "Will we see you again?"

"Of course, George. Although, next time I may be one of my sisters," Lucy said with a smile.

"It was nice meeting you, Mr. Night," George said.

"The pleasure was mine, George."

The kids went to say good-bye to Mr. Neptune and were disappointed when he told them that Cavendish needed far too much work to go home with them right away.

"I don't need that much work! I just got a little wet, is all. You can send me home with them!" Cavendish said.

"Um, that isn't all that happened," Caleb said.

"Yeah . . . there's something we need to tell you," George said.

"What is it?" Cavendish asked. "Did you drop me while I was turned off?"

"No."

And over the next several minutes, they explained to Cavendish, with many apologies, what had happened in the tunnel with Nero.

"Well I NEVER," Cavendish said when they had finished.

"We think that's why he wasn't working in Obsidia, Mr. Neptune," Mikal said.

"Yeah, it certainly isn't because I beat up a bad guy with him," George said.

"You should be more careful with such advanced technology," Mr. Neptune said. "But with a little troubleshooting I'll be able to fix him. I'll send him to you at Snaffleharp Lane as soon as I repair the water damage and the cracked casing."

"But I like my cracks!" Cavendish said. "They're my battle scars."

Then George perked up and looked at Henrietta. "Aunt Henrietta, Mikal and I have to know what a Snaffleharp is!"

"Why, it's a singing hen, dear," Henrietta said, tucking a curl behind George's ear.

George squinted thoughtfully as she tried to imagine a chicken singing opera. Then she smiled and shook it off.

"This is our stop," Constantine said, though nobody had felt Chrone Cottage move. He lunged up the stairs on his long legs. When he reached the shed, there was a great clattering noise. "Confound all these shovels! I'm too tall for this nonsense!"

"Oh my. I'm coming, dear!" Henrietta said, going after him.

"Map, check the weather forecast. We need a mud puddle," Mr. Neptune said.

"*Map*?" Cavendish said indignantly. "I'm a member of the Council, and you call me *map*? I'm the Guide. I have a name now. I have a name, and I am much too important to be—"

"All right. All right! You have a name!" Mr. Neptune said, then muttered under his breath, "Who would name a map anyhow?"

"The Snaffleharp Company named him, and his *name* is Cavendish," George said, tossing the end of her scarf over one shoulder.

Mr. Neptune gave a long-suffering sigh and trudged up the steps, Cavendish keeping up a steady stream of chatter.

The children waved good-bye to Lucy and Mr. Night before following after. When they reached the shed, the others had gone on and it was empty.

They walked through the garden and out under the pomegranate arch. Before them was Snaffleharp Lane, and the boys ran eagerly ahead.

George paused next to the mailbox. It had been battered by meteors, and the metal door was caved in and hanging from its hinges. She tilted her head curiously and looked inside. There, in the shadowy recesses, was a tiny blackened orb surrounded by sparkling powder.

George retrieved the dark sphere and brushed the dust into a handkerchief for safekeeping. It would make a fine *hikaru dorodango*. Then she looked up at the fading Victorian cottage with its cobweb-covered windows. It was shining with so much light the gossamer nets seemed to glow like moonbeams.

She felt a familiar quiver of anxiety, but it wasn't the same as the first time she had stood here. There was nervousness, yes. So much could still go disastrously wrong. But underneath that, bubbling up to the top and taking over, if only for the moment, was something warm and radiant. It was something she hadn't felt since before that day in Istanbul. She had found people to belong to, and together they would get back what she had lost. She tucked the star into her pocket, and as she climbed the steps, she began to count.

"One for Snaffleharp Lane."

ACKNOWLEDGMENTS

I would like to thank Amy, who was a bright spot in the monotony of revisions; Daniel, ever faithful sounding board; Happy, for reminding me that I really wanted this; Jacob, who told me I was a writer when I needed to hear it; Jamie, always vigorously supportive; Mrs. Bone, because I still remember her; and Kay and Samantha, the first people to read this book who didn't *have* to.

Boundless appreciation to my copyeditor, Ana Deboo, who defended this manuscript against a multitude of *silentlys*; my editor, Christy Ottaviano, for asking the right questions in the right way; Jaime Zollars, whose illustrations provided me with the first physical glimpse of characters who have been living in my head for the past decade; Liz, for believing in *Enter a Glossy Web*; my agent, Robert Wilson, who knows what he's talking about.

Finally, I am thankful for my niece, Junebug, who informed me that the chicken shed where I do my writing *is* a magic place.

COMING SOON!

ESCAPE THE SILKEN THREAD

BOOK 2

IN THE GOSSAMER TRILOGY